B.D.PEDERSEN

Alien Dig

SECRETS OF THE CUBES

Edited by

Shannon Lynam
Samantha Thompson
June Pedersen

Cover Design
Mike Lynam
Red Fence Productions

Prologue

Who would have known I was a genius? I had no idea of it myself. But, as things developed and each situation manifested itself and then became fully matured, I came to realize I was, in fact, a genius. After all, they wouldn't be putting me through all this crap if I weren't.

Well, anyway, I think I am. Who would have known a simple deep soil radar scan would create such a stir? Agreed, the head of the survey team did the right thing and actually gave us everything we needed to get this whole mess started.

So, I find myself deep in the Brazilian forests at the eastern side of the old Guiana Mountain foothills, running a dig that would eventually bring the whole of the world to the edge of total war. Oh, did I mention they set a nuclear bomb off at our dig site? Come on people, it's just a stupid archeological dig and nothing more and you hit us with a nuclear bomb.

It started out as a simple dig, looking for what I thought was a tunneling machine, only to discover we were right on top of an alien outpost. Did I also mention we were noncombatants? That's right. No military within five hundred miles and they hit us with a nuclear bomb?

Yes, we're all right. The cubes saw to that, but what they did in return I prefer not to think about. The only thing I can say is these things, the cubes, are the nastiest thing you could ever wish you had not crossed in any way, shape, or form.

We were trapped, all we could do was to stay put and sit it out and hope for the best. Have you ever had that feeling one gets when things are going on around you and you can do nothing about it? You have no ability to even communicate you would prefer not to be there and would welcome the opportunity to get the hell out.

Well, this was fifty, a hundred, a thousand times that. We have the Brazilian military coming at us, the cubes, who have already killed two of our team, keeping us inside the only shelter in the whole of the dig area, and the United Nations trying to formulate peace between the warring parties.

In a nut shell, everything has gone crazy as hell and we're stuck dead center in the middle. The Brazilians want to take over the site, the United Nations want them to stay out of it, and the aliens are coming back to claim that which is theirs.

Me? I'm just a guy who was asked to take part in the dig and to supervise and oversee the actual process of digging out this monster machine. Just bare the machine so the experts can get to it and figure out what it is and why it's there. That's it. And, all hell busts loose.

Aliens, for the love of might, how did they get involved in this thing? The whole story is crazy, but if you're ever going to understand just what brought us to this time and place, I need to fill you in on the details. Please, hear me out and maybe you'll be able to grasp what has happened and what is coming in the not-too-distant future.

I can only tell you, unless you hear me out, you're never going to be able to deal with what is coming. Believe me when I tell you they are coming and they can't be stopped, the cubes will see to that. You have no idea what they can do and based on what I have seen and what has already taken place I don't think there is much they can't do.

Please, hear me out and you'll understand once I have told you everything. Just be patient with me, this is really not easy.

Chapter One

THE DISCOVERY

Melanie had sounded so insistent and yet controlled I knew there was something really bad waiting for me. I pulled up to the big road cat sitting there with its engine idling, coming to a sliding stop.

She was standing there with the cat operator and the site archeologist and as my rig came to a stop she turned and started walking toward me. As I got out of the rig and walked to meet her, my eyes fell on the scene just beyond where the operator and archeologist were standing.

All I saw were his legs sticking out from under the treads of the big cat. I didn't want to see that. My day had just gone from hard to impossible. God, I didn't want to be here right now. If only I could find myself someplace else, anyplace as long as it wasn't here.

I felt old like I had been here in this place for a hundred years. So much has happened over these past few weeks and still things keep coming up and happening. It makes me think someone or something is really trying hard to ruin my day, my life.

How could things get any worse? What I didn't know was things were just starting to happen and it was going to get much worse. It wasn't so bad when I first got here which seemed like many hundreds of years ago. It was exciting and something new and challenging. It was almost like it was yesterday when I stepped out of the helicopter.

It was August 3, 2035; I would have never thought I would be standing in the foothills of one of the oldest mountain ranges in the world. Yet, here I was and what I was about to learn and see would change my life and future of the world.

Me? I'm a designer of some of the world's largest machines. Machines that tear the earth, move massive loads, launch payloads into space, and crawl across the ocean floors. The question that must be asked is, why me? I guess over the course of my career I have gained a reputation as a top-notch engineer. I have the usual degrees and a number of special awards that declare me to be something of a master in the area of engineering and building. I have reached a point in my life where I was the first name to come up when an especially difficult or complex engineering task was at hand.

It was not surprising to me I would be contacted in regards to the moving or excavation of a mountain range, but the manner in which it was done was a new one to me.

I was there under a presidential order. My experience with this process was limited and so I learned firsthand you simply go along with those who were shipping you to wherever they wanted you. It was not a comfortable process, but it was effective and fast.

Why am I here? To go one question further, who are these people who have summoned me here? On top of that, who are these other people here with me?

There's nothing out here. They brought

me to this place in the rain forests of Brazil, about half way between Normandia and Uiramuta, Brazil, in the eastern foothills of the Guiana Highlands, located between Brazil and Guyana. These mountains go back some two billion years, just the remnants of a mountain range standing in front of me. Oh, one other thing, there is a small tent city sitting out here in this nowhere, this no place.

As I left the helicopter a Mister Dennis met me. "Joe Nash? You are Joe Nash, right?"

"Yes, I'm Nash."

"Joe, welcome to Base Majestic." As he reached out and shook my hand.

"Leave your equipment and luggage here. A team will see that everything gets to your facilities. Right now, we need you at the project meeting which is going to start in just ten minutes."

He was almost shoving me toward the Jeep. "Sorry for the inconvenience, but you'll understand why shortly."

He turned and directed my attention toward a young woman standing just a few feet behind him.

"Oh yes. I want you to meet your assistant." He was waving her toward us and trying to move me toward the Jeep. "Joe, this is Jennifer Welding. She will assist you in everything and anything you need while you're here. She will also maintain an ongoing log on all your activities. Are there any questions at this time?"

"No sir Mister Dennis. Oh, by the way, what is your first name?"

"It's Mark, Mark Dennis. Is there anything else?"

"Not now thank you."

He continued. "I know we are pushing things right now, but you'll have ample time to settle in and get to know your assistant after this meeting."

I had gotten into the Jeep and Miss Welding was in the back seat as Mark ran around to the driver's side, started the Jeep, and headed for wherever.

As we headed for the meeting location I asked. "Mark, how many people are here for this meeting?"

He was half way looking at me and the road ahead of him. Well, I guess you would call it a road. "Well Joe, there are thirty-one people covering almost every scientific and engineering discipline, and that's not including the support personnel. Support personnel number sixty-five. Again, you will have ample time to meet and socialize with the others once this meeting is over."

Just then, we pulled up in front of a large tent. As I entered the tent, I noted it was divided into several areas with floor to ceiling partitions which separated several locations within the tent. I could smell hot coffee and pastry whiffing out of the entrance to what turned out to be the dining hall and meeting room.

I barely got a coffee and a couple of donuts when the meeting was called to order.

Just then a man stood up at the front of the room. That would be the opposite end of the room from the entrance and coffee and donut tables. "Ladies and gentlemen, my name is Stanley Davenport." He waited while the stragglers got in their seats and let the name sink in. "I am the director and lead scientist on this project, Project Majestic.

"To my left is Bob Hammer, second in charge." Mr. Hammer stood up and bowed his head toward the group. "Bob will be your primary contact person once we get everyone organized.

"On my right is Terry Huntington, our logistics coordinator." Mr. Huntington stood up and bowed his head and then sat back down. "He's the guy you go to for any equipment or other needs while you're here. Please, use him. I can think of nothing we would deny you if it will assist your assigned activities while you're here."

Stanly then shifted from introductions to describing what we were doing there. "Our purpose here and now is to layout the organizational make up of this project and to give you a brief overview of why you're here. What has happened to bring you here, and what we have found?"

I found myself thinking, this would help a lot in that I know absolutely nothing as to why I was there and what the hell I would be doing.

Stanley continued. "I know this is your greatest interest at this time. Right now, you can refer to the hand out given each of you." Stan held the handout up for all to see. "This will tell you what section and team you're assigned to. Some of you are on your own and others will be teamed with several fellow scientists." He paused to see if there were any questions.

He appeared to be a well-organized individual and also seemed comfortable in front of groups of people. As he gave us the chance to look the paper work over he was turning to Mr. Hammer and saying something. I had the feeling this whole gathering was something that had been in the fast lane for a while and we were about to get several weeks of activity dumped on us in just a few short minutes.

He then turned back to the group. "So, let's get started. Five weeks ago, a minerals survey crew was working the foothills of this old mountain range, the Guiana Highlands, when they found a strange reading in their data from the day's sounding process. Normally, they would simply note the fact and set up their next day's schedule, except these reading was off the chart with readings they had never seen before. In fact, they could find no records of any reading like these before.

"They indicated whatever was causing them was in a near surface position. But the real kicker was the size the data indicated. The data told them there was an object below them. It was not natural and it was huge."

At this point a projector came on and a diagram of the region and location of the object was projected onto the main screen at the head of the room.

Stan continued. "Current predictions indicate the object is at least two hundred seventy-four meters long and close to twenty-eight meters wide." He was pointing each feature out with a long pointing stick. "The mountain range runs north and south in this area and the object is sitting ninety degrees to that of the mountain range, exactly east to west.

"The survey crew had no way of excavating the location, so they made a number of additional soundings and then brought their findings back to our institution in Los Angeles. We then ran an extensive analysis of the data and have come to the conclusion the object is manmade. A series of charts were then projected on the screen. Ladies and gentlemen, all we can say is whatever it is, it is not natural but is an object built by someone, who we do not know as of yet."

He then nodded to several people standing at the side of the main screen. "Each of you is being provided with a laptop, loaded up with all the data involving this object. Please make sure it has your name on it." They started handing out laptops to everyone in the meeting. "We are here to excavate this object and determine what it is, who made it, and what its purpose was. What we need from each of you right now are your ideas as to how to progress in this process.

"By that I mean, what direction we should approach from, how large an initial bore should be and whether we should use machines or hand dig?" Stan waited while everyone got their laptops and had turned them on. "Please, review the data and then, by your laptops, provide your interpretation of the data and your best call on direction and methods to take in approaching the object, any questions?"

Questions hell, I didn't even know what I had just heard let alone what their data would show. Everyone was in the same state of shock, confusion, and wonder.

For the most part the meeting only lasted about twenty minutes. It was just two o'clock in the afternoon and everyone started meeting and talking to each other. It was obvious many knew each other and they were making up for the times they had not seen one another. Others were strangers to the rest and were wandering around meeting one another and exchanging small talk. I was in the latter group.

About this time Jennifer rescued me and we started getting acquainted. She was a graduate student at U.S.C. and was working on her thesis for her doctorate in Archeology. I would guess she was around twenty-eight years old and of average height and weight. She was a rather striking woman well-built and proportioned. I know, only a man would think of that, but she was and why not recognize it?

I noted she had a line of freckles running across her face just below her eyes and across the bridge of her nose. It was just enough to add interest to her face and give her a youthful appearance.

She seemed to be a bright person and eager to assist in any way she could. So, we sat down and turned my laptop on. As the data started to fill the screen, Jennifer noted the type of data was unfamiliar to her.

As I watched the flow, I started to recognize its characteristics and sequence. It was scanning a metal object. Type and age of the metal was not evident. Clearly there was little more than that. Not much there to help us to determine its purpose or age or anything else concerning its purpose and nature.

What really caught my eye was the size

and proportions of the object. Just the fact it was sitting here at the foot of a mountain range, and because of its length and width it hit me that it could well be a tunneling machine. One hell of a big one, but I was sure it was a tunneling machine none the less.

I advised Jennifer to make that notation and include it in our report to staff.

I had worked on subterranean projects many times and knew the shortest distance to any underground target was not always a straight line, not always the best, quickest, or safest. With that I concentrated on the makeup of the ground around the object. The survey crew leader had been brilliant in determining what the general layout and makeup of the mountains and land around this area would be needed for any workable analysis. He was right on and it was paying off now.

With that we had a problem. The age of the mountain range was not going to help us. Over time, wind and water erodes the land and this, in simple terms, causes the mountain to break away and fill in the valleys. The filler which is left is a loosely packed fill that would be impossible to drill, dig a shaft or tunnel through. Our best bet was an excavation in the shape of a horse shoe, digging out the side of the slope and baring the object.

It was obvious. This was not going to be a simple dig, finding the object and then taking it home. This was going to be a massive excavation. Because of the size of the target and its location this would take time and would clearly be a most difficult task. I felt sure the actual excavation would take anywhere up to a year and would require the removal of at least eight tenths of a cubic kilometer of earth maybe even more depending on the reaction of the ground to our excavation activities.

This, however, created additional problems. The mountain would continue to fill in the excavation, which would require us to excavate an area three or four times the space needed to uncover the object itself. In addition, the rain forests that grew up the side of the mountain slope would need to be removed from a fairly large area up the side of the mountain. No, I could see this was not going to be a simple or quick project.

When we get to the object, there is no way of knowing the condition of this thing. We could tell it was large by any standard, but what it was and how it got there was something we could not speculate about at this time, yet I couldn't help but feel it was a tunneling machine.

Metal does not hold up well underground. As the water and soil contacts the metal, it degrades it. How badly depends on the type of metal and alloy design. Care would have to be taken to ensure the welfare of the object.

We would need to open up the whole flank of the mountain. It would be a massive operation. In doing that, it would also expose the object to the air and this in turn could cause considerable problems.

I submitted my observations and recommendations and went to my quarters and settled in. My mind was running over all that had been said so far and frankly, not a hell of a lot had been said. They were asking us to make determination on the most meager of data and I would expect the whole gambit of speculation would follow. Meanwhile Jennifer followed up with the details of my suggestions. I had put together a series of calculations and the impact of each and every process as it was implemented.

I had no doubt my observations and suggestions would run counter to those of many of the scientists who were present, but the need to remove a massive amount of mountain would clearly limit their usual methods and means of excavating a historical site.

Anyway, I had finished my review of the data provided and I really needed to lie down and get some rest. The flight to Brazil, the helicopter run here and then the meeting had sapped my energy and I needed to rest.

That was the last I remembered until the next morning. I had fallen asleep and was still in the clothes I had arrived in. The fact was I needed a shower and shave and I needed them badly. I finished getting ready and wandered out of my tent and over to the main tent for something to eat. When I entered the tent, Jennifer was already there. She waved her hand at me and then moved over giving me room to sit.

I set my stuff down by her and went and got a plate full of whatever they had to eat. I'm not a picky eater and will usually eat anything and everything put in front of me. I returned to the table and sat down and started to eat. She finally started to fill me in on what was scheduled for the day and where I needed to be in the next hour or two. It was going to be helpful having her available to help me keep track of where I needed to be.

The rest of the and the following days were a series of meetings and conferences between the many disciplines present at the site. It was exhausting to say the least. We poured over the data and ran additional tests on the lands and environment around the site.

By this time, I was gaining a complete understanding as to the reason for the presidential order and the speed in which it was carried out. There was something here that was outside the normal human experience. It was way beyond one individual or corporation. This was something I would learn later on carried all the ramifications of direct nation to nation confrontations.

At first, my recommendations were rejected due to the massive amount of earth moving that would take place. The process would eliminate any attempt to systematically work the area layer by layer as was the normal operational procedure in an archeological dig. Yet, as they worked the area and determined the magnitude of the project, they gradually started to lean toward those recommendations.

What came out of the process was a

system in which the forest around and over the site would be systematically logged. The process would give the scientists the opportunity to view the area in detail and determine if there were any structural anomalies or items of antiquity they may wish to preserve.

Next, would be the removal of all surface material which included all the undergrowth, loose soil and rocks, bringing the area down to a clear and solid foundation. This would give the archeologist the ability to observe and stop any activity if they discovered anything of historical value. It would be during this process when our first surprise would make itself known. More will be addressed on that later.

Next, we would start the actual excavation and, in doing that, we would work the area in a pattern method give the scientists the ability to be present and observe any artifacts which may be uncovered in the process. Though this would slow the excavation down, it did give us a chance to observe and recover anything that may aid in the identification of the object we were targeting.

It was a good workable plan but what

we did not know was our plan would be blown apart time and again by the unexpected. This was not going to be a cake walk and in time we would come to realize we just may have bitten off more than we could chew.

Over the next three weeks, we managed to work out all the rest of the concerns and logistical needs. During this time Terry Huntington was being overwhelmed by requests for equipment and supplies needed to proceed with the excavation.

In short order, a small city was growing in the area of the project. Equipment and supplies were arriving daily and were stacking up on every square meter of flat space available in the immediate area. We cleared an area just outside the small valley we would be working in while excavating. This became our staging area for all our equipment and supplies.

Several Quonset huts were brought in and set up as our maintenance facility, supply storage, and artifact storage facilities. The huts were all around ten by thirty meters in size, which was ample for the maintenance and supply facility. The artifact storage hut was probably way over sized, but you never know.

When looking over a map of the immediate area, I noted there was a service road which came north out of Normandia. All the heavy equipment and supplies came by this road. This was the road that linked Normandia with Uiramuta to the north of our location. It was basically a black top road with little or no service facilities located anywhere along its length between the two cities. They had run a gravel spur off this main road into the staging area when they first arrived. All personnel were brought in by helicopter.

A considerable amount of prep work had gone into this location before they started bringing in the scientists and engineers. The general terrain was rain forests and mountains. The object was located at the far end of the valley from the staging area, maybe one and a quarter kilometer or so.

On the first day of week four, Mr. Davenport called me to his office and informed me there was a consensus that I should lead the excavation part of the overall project. Due to my experience and overall knowledge of these types of projects, it was felt my skills should be put to good use. I agreed, but on one condition, that being the need for a second assistant, which was granted.

The new assistant showed up three days later. Her name was Melanie Stanford. She was completing her engineering degree when she was contacted and given the opportunity to take part in this project. Melanie was twenty-six years old. She was average height for a woman, fairly husky in her build, but still an attractive young lady.

Because Jennifer was specializing in archeology, I kept her in that position as the liaison between us and the archeological element of the overall program. Melanie would become my direct assistant in the engineering needs of this project. There was little doubt the three of us were going to be working close together and would become highly dependent on one another.

On the Monday of the fifth week, we officially started the excavation. I had designated a boundary area of five hundred meters around the object and ordered all forest in that boundary area to be removed down to the last stick. Everything was to go.

The loggers moved in and in less than a week had every tree down and eighty percent of them removed. During this time, we had built three roads into the area for access by the loggers and access by the heavy machinery which would be following. With a cleared forest area, we were ready to start the second phase, the removal of all the undergrowth and loose soil and rocks.

When the roads were finished it automatically cut the area into three sectors and each sector was attacked by a separate crew of earth movers. The terrain was not that bad, but there were several shallow gullies or depressions at the entrance of the small valley and these would need to be handled carefully to ensure that nothing of importance was damaged or lost.

It had been noted the gullies, though shallow and somewhat manicured ran across the whole of the entrance to the valley. When we laid it out on the map it was clearly a boundary issue. It cut the valley off from the rest of the area making the valley a select or primary area. We determined we would honor that layout and set the boundary for the dig at the gullies.

It was while working the largest of the gullies our first major discovery came about. As the earth mover bulled into the gully entrance, a quick eyed archeologist spotted what he thought was a structural anomaly on the left side of the gully. Per our operational criteria, the project was halted until scientists could evaluate the observation and make a determination as to its validation.

What we found was the remnants of an old road. This was not a four-thousand-year-old road. It was much older and of a much more advanced design than anything we produced today. This was the first mind buster of our excavation, a process which would not stop throughout the entire excavation.

The surface of the road was tight and well maintained. It appeared to be like concrete, but was of a much closer aggregate than the concrete we use on our roads across the world. There were no cracks or other anomalies on the surface. Once cleared, it was determined the road was fully eight meters across. The edges of the road were square and pristine. Something that is totally unheard of in this day and age.

As we excavated the roadway, we were able to obtain samples of the road surface which turned out to be one heck of a task. Every tool we used either dulled or broke as we tried to chip a piece of the material away.

It would have been easier if it had been made of steel. Finally, we were able to scrape a small sample off the face of the roadway and send it off for analysis.

After the analysis of the samples, an emergency meeting was called by Mr. Davenport. It would change everything and everyone's attitudes and sense of importance. I knew from my own experience, and before any analysis happened, this roadway was far beyond anything ever built or used across the world.

"Ladies and gentlemen." Stan always started his meeting that way. "We have just hit the mother lode. The samples that were received from the excavation of the mystery road have been completed. What we are about to reveal to you is something so revolutionary we are at a loss as to just how to present it. So, here it comes.

"The material we received was analyzed and we found it was a form of concrete, but a concrete no one has ever seen before. This concrete is made up of all the usual ingredients except it also includes metals. It will take further analysis to determine the amount and makeup of the metals, but suffice to say it is a metal roadway. We have dubbed the material with the name 'metalcrete'."

I had not expected the results of the analysis. It confused me for about thirty seconds and then I excused myself and headed for the excavation site of the roadway. Jennifer and Melanie accompanied me. I wanted to view that roadway myself and see if I could determine as to the load rating of it and whether it was a major arterial road or a service type road.

When we got to the roadway I stood there and looked at the terrain and position of the roadway. I was trying to determine the reasoning for its placement in this particular location and the lay of the land around it. As I looked at the area, a strange feeling started to come over me. This was more than just a roadway. This was something the world had never seen before and was so far beyond our technology it staggers the imagination.

"Mr. Nash, what are we looking at anyway?"

I guess I must have spaced out or something because I had forgot the two assistants had accompanied me.

I turned to the two of them and then focused on Melanie. "Melanie, I'm not entirely sure, but I am sure about one thing, this is beyond anything anyone in this world has ever seen. And by the way, call me Joe."

She appeared to be even more puzzled after I had made the remarks. There was a look of disbelief on her face a small but noticeable down turn of the corners of her mouth. "Yes Sir. But, if it is a metal concrete, who made it and most of all how old is it?"

Actually, I was rather pleased with her response and expression. It told me this was a thinker and she was just what I needed. "That my dear Melanie is the big question of questions." I turned from her and walked onto the roadway and scrapped my boots along the surface. "Right now, we do not have the answers, but one thing I can assure you, this has changed the whole scope and process of this project. Let's get back to Mr. Davenport and Hammer I need to talk to them."

Twenty minutes later I entered Hammer's office and found Davenport there as well. Jennifer and Melanie had gone off to set up their schedules and expand the scope of my plan.

"What's up, Joe?"

I walked over by the fan that was running at full speed and stepped in front of it letting the air run up my shirt and around my body. "Well Stan, we need to talk."

He looked at me a second or two and sat back. "Have a seat and let's get talking." He said pointing at a chair.

I moved over and took the chair across the desk from Stan. Bob was sitting to my left. "Bob, Stan, you both probably know why I'm here?"

Stan looked over at Bob and then sat forward putting his elbows on the desk top. "Yes, we think we do."

I was looking at both of them with my hands pressed together and the tips of my fingers touching my lower lip. "You know these changes everything, don't you?"

It was obvious they were clearly up on what I was approaching them on. Stan nodded. "Joe, we were just talking about it, what are your feelings about this whole thing?"

With that I got up and walked over to the wall map. "I have just come back from the roadway site and after looking the terrain over I have determined we need to concentrate on the road and following it." I let that sink in before I continued. "Not just toward the object but to follow it away from that location as well. As I looked at the location, I noted there were no trees between the place where we found the road and the base of the mountain. That tells me the road continues on to the mountain and the location of the object." At this time, I was tracing the road location on the wall map and emphasizing the need to pursue the road.

I continued. "However, when I turned and looked east, I noted there were no trees growing in the area due east from where we first found it. I can almost assure you there is road there as well." I was now marking the locations on the map as I explained my ideas. "We need to know where it is coming from as much as we need to know where it is going to."

I paused long enough for them to take in what I had just said. "As we cleared the jungle off the road, we actually found a structure, a roadway, for all intent and purposes could have been built last year. The engineering of that road is beyond anything I have ever seen. There are no expansion joints in it either running length-wise or across the road. This thing was laid in one continuous pour, for how far I have no idea at this time. Hopefully we will be able to determine that once we clear the rest of it, wherever it goes.

"Right now, the road is the key to everything. Once we found it that changed everything." I had returned to my chair and sat down. "The makeup of the road is unlike anything I have ever seen or been involved with. This is our first major find and we need to pursue it to wherever it goes."

They sat there a few seconds and then Stan nodded his head. "Joe, Bob and I agree with your view point, but what about the object?"

That was the issue I needed to get straight with them. The object was our primary target, but sometimes you have to set the target aside while you're building a system that will bring you there from a different direction, and many times a much faster method overall. "Stan, it's not going anywhere. In fact, if we follow the road, we will eventually come to the object. My attitude about this is that we need to scale it out."

"Scale it out? What do you mean by that?"

"Stan, it's just a term I use when I'm ready to get something moving. I get amped up and want to see things start moving but moving in the right direction.

It was obvious I had lost Stan and probably Bob somewhere along the way. "So, you don't think we need to excavate everything as you first suggested."

"No, Stan, I mean we start from a different direction." I turned back to the map. "The topography here will dictate where we dig and it will be no different than what I projected. I am just saying we come at it from a different direction. Follow the road."

Chapter Two

ROADS AND BUGS

Over the next three days we moved our excavating equipment in to the area of the road. I continued to have the terrain around the area cleared and prepared for the major excavation job that would eventually come. But, for right now, we were going to concentrate on the road, in both directions.

We set up two teams, one working into or toward the mountains and the other working out or away from the mountains. Next, we set up the tracked equipment with rubber treads in order to protect the road's surface. The objective was to clear the road surface and a space thirty meters wide on both sides of the roadway.

Each excavation team had an engineer and an archeologist with them to observe and save any artifacts which may surface during the procedure. Melanie was assigned to oversee the whole of the progress of the excavation. Once the two teams were separated by a distance that was more than she could keep up with, we would assign a third assistant to me and that person would work one end of the excavation.

Working toward the mountains was progressing well until the terrain became steeper on the mountain side of the roadway. The sides of the excavation started to slide into the cleared areas. We had to widen the excavation to ensure the ground slippage would not become a major problem.

On the other hand, the outgoing team needed the services of the loggers again in order to clear out the trees and clear off the landscape of the undergrowth and loose rock on both sides of the road. Once set up and working it looked like a progressing caterpillar, each segment moving as the next progressed.

It was not long before the first of the artifacts started to show up, mostly in the form of tools, but some of the oddest-looking tools you have ever seen. And, to top it off, they were old. Not just old, but real old. Our metallurgists found the makeup of these tools was unlike anything on earth. On top of that, the application of the tools was a mystery as well. All in all, we had a pile of tools and objects and not the slightest idea as to what they were used for or how they were used.

I was beginning to have second thoughts about this whole situation. There was just a feeling we were not connecting with this place. It was a feeling there was something there waiting for us and I was not too sure I wanted to find out what it was.

The first structure was located two days later on the outbound road. When I got the report, they had just located the corner of a building of some kind and were in the process of setting up a full archeological dig on that sight. From the first contact it was clearly determined this was old beyond anything we had experienced. The structure was sitting just off the road, maybe nine meters or so. What we could see of it showed a squared corner that was sharp and precise and it was made of the same material as the road.

When I arrived at the scene Melanie was standing on the roadway directly out from the object. She was talking to one of the cat operators and shaking her head while pointing in the direction of the mountains. The operator was nodding and then left and returned to his cat and put it in reverse and backed down the road about fifty meters. Melanie looked over at me and smiled and walked over. She nodded her head in the direction of the cat. "He wanted to clear the area away from the object with his cat."

The team of scientists who were going to clear the area and reveal the object arrived and started setting up their equipment. Almost thirty minutes later they were ready and then approached the object.

Once they started the excavation of the corner, they determined it was not a structure at all, but appeared to be some kind of marker or something of that nature. It was a cube measuring exactly one meter on all sides and made of the metal concrete the road was made from. The only real difference was this cube had markings on it, markings that were unlike any found anywhere else in the world. It simply screamed old.

By this time, every scientist in the area had gathered at the cube and was starting to analyze the markings on it. As one of the scientists was walking around the cube, his shadow passed over its face and something amazing happened. The markings lit up. That's right. As soon as a shadow moved across the markings, they began to glow a light blue color. As soon as his shadow moved off the markings they went back to normal.

Almost within seconds, we had a tent up over the cube and darkened the interior of the tent completely. Every mark on the cube was lit up in a light blue color. When checked for temperature, there was none. The cube remained the same temperature with not a fraction of a degree change or variance. Also, the edges of the cube were absolutely perfect, not a chip or mark, almost like it had just been built and the forms taken away.

Something struck me in the back of my mind and I left the tent and started walking around the area and taking a close hard look at the ground and surrounding landscape. We were about three hundred meters from the location where we first discovered the road.

I turned to Lloyd, that is Lloyd Stapleton, one of the leading archeologists present. "Lloyd, I need you to start a dig across the road from the cube." I was pointing in the direction north of the cubes position. "If I am right, you will find a foundation or something related to a structure in that location."

Lloyd looked off in the direction I was pointing and then turned his gaze along the ground, across the road and to the cube. "How do you know that, Joe?"

"Lloyd if I am right, I believe the cube is a sign marker for the entrance to a construction site. I think I'm getting a feeling for this place and if this proves out then I know what our next step needs to be."

He nodded his head in understanding and immediately started to pulled together a half dozen people to carry out a survey of the area I had indicated and set up a grid system to start the excavation. Within four hours they hit pay dirt.

Lloyd called me and told me they had a foundation and for me to get there on the double. "Joe you were right, we have a port of entry station here or something similar." He was looking around at the ground and was clearly excited about the discovery. "How did you know?"

I walked over to the layout they had been working on and swung my arm in a half circle from the cube around toward the mountains and back to the layout. "Lloyd, it was the layout of this whole thing. It just screams construction. I will bet my bottom dollar the object underground is a tunneling machine."

Lloyd snapped his head around toward me, almost losing control and falling down. "How the hell can you stand there and based on the few things we have discovered make a quantum determination like that?"

It's kind of set me back and I had to quickly adjust my position and then explain it to him. "Relax, kick it down, it's my experience I am leaning on. I could clearly be wrong, but everything points to that scenario and besides I think I'm right.

"Lloyd, we need to expand our attack on this whole thing. I want to continue to follow the road toward the object and out and away from this location. Only now I want to expand our search and take two routes ninety degrees to the line of the road from the point of the cube. If I am right, we will find more markers and possibly indications of other artifacts."

About this time Stan, Bob and Terry pulled up. Stan was in the front passenger's seat and was the first one out of the car and walking toward me. "What's going on Joe?"

I walked toward the three of them and gestured back toward where Lloyd and his team had been working. "Stan, we have hit pay dirt and I mean that in capital letters. I have expanded our search in two more directions from the point of the cube and ninety degrees to the main road."

Bob and Terry were walking around the area between the road and layout where Lloyd and his team were working and taking a general look around. Stan stopped by me and was scanning the entire area. "Man, Joe, this is getting a little complex."

About then, Bob turned and walked back to the two of us and jumped in to the conversation. "We have to start considering a budget somewhere along the line."

You could see his accountant mind working as fast as he could make it go. "We may have to cut some of these activities in favor of targeting the object."

I started to shake my head. "Gentlemen, what is taking place here is so monumental we would be foolish to limit ourselves." I turned more toward Bob and continued. "We are working ourselves toward the object and we will reach it in due time. The importance of this road requires we pursue this route. I have a feeling there was one massive facility located here, just what, I don't really know."

I turned and pointed out the location of the cube and the new foundation we had just located. I then returned to the road. "We have been following the road away from the object and have found a port of entry gate and a cube which is clearly marked, but in a language, we have never seen or even resembles anything on earth."

Whether it is actually a port of entry is a guess on my part. "We have turned and added a third and fourth run and have already found the foundation of the port of entry building. No, we are not even close to over extending ourselves on this. We are just beginning."

I then turned directly at Stan and continued. "Stan, I do not expect the two new routes to pan out, but we must take a look anyway. I want to keep at the two main projects following the road out and in toward the object. Any background we can find will be helpful when we get to the object. Already, we have found a language we have people working on right now to try and interpret what it is saying, giving us a working guide when we reach the object."

I have to admit I was a little amped up on this project at this point, but I also knew we were working on something unique and earth shattering.

Stan turned and walked away from me toward the cube, where Bob and Terry were standing, and when he got to the edge of the road he stopped and turned back toward me "Joe, can I ask you one simple question before we continue on?"

I walked over to where Stan was standing. "Sure, what's your question?"

He looked around to make sure there was no one standing close by. "Are we dealing with an alien race here?"

When Stan asked that question Bob and Terry stepped over closer to Stan. At the same time, I had walked up to Stan. Both Bob and Terry were obviously surprised by the question Stan had asked.

How was I to answer it? I'm no expert in this area, I'm an engineer. "Right now, Stan, I cannot say for sure, but I have a strange feeling this is not alien to this planet, but originated here."

Good answer, I had no idea what I had just said and was really trying not to jump into a conclusion I could not support or knew nothing about.

By now Stan was starting to crank it up and I knew damn well he was serious. "Joe, this simply screams mystery, worry, fear and every other human emotion. If it is Earth original, then it is a society we have never heard of and one that appears to be advanced over us. How the hell can that be?"

Frankly I was starting to look around for someone else to dump this conversation on, but there was no one and so I forged ahead. "Again Stan, I can't say. All I can tell you is this is probably Earth originated. That is why we need to expand our search and reach out in every direction we receive evidence from. These roads and buildings were going somewhere for a reason. Again, we need to pursue it at this time."

He stood there looking at the ground and scrapping his foot through the dirt forming a small pile of dirt and then stepping on the middle of it and spreading it back out. "Yup, you're right."

Stan turned to Terry. "Terry, you need to get yourself back to your office and do your thing. Get them anything they need and keep it coming. I need to make a trip to Brasilia. The government needs to be filled in on this situation now."

I nodded in agreement with what he had just said and then added. "Stan, may I suggest you make a second trip to Georgetown, Guyana and fill them in as well. If I'm right, the road will cross into Guyana in short order."

He looked off toward the east and Guyana. "You really think so?"

I kept my eyes on Stan. "Well, its heading that way and it's only thirty-five kilometers from the foothills to the Guyana boarder. We are here as a representative of the United Nations and it is our responsibility to keep the political interests in this part of the world informed and aware of what is going on."

Stan was looking the area over and nodding his head in agreement to what I had just said. "The next question that needs to be asked is should we tell them everything or just a short cover story?"

I knew Stan was experienced in this area of political relations, but right now he seemed to be a little disjointed. My experience has taught me you lay it on the line, no bullshitting with those people in decision making positions that was only inviting trouble.

"Stan, I think you need to lay it all out. No secrets in this thing. Cover it all and give it to them straight."

"What if they deny us access to Guyana?"

What was going on here anyway? Stan was the man in charge and it was his responsibility to contact these leaders and brief them on our progress and here he was second guessing everything he should be doing. "Then you turn it over to the United Nations and let them do the trouble-shooting. Stan, come on, you're in charge here. You know what you need to do, so do it."

Stan turned and walked around the rig. "Yeah, you're right it's just that, with everything happening so fast I was just not concentrating. I'm going to leave the excavation to you and go do my job." He stopped and turned toward the others. "That goes for Bob and Terry as well. Got it guys? okay, let's get to our jobs and make this thing happen."

He then turned back to me. "Joe, please keep us all fully informed as you progress. I'm going to need that information as I deal with the powers to be down here."

Finally, I felt like we had just turned the page and things were finally falling in to place. "All right Stan, I'll have Jennifer set up an auto notification trailer for you guys and keep the information coming on a minute-by-minute basis. You'll be able to access all the data any time and any place. Work with Jennifer and she'll see the system is up and going before you leave this afternoon."

I turned to Jennifer and got her attention. "Jen, you got that?" She was already starting to bring up the briefing protocol and working on it.

She hardly looked up at me and nodded her head. "Will do, Joe."

I don't know if Jennifer liked my using the nickname, I had just given her, but for the time being that's the way it was going to be. She showed no sign of disliking it, so I left it at that.

Meanwhile, Melanie was working her way into the oversight position for the two new search routes. She walked over to me. "Joe, should I make my own decisions concerning issues as they come up or refer all of them to you?"

I turned toward her and saw she was almost asking as a matter-of-fact thing. She was looking at her laptop and holding her radio in the other hand. "Melanie, listen to me, I am up to my ears with decisions right now and the fewer I have referred to me the better." She had now turned her attention to me and what I was saying. "No, you go out there and run this project and get it done. You know our criteria and protocol. Do your job. Do it safe, but do it hard."

She smiled, "All right Joe." Then turned and walked away while taking her radio and called on the two teams working the new routes to get started. She would be overseeing all their activities and they were to call her directly if anything is found or any problems come up. I had a feeling the new routes were in good hands.

We were fully involved in tracking the two road directions and I needed to get back to the object site and take a closer look at the surrounding area. There was something stirring in me and I could not figure out what it was. I got in my rig and headed back up the road to the main dig area. As I got to the dig area and stopped, I got out of the truck and just stood there looking.

The road was located to the left on the southern side of the valley. Overall, the valley was a full one and a quarter kilometer wide at this point. The road ran the south side and up against the slope of the foothills in that area. As I looked across the valley to the other side, the first thing I noted was how flat it was. Then it dawned on me there appeared to be no water resources in this valley.

It is common for small streams to run down through these valleys and this had none. Also, it was common for these valleys to have terrain in them. By that I mean highs and lows, but it was flat as far as I could tell, except for the shallow gullies which ran across its mouth, strange.

The crews had managed to clear about two thirds of the valley floor by this time and still it had no signs of highs and lows. It was truly flat as a griddle. I walked across the cleared area to the logging crew superintendent. He saw me coming and started walking toward me. I signaled him to stay there and continued my walk to him. I was looking down at the ground and then it dawned on me.

The ground, what was it that was different with the ground? I stopped and stood there. The ground, there was something right there before me and I could not get a handle on it. I continued my walk over to the super.

As I approached him, he asked. "Do you see it too sir?"

I looked at him. "See what? I know there is something I am looking at but it is not registering for me. It's wrong. It's different. But I can't put a finger on it. What do you see?"

The superintendent swept his arm in a semi-circle. "There's no insect life in the soil."

It took several seconds for his comment to sink in. I stood there looking out across the valley and then down at my feet. How stupid could I be? "Damn, you're right. That's what I was seeing, well not seeing. Is it that way all over this area?"

He was scraping his foot over the ground. "Yes sir, so far there is not a single bug anywhere in this valley. Not one. On top of that there are none on the trees or in the branches. There are none flying around either."

All I could do was stand there and let it sink in. This was unheard of. I turned to him. "What's your name?"

"Larry, Sir, Larry Hanover."

I was now looking directly at him. "Well, Larry, when did you notice this anomaly?"

He was getting a little uncomfortable about this time. "Two days ago, Sir."

I looked down at the ground and dug my boot toe into the soil. "Why didn't you tell someone about it?"

There was a fairly long pause as he prepared to answer me. I had not made eye contact with him as yet, but it was about to come to that. As he spoke, I looked up at him. "I don't really know. I guess I thought they were missing because of the fast pace of the logging going on in the valley. It did not settle in until just about twenty minutes ago and then I saw you coming."

When he finished, I stood there looking the logging show over. "Okay, what do you think about this anyway?"

He was now standing there with his hands on his hips and looking off toward the mountains to our west. "I'm not sure. I have never seen anything like it before in my life and I've logged all over the world and the bugs are always there. I just have no idea as to why they are not here. Do you think it's significant?"

I took several steps away from him looking at the ground and then turned back to him. "Larry, we are standing on a unique piece of land here. I know of no land, except maybe that of a new lava flow that is as totally empty of insect life as this. A lava flow will have insects on it almost as soon as it cools down enough so they can walk and fly over it."

I walked back over to him and stopped beside him. "Significant? Yeah, this is more than that. How extensive is this lack of bugs and how long has it been this way?"

I was kind of pissed off a little with the fact Larry had not thought this significant enough to take some form of action. For that matter why had no one else recognized this? "Has anyone called for an entomologist to take a look at this?"

He repositioned himself. "No sir, at least I haven't called for any."

"Well, Larry don't you think maybe we had better take that step right now."

He nodded his head and pulled his radio out and made the call.

"Gees, no bugs!" All I could do was stand there and shake my head. I pulled my radio and called Melanie.

"Melanie, Joe here."

There was a pause and then she came

56

on line. She had to yell over the noise of the cats working in the background. "Yes Joe?"

"Kid, take a look around you and tell me what you see or don't see."

She came back to me immediately and seemed to be a little irritated. "First of all, I'm not a kid. Second, what do you mean take a look around?"

I decided to give her a halfway apology. "Okay, Melanie you're not a kid, sorry about that. Now, look at the ground and tell me what you see. Be analytical and look at everything. What don't you see?"

She was quiet for several seconds and then started telling me what she was doing. "Well, I see rocks, soil, some grass and bushes. I'm not sure what it is you want me to determine, but, wait a minute."

"Joe?"

"Yes?"

"No just a minute."

"Take your time Melanie, take your time."

I could just see her standing there and straining, trying to see what is not there and not yet realizing it. If this goes right, she should be responding in just about ten seconds, just about now.

"Bugs, I can't find any bugs. Joe, you get that?" Her voice was edgy and surprised at the same time.

"That's right Melanie, there are no bugs." I kept my voice calm and controlled.

I could tell she was in a state of excitement and puzzlement as well. "But, that's impossible. There has to be bugs. I hate bugs and there are none. Why didn't I see that right off the bat? No bugs, that's impossible. No bugs, not a single one anywhere."

There it was she had hit on the main concern I was having. No one recognized the fact there were no bugs and when they did, they acted as though it was no big deal. "What's getting me Melanie is that no one noticed it until now and they have been gone all the while we have been here. They have been gone for a long time. In fact, I would bet if we inspect the trees, we will find no evidence of them ever being here."

It got dead quiet from her end and I waited for her to respond. Finally, it came, subdued and fearful "Joe?"

"Yes, Melanie?"

She was clearly concerned and seemed to be taking each and every step in a careful and calculated manner. "Have you noticed there are no animals as well?" There was a pause. "Joe, as I was leaving Normandia, I noticed a lot of monkeys in the trees as we flew over them. And, there were birds all over the place. But, here, there are none. I have not seen a single bird or monkey anywhere, none."

I turned around and looked at the trees out beyond the staging area and there was nothing moving in them. The sky was empty there was nothing, not a bird, not a bug of any kind.

It was like a veil had been pulled away from my eyes. She was right there were no animals of any kind besides the bugs. This was unreal there was something really wrong here?

I called Terry and asked him. "Do we have anyone on site who was an expert on bugs an entomologist?"

It seemed like an hour before he responded. "What do we need an entomologist for?"

It was obvious he had not the slightest idea as to what was going on with the bugs and wildlife in this area. "Terry, how long have we been on site?"

By now he was sounding puzzled.

"About six weeks now Joe, why?"

I waited several seconds so that I could organize what I needed to ask. "Okay, and in all that time has anyone complained about bugs or seeing bugs?"

He was starting to figure something was going on. "I've received no complaints at any time about bugs."

He hadn't a clue as to what was going on in regards to the bugs and wildlife around here and that bothered me. Why had he not seen this before now, it was so obvious no one should have missed it? "Well Terry, that's because there are no bugs here."

I could almost feel his reaction. The line went quiet. I could almost see him sitting there trying to grasp what was being said. Finally, he replied. "Joe that's not possible. There have to be bugs. The world is covered with them." Again, there was a long pause. "Where are you at?"

That got his attention. "Terry, I'm at the end of the road toward the object with the logging supt.

It sounded like he was moving as fast as he could. "Wait for me there, I'm on my way."

Five minutes later, Terry pulled up and

got out of his rig. He was looking everywhere, the sky, and the ground, himself, on his car. He had a puzzled look on his face and a little tinge of fear in his eyes.

As he was walking up to me, he was looking right at me. "Joe, what's going on here?" He kept looking around the area straining to see that which was not there.

"I don't know, Terry, I don't know. There has to be a reason, but it simply escapes me right now. Let me ask you this question. Has anyone said anything about snakes in the time we have been here?"

He stood there thinking and looking at me. "No, not once."

That figured, no one recognized the absence of the obvious. "Well Terry, there are three hundred sixty-six species of snakes in Brazil, with fifty-six of them venomous. These forest lands should be full of them, but we have seen none and if we tried, I don't think we would find one either. If you walked these woods for the next week, you would not find a single one.

"And, what about the birds, monkeys, predators, and any other life form that is common to these forests? None of them are here. This land is completely empty of any living creature except plants and those of us here for this project. There aren't even any native humans anywhere near this place. Why the hell is that?"

Terry reached up and ran his hand through his hair. "That's where the stories are from." He turned looking at me with this expression of disbelief in his face.

That brought me around and I looked at him. "What do you mean, Terry, what stories?"

He stopped and brought his right hand up to his jaw. "Joe, there are local stories of a place where no living creature lives. This is said to be a forbidden place because it is cursed. As a result, no natives of this region will set foot into this area for any reason. It is off limits to everyone and anyone who values his or her life."

The questions were exploding in my mind. No one saw the absence of all living life forms in this area and the fact they were missing was obvious. Why the hell was that anyway? No, I was convinced there was more going on here than any of us could possibly think of. "Terry, I think we need a meeting, now."

Within an hour everyone was gathered

at the meeting room. Terry had me do the presentation and we had set up an internet link with Stan so he would be in on what we would be discussing.

"Okay everyone, listen up." It took a couple of minutes for everyone to calm down and concentrate on what we were doing. "About two hours ago something was brought to my attention that we all need to consider. It all began as I was going to the clear cut at the end of the road to the object.

As I walked across the ground, I started looking at the soil and it came to me there were no bugs. When I talked to the logging foreman, he told me he had noted that a day or two earlier, but was not sure if it was just an anomaly for the area he was in or something else."

I waited so that the meaning of my first statement could sink in with everyone. I then continued. "As we talked about it, we came to realize they had not seen any snakes as well, nor monkeys, nor any other animal other than those of us here working on this project.

There are no natives of any kind in this area either. This place is completely void of any living animal or insect-based life form of any kind. In addition, the local natives have designated this place off limits because there is no life here."

I again stopped and watched for their reactions to what I was telling them. I could see the realization starting to register on their faces.

The reaction moved across the room and then people started looking around at one another trying to come to grips with the reality of what I had just said. I then continued. "A bunch of scientist and not one of us made the link that all living life forms, other than plants, were absent from this area. For how far out from this valley that goes, I don't know, but somehow, we missed this most obvious of events and I want to know why."

"Joe, Stan here. Are you trying to say that somehow something kept us from observing that fact?"

I was watching the people in the room react as Stan asked that question. "Stan, I think you expressed it just right. I don't think it was a failure on our part. These people are too talented to fail to see something as obvious as this. No something had to be influencing us. I don't know what, but there is something more involved going on here in this place and we need to determine what it was before we get to that object."

"I agree Joe. Is it your opinion we need to pull another team together to go after that issue?"

I was concentrating on Stan's question at this time. "Stan, we need to put together a blue-ribbon team with top priority to pursue this issue and do it now. I have no doubt there is an influence here which may or may not be hazardous to us. We need to answer this question and it needs to be done stat.

"In addition, I want that team to make a determination if any of our personnel are experiencing any health or mental problems, they were not aware of or had prior to coming on scene here. If there is an influence in this place it could well impact us physically or mentally."

"All right Joe, I think you're right."

"Bob."

"Yes, Stan."

Stan then laid it out. "You see to it that a team is formed. If we do not have all the right disciplines present to pursue this issue, then get them here by tomorrow this time. Put that team on this issue full time and keep Joe and me in the loop as they address this issue.

Got that?"

"Got it, Stan."

Stan continued. "Joe, do you think we should hold up on our excavations or continue on?"

Good question and right down my line. I am a go-for-it personality and I wanted to keep pushing ahead. "Right now, I think we can continue on, Stan. There has been no adverse effect from this issue as of yet and there have been no indications there will be resistance to our pursuing our objectives. No, we need to continue on with the project."

Stan paused. "Okay, we'll do that, but be ready to stop and clear out if the team comes up with anything adverse or problematic."

"I agree Stan. How about you Bob?"

"Got it, Joe"

Bob then turned to the meeting. "Okay everyone, we need anyone who feels they would be of assistance on the research team dealing with this issue to step forward and join the team. In addition, if there is anyone you know or have heard of who would fit into this team, please advise us so we can bring them on board. Everyone else will return to their regular duties and continue on with your projects until further notice any questions?"

Within minutes five people stepped up and advised they felt they would be a benefit to the research team. Each was asked to give their first impressions as to the reason for this anomaly. All five fit in well and were transferred to the research team.

One name was brought up by the group. It was a member of the faculty at MIT by the name of Herman Blumfield. This was passed to Terry and he set to work on bringing Professor Blumfield on board. Terry did the research on Professor Blumfield and upon seeing his qualifications Terry was certain he was of major importance to this research team.

He then contacted Stan and myself and advised us he would be tapping Professor Blumfield for this job, but we had better be ready to receive a rather pissed off and ready to fight man when he got here. Going through the White House to have someone drafted into this project was not that pleasant an experience.

The process was rather unique. Terry called the office of the President of the United States and advised them of the need. A Presidential order was then issued and a team of secret service agents were sent to the professor's office and home and when they found him, he was, more or less, kidnapped and shipped off to us.

There was no ceremony or special invitation. The fact was he had no choice. One minute the poor guy was sitting at home reading a book and the next minute he was being hauled to a car and driven away his wife standing on the steps wondering just what the hell he had done.

Meanwhile, the secret service is man handling him out of their car and on to a plane and not telling him anything about what was going on and why. He even took a swing at one of them as they were moving him.

Professor Blumfield kept asking. "Where am I going and who are you?"

"Mr. Blumfield, please, we are the secret service and we have Presidential orders to take you into custody and deliver you to a designated place by a designated time. We have no choice and you certainly have no choice, so please try to relax and cooperate. In time you will be informed of the whys and wherefores of this trip."

The professor was still not buying it and continued to demand more information.

Then he asked. "But, what about my wife?"

The agent in charge was doing his best to ease his mind. "We are certain you will be able to contact your wife and explain everything to her when you get to your destination. Please understand this is a national emergency. Presidential orders of this kind do not happen just by accident. They are specific and they are strict and require us to act with speed and deliberateness."

By five o'clock the next morning Professor Blumfield was standing in front of the main tent wondering what had just happened. As I walked up to him, he looked at me with the look of a man just about ready to let loose with everything he could muster up. "Who the hell are you?"

I took special measures to remain calm and matter of fact as I answered his questions. "Professor Blumfield my name is Joe Nash. I am in charge of a good part of this program you have been brought into. I welcome you to it."

"What do you mean 'Welcome me to it'? Who the hell do you think you are bringing me here this way?" His voice was sharp and most degrading.

This guy was mad, not just mad, he was

69

mad as hell and I knew I would be spending a good part of the forenoon and possibly the afternoon trying to calm him and answer his questions. "I'm sorry sir, I can see you're really amped up by the methods used, but they were beyond my control. You're here by a direct Presidential order and there is nothing I can do about it."

All I could do at that point was try and help him deal with his change of scenery.

"However, I can inform you as to what is going on here and why you find yourself here. Perhaps this will help you in dealing with the sudden change that has taken place. If you would follow me, I'll explain everything to you."

He stood there looking at me like he wanted to say something else and then just shrugged his shoulders. "Well, all right, but I'm still mad as Hell."

"Professor Blumfield, I understand."

I gave the professor everything we had done, seen and heard up to that moment in time and the setting up of the research team to work on the anomaly we had identified and brought him there for. When I was done, he sat there and looked over the data again and then leaned back and looked at me.

He sat back up and looked the data over for a few more minutes and then sat back and looked at me again. "How long have you been working this site?"

"We've been here approaching eight weeks now and each day something new pops up." I was trying to get him to see the importance of his being here. "We could really use your help."

I was trying to be as sincere as I could and not make it look like I was begging. Truth was I was begging.

"All right I'm with you on this. I'm still not totally happy because of what this is doing to my wife. Before we do anything, I would like to call her and let her know that I am all right."

Crap, I totally forgot that. I should have addressed that issue before everything else. I pulled out my phone. "Professor, here is my phone and please take as long to talk to her as you want. The only caution I have is you cannot tell her where you are or what you are doing. You can advise her you are not allowed to give her that information and you will keep her informed as to how you're doing while you're here."

He looked at me with a rather obvious

smirk on his face. "I understand Mr. Nash. I've been on these ventures before. It's just that I never came into one quite this way before."

Almost fifty-seven minutes later, Herman bid his wife goodbye. "That is the one thing I will find it hard to forgive, the way they took me and what it did to her. Someday I'll have the opportunity to look someone in the face and tell them what I think of them."

I couldn't imagine how it had felt for both of them. "Herman, I'll see that you get that opportunity."

With that done he handed the phone back to me and stood up. "Thanks Joe. I think I'm all right now. I'm calming down and the anger is just about spent. I am ready to shift back to the scientific mode I was brought here for. I can see the magnitude of the project. I'm pleased to be a part of it. Where do you want me?"

I felt the relief wash over me and Herman finally set his anger aside and redirected his efforts toward the project.

"First of all, Herman I would like to take you on a tour of the project so you can have an overall picture of what is going on here. We will start at the original excavation site and then move on from there."

"That sounds good to me."

As we toured the area, he became more and more interested in the overall project and, in particular, the anomaly that had brought him here. When he saw the land and its absence of any insects or other living creatures, he knew something special was going on in this place.

"The land is never void of creatures of this Earth, Joe. If it is then it must be for a reason. Either the land is poisoned or something else is happening. Can you answer me this? Do you know how long the land had been void of insects?"

"Herman, we can't give you a true number, but it appears they have never been in this place for as far back as the geology tells us. It appears to be millenniums."

He turned to me and started to shake his head. "Mr. Nash, you have got to be kidding."

It turned out the Professor always got formal when he was stressed or surprised.

"No, Professor, I am not. By the way, please call me Joe and I'll call you Herman. No formalities here."

"Okay, Joe, continue please."

"Herman the soil appears to be void of any indication of insect or any other biological life forms. On the other hand, the soil is rich and well suited for plant growth. The forest here is well established and healthy and strong. Does that give you any ideas?"

He was pursing his lips as I related our activities to him. "Yes, it does. It tells me we are dealing with a unique and special situation that has never been seen or experienced in all recorded history. Right off the bat it leads me to a unique theory that appears to fit all the data to date."

"And what is that?"

"From first look Joe I would say the Earth was home to another time and occupation by another race of beings. Another time before the first humans of this time even walked the face of the Earth. Another time which came before all else we know of, and for some reason was destroyed and then erased from the world before we came on the scene."

That got my attention. "God, Herman that is one hell of a theory."

He smiled a sly and knowing smile. "I know, but it fits all the data we have seen so far. My friend we are on the verge of a discovery that will change the entire human race from now on. Not only that, it will tell us we are not unique and we are but another line in a series of other times and cultures. How many, I have no idea.

"All this was before the Cenozoic and Phanerozoic periods and may well have been as far back as the Proterozoic period. This happened so far back in time the whole face of the earth has changed."

He was making a good logical story, but I still felt he was jumping the gun and we did not have that much evidences to support what he was saying. "But, how did this survive."

"This was here at the end of the prior civilizations presence and as a result their facility stood the time."

"Well, I don't know, Herman, but we will see. Theories are theories, you know and any little thing can disprove them at any time. I guess when all else is considered, this is well before anything or any consideration of current man was evident.

"And, that brings up another point. How can a prior culture exist and then be so completely destroyed there is nothing left of them, not one single stone or mark on the face of this world? Yet, it appears they were well advanced and may well have been here for many millions of years. It's almost impossible to tell."

"Hopefully Joe we will find evidence that will clarify everything for us.

"It appears the mere presence of this mountain range was the key that explains the longevity of this place. When mountains reach this age, they are really rather stable, and unless the whole of the face of the world goes through a full reconfiguration, they will remain as they are, slowly eroding over time.

"Even the changes of the continents would not significantly impact this region. Pangaea and its break up would not touch this region. No, this has been a stable region for millenniums and that is the key to our being here.

"This place is not just old Joe this place is old beyond anything we could ever imagine. This place will stretch our souls to try and come to an understanding of it. Joe I just feel those who left this place where wise beyond our level of understanding by hundreds of thousands of years, if not millions."

Chapter Three

ROAD TO THE CUBE

Well, let's see where we're at. We have found a road on the south side of a small valley about one and half kilometers wide, the valley that is. We started the excavation of the road in both directions, toward the object and away from it.

We then found a cube made of the same substance as the road. It appears to be a combination of concrete and metal (metalcrete), the makeup of the metal is still unknown at this time. The cube was one meter on all sides and had markings which illuminated when darkness hit it.

We started an excavation at ninety degrees to the road and headed both north and south. On the north side, across from the cube, we found the foundation for a small building thought to be a gate house or port of entry building of some kind. This led me to believe this was a boundary of some kind which had been placed around or across the valley to restrict access to the construction site or the valley itself.

Finally, we had determined there was no insect life or any other forms of life living within the boundary area. The fact that no living matter, other than plant life, was in this area caused us a high degree of concern. As a result of this concern, we brought in a new team of researcher led by noted MIT Professor Herman Blumfield. The team had just started its work to try and determine the cause and effect of this anomaly.

I ordered the continued excavation of the road toward and away from the object, and the two new north and south bound jobs. For the next two days nothing seemed to change as far as the environment was concerned. Weather had not changed it was just as hot now as it had been. We still had late afternoon rain and balmy nights.

I was beginning to feel comfortable in the whole situation when I got a call. It was from Melanie. "Joe."

"Yeah, Melanie, what's up?" I was standing outside the maintenance shed talking to the foreman.

"Joe, you better get down to the road excavation moving toward the object. You better get here as soon as possible." I had never heard Melanie's voice sound like that. It was subdued with a rather high level of shock. She was definitely under heavy stress.

I turned and walked away from the foreman and lowered my voice. "What's going on?"

She paused. "I better not talk about it this way. Just get here and get here fast."

The distance from the maintenance shop and the spot where she was at was just under a kilometer. As I came sliding to a stop at the excavation, Melanie and the two equipment operators were standing by the back end of the big D-9 cat. When I saw her face, I knew there was something really bad in store for me. As I walked up to her, my eyes fell on the ground just past where she was standing. All I saw were his legs. The rest of his body was under the treads of the caterpillar. It stopped me dead in my tracks.

Next thing I knew you could hear me

yelling at her, the anger was blasting into and through me. "God, how did this happen? Who the hell screwed up?"

Melanie lowered her head and started walking straight at me. She raised both of her hands and started waving them at me. "Joe, hold off. This is not what you think." She was like a bulldog coming at me.

By now my face was flushed and my eyes were like pointed spears zeroed in right on her. "Melanie what the hell do you know what I think?" I could see my words hitting her, but she held her ground and kept coming at me.

She walked right up to me just inches away from my chest, standing on her toes and forcing her face right into mine. "You think this was a work site accident and we're here to tell you it is not." Her eyes were hard as nails as she stood there waiting for what she had said to sink into my brain.

That stopped me again. I held both my hands out and shrugged my shoulders. "Then what else could it be for crying out loud?" I was still yelling.

She stood her ground and in a soft and direct voice said. "Suicide, Joe it's a suicide."

I felt the anger wash out of me and that

was followed by an overwhelming sense of fatigue. "No way!"

She stepped back and took a deep breath. "Joe, it was witnessed by four people. They all saw it happen and all said the same thing."

By this time, she was walking in a small circle with her right hand on her forehead. "This man was out here spotting for the cat driver. He was over there where his hat is laying, clearly nine meters clear of the cat. Then for no reason, he took off his hard hat, set it down on the ground and walked over in front of the cat and lay down in front of the treads. The driver lost view of him and tried to stop, but by the time he did, it was too late."

Melanie looked over at the man and then back at me while pointing at his body. "Joe that man literally walked over to the machine and lay down in front of those tracks. The witnesses stated he never made a sound. It was that quick. In talking to them, each one said there had been no indications of a problem."

She was still walking back and forth while telling me about what had happened. "This man was newly married and was

81

excited about having the opportunity to work on this project. He ate well this morning and was okay and having a great time. There was nothing to indicate a problem. He was doing his job spotting for the cat driver and then walked over and laid down under the tracks and that was it."

If what Melanie was telling me was actually fact, then there was something really dangerous going on here. "Why would a young man do something like that?"

By this time, I felt like someone had used me for a punching bag. I could hardly think let alone talk. "Okay, let's stop right here. Lay this thing out for me. The cat was sitting exactly where it's at right now. Where were the victim and everyone else working this area? Let's place markers in each place. I want to see a clear and accurate layout of the place just before the accident happened."

If we were to understand what happened we had to know exactly what took place second by second. We were going to be answering a lot of questions on this one and we had better be ready for them and the answers had better be correct.

As the markers were being placed, I walked to the center of the excavation site so I could get a good overall view of the area. Each marker started to tell me a story as they were placed. As it turned out the victim was the closest person to the location of the object we're excavating toward. No one else was closer than eight meters to the victim and away from the object's location. I immediately closed the site down.

I waved at Melanie and motioned her over to me. As she walked up to me, I reached out and put my hand on her left shoulder. "Melanie, he was the closest person to the site where the object is buried, that may be the key. Get the research team in here now. They need to see this layout and see if they can discern any anomalies that could be linked to this death.

"Let's get that man out of there and off to the medical facilities. I want a complete autopsy of him, top to bottom. I don't want any shortcuts on this one. They have to cover everything they can think of."

There was little else I could do at that point in time. Melanie and the scientist who had been with her were doing the layout and measurements and a medical team had arrived and were removing the body.

I walked back to my truck and when I

got in to the truck, I remembered I needed to get a hold of Stan and fill him in, and it needed to be done now.

I left the area in Melanie's hands and headed back to Bob's office. I filled Bob in on the situation and then in his presence called Stan. He took it hard. He knew the young man who had been killed. I then filled both of them in on what I felt and was thinking.

"Look guys, we are working with a huge unknown here. After finding the road, then the cube and the foundation, I'm a little more than worried about what is going on here. We have no animal or insect life, so that tells me this environment is hostile to us. How? I don't know, but there is something wrong, and we need to find out what it is before we move on."

I paused trying to get my thoughts together so I could continue. The others stood by as I got organized. There was a heavy feeling in Bob's office. I really did not want to be here and I surely did not like the idea of talking about that boy's death.

"Stan, Bob, I've closed the excavation toward the object down for the time being. I think we need to keep going on the other three excavations. They may tell us what we are facing or at least give us some clues in that direction. Are there any objections?" I sat there waiting for Bob or Stan to say something. Both were silent.

It lasted for maybe fifteen seconds when Bob started to talk. "Stan, Joe, we have a time issue as well. We need to get into that object as soon as possible. There needs to be some results from the money we have spent so far. Any delays could be hazardous to the whole of the project."

Finally, Stan spoke up. "Bob, I agree, but I also think Joe is right on this one. This death is not normal. It is so out of character I'm worried to the extreme. No, we'll go with Joe on this. The excavation toward the object is on hold until the research team can come up with something that will give us assurance there is no unknown hazard facing our personnel."

Bob was nodding his head in agreement. "Okay, Stan. We're with you on this. I'll give Joe everything he needs to move along on the other jobs. The research team is already on scene and digging into the situation. We'll keep you notified as things develop."

I could pick up on the emotions Stan

was feeling. "Thanks Bob, I'll be back there sometime within the next forty-eight hours."

"Got you, Stan, we'll keep you informed."

Bob cut the connection and turned to me. "Okay, Joe, it's all yours. What can I do to help?"

I can tell you here and now I was emotionally spent after that session with Stan and Bob. Those events are few and far between, but they wring you out. "You have already, Bob. I'll stay on top of this and let you know if and when anything comes up. Will you advise Terry of the change in plans?"

Bob was clearly having a hard time with the loss of our man but he was also nodding his head toward me. "Yeah, I'll let him know. Do you want the cat left at the scene or can we move it to the staging area?"

I couldn't think of any reason to keep the cat there and felt it would really help if it was out of there. "Go ahead and move it, we have it marked for future reference."

As I got back to the death site, I saw the research team setting up an array of instruments and surveying equipment. Herman was in the thick of things when I pulled up. We met half way between my truck and the team. "Hi, Herman, how's it going?"

Herman was writing something in his note pad as he walked up to me. He finished and placed the pen inside the book and closed it and placed it in his jacket pocket. "Going fine Joe, we have marked off the position of the victim and have set the area beyond as a no man's zone. We don't want anyone venturing beyond that point until we know it is safe." Herman was pointing at each position and area as he filled me in on their progress.

He then turned to me. "Joe, the team was talking as we started to set things up. It came to us the cube found on the road may be a part of this overall situation." He then looked over at one of the crew members as he was trying to calibrate an instrument, "just a minute Joe."

He walked over to the man and helped set the instrument up and then returned to me and started where he left off. "We came to our conclusion because of the markings on it and the way it reacted to darkness. We think it's not just an informational sign, but it's a warning sign."

"Warning sign?" I looked at Herman and knew immediately they had hit on something big. Damn, why hadn't I thought of that? Of course, it was. It had to be.

I stood there looking off toward the mountains. "Okay, the sign is yours. Do you want it here or should we leave it there?"

He shook his head. "Leave it there and we will work a crew over to it. We want those who have been working on it to remain and assist in our observations."

"You have it."

I started to walk away and then stopped and turned back to Herman. I found myself searching for the right words that would emphasize what I was trying to relate to him. "Herman, this is big. Do you understand? We are dealing with an unknown here that is beyond anything we have faced anywhere on Earth."

I had my right hand gripped into a fist as I tried to emphasize my feelings. "I don't know how, but this thing is from a time before our current history of the world. Our world is something like four and a half billion years old. Who knows how many civilizations have lived and then vanished over that time?"

Herman followed me toward my truck. "Joe, that is all speculation right now, we have nothing that even so much as hints to that theory."

I nodded and held my ground. "I know, but you were right when you mentioned it in our general discussion. I think you're right on this whole thing. I'm a logical man and this is my own logic talking, but it's a theory which fits everything we have seen to date. I think this is all terrestrial and not alien. I just feel it. Don't ask me how and why, I just feel it."

Just then, one of the researchers ran over to us. "Herman."

Herman turned to him. "Yes, Larry?"

Larry looked to be a little excited about something. "Herman, we need to move everyone back."

Herman could tell Larry was concerned. "What do you mean?"

Larry was looking back in the direction he came from and I could see both his hands were shaking. "We started our instruments and started getting these readings. They are strange as hell and coming on strong. Herman, the front edge of those readings is moving toward us, out from the object. We have no idea as to what they can do to us or how they can affect us. With that we need to move back so we can figure this out." There was an edge of panic in his voice.

Herman slowed everything down. "How fast is it moving?"

Larry stopped and focused, he seemed to relax at that point. "Not too fast, maybe six-tenths of a meter an hour, but they are moving outward."

Herman smiled at Larry and then turned to me. "Joe, you got that?"

"Yeah, I do, but how far back should we move?"

"My suggestion is back to the cube."

I looked around the area and noted the others were moving away from the object area and then agreed. "Back to the cube it is."

With that, the excavation site was closed back to the cube and everyone repositioned there. I then advised Bob and Terry of the move and the findings of the research team. One look at Herman and I knew this was not an insignificant situation. This was big time trouble and I knew it.

The following morning when I returned, I found the tent around the cube had been removed. Herman was standing on the east side of the cube looking at a pack of data on his computer.

I parked, got out of the truck and walked up to him. "Hi Herman, what's up?"

Herman looked up at me and then back to his computer and then said in a rather subdues manner. "Well, Joe, we have had a rather interesting night here."

I had noted the tent was down and had not remembered anyone saying they were going to take it down. "Why did you take the tent down?"

He looked over at the tent laying there on the ground in a rather unorganized pile. "We didn't. It came down all by itself. No, that's not right. It was thrown off the cube by a force we could not measure or feel."

He then nodded his head toward the cube. "As you can see, the cube is lit up bright red at this time."

My mind just took off. *'Red' No it had not been red before it had been blue, but what would cause it to be that way?* "Wait a minute it was blue before. What caused it to go red?"

Herman looked back at me and shrugged his shoulders. "Joe, if I were to guess, we caused it to go red. And you know what red means."

I felt my eyes get large and a chill run down my back. "Yeah, stop."

"Joe, if I were to guess I would say the cube is restraining itself." He still had that flat emotionless tone to his voice. "I have no idea why and for what reason, but for all intent and purposes, that thing is resisting getting physical with us."

Just then my temper flashed. "That, Mr. Blumfield, is a bunch of bull. That thing killed one of our people. That thing is as dangerous a piece of whatever I have ever seen. That thing is also the key to this whole mess and we have to figure it out one way or the other."

Herman turned away from me and stood there looking at the cube. "Joe, I agree, but it does not mean it is not restraining itself." He turned back to me and raised his hands. "Look how it killed that boy. It could have blown half this operation away in one blast, but it tried to push us away. It did not know how we would react to its actions and now it does."

I was not yet buying his argument, but I knew the more we talked the closer we got to an answer. "Herman, can you determine when the cube turned red?"

"I don't know. It was red when we got here. Let's check with the other team and see if they recorded it action."

When the team was assigned primary

responsibility of the cubes analysis was checked they advised they had been viewing the cube when it went red. The time was exactly three twenty-five yesterday afternoon. The whole place went quiet.

I looked at Herman and the look on his face said it all. "The death took place around three twenty-five yesterday afternoon. There is a connection."

Herman turned and looked at the cube. "Okay this is our target. Bring everything we have to bear on that cube. I want every measurement possibly made of that thing."

"Herman, do we know where we're at with the interpretation of those markings?"

"We don't know Joe, but we'll get that team here as well."

"Okay, I want everyone to gather round, I'm going to set up a large tent right here by the road east of the cube. I want everyone who has had anything to do with that object in the tent no less than ten minutes after it is up. By everyone, I mean everyone, the crews who found it, those who cleaned it, and so on."

Within an hour everyone was present in the newly raised tent. Dr. Blumfield started the discussion and led the program.

Everything we had and everyone we felt could aid and assist in the deciphering of the cube was there and ready to work. It was the cube. That was the key to everything here.

As people moved around finding chairs and getting their laptops ready, I thought back to the first time we saw the cube. At the time we saw no colors until after we had cleared the underbrush away. In fact, nothing showed up until someone's shadow passed across the cube. Until then we had been moving around this thing for maybe an hour and it had done nothing. It wasn't the shadow; it was something else that woke it up or initiated its activation.

I walked over to Herman and took him aside. "Herman, I've been thinking about the first day when we found this thing. Once it was cleared of any covering, we were working around it for maybe an hour before the lights came on. We thought at the time it was caused by a shadow of one of the people who triggered it, but I don't think so now. Something else triggered it and we need to know what that something was."

Herman was nodding his head as I finished advising him of the event.

"One other thing, I've been running

around here guessing about a lot of things, and right now I think I'm all wrong about everything. I took a simplistic attitude toward this whole mess and it has hurt everything we have done. I personally am beginning to take this fatality as my responsibility. I should have looked harder at what we were doing and finding and I didn't. The end result was a man's death.

"The technology behind this place is way the hell out of our domain. That thing is so far beyond us it's pitiful. That should have been a warning to us, but we failed to see it. We came in here like a bunch of kids finding a new toy and did not pay attention to what we were really walking into. I take full responsibility for my part in this and it was a big part.

"If after this meeting is over and it is felt I should be replaced, I will have no problem resigning. My most sincere concern is for the project, but even more important is for the welfare of these people. It's now one lost and it can't get any worse. So, I'm not looking for a scapegoat situation here, but if you read the general consensus is someone else should be in charge of this project, I will back out and leave the project."

Herman shook his head and turned toward me. He had a stern look on his face and then looked directly into my eyes. "Joe, we're not going to have that here. Every point in this project has been reviewed and discussed by everyone before we moved. You have held nothing back from anyone and everyone knew what we were going to do before we took the next step. What we don't need at this time is a quitting attitude from anyone especially you, got me."

I should have known you never under estimate a mild-mannered scientist. This he was not. "Right Herman and thanks."

It measured exactly one meter on all six sides, not a fraction of a meter less or more. It was metallic gray in color, but was clearly made with concrete and a metal substance.

The four vertical sides had markings of some unknown language on them and when it turned dark, the markings would appear with a light blue light. When a light passed over it the lighting would go off and return when it was dark again.

The top of the cube was flat with no marking or anything else on its surface. To the touch it was smooth as glass and even in temperature. The edges were sharp and true with no damage what-so-ever. You would think after being in the ground throughout this time, however long it was, there would be some kind of wear and tear, but there was not. It was in perfect condition on all sides.

At this point, no attempt had been made to move the cube. Everything that had been done had been by observation and measurements and no physical attempt to move it had taken place. Then why had its lighting turned red?

Everyone, a total of twenty-three people stood there looking at this thing, wondering what to do next. If we tried to move it, would it initiate something? An explosion, some kind of defensive weapon, or cause the effects that killed the worker to spread out and hit us all. Everyone stood there looking at the damn thing.

Someone finally said. "What the hell, let's move it."

It was like someone had hit a button, everyone started moving all at once. About ten of them walked right up to the cube and grabbed hold and tried to slide it from its position, nothing. Next, they looped a rope around it and tied it to a jeep and tried to pull it, nothing.

Someone brought a long metal bar with a large piece of wood and stuck the bar under the bottom of the cube and placed the wood against the bar and then tried to pry it up, nothing.

Finally, after a number of attempts, everyone stepped back and stood there looking at it. About this time Herman stepped forward and placed both of his hands on the top of the cube about twenty centimeters apart and leaned over the cube. He was just looking at it when the lighted markings changed from red to amber.

All you could hear was gasps as everyone sucked in at the same time. Immediately, he stepped back and then turned looking straight at the group. "The other day at three twenty-five, what were you doing around this cube? Come on I need to know everything. Was anyone touching that cube?" He was looking at everyone and waiting for a response.

"Listen people we need to know. If you're thinking you may have been responsible for that man's death, get that out of your mind. You were not. We are working with unknowns here and anything we do that result in anything else happening is vital to our understanding of what is going on here. Now, did anyone touch that cube around that time?"

The team leader on the cube research stepped forward. "Yes, we were just then trying to determine the type of light the cube was emitting. Only one of the team members touched the cube. She did that with her left hand and was placing the scope over one of the markings to make the measurement. By our records it was the exact time of the incident. When it happened, the light blue light changed to red."

"Okay, will you recreate your activity again right now? The light is currently amber, we have no idea as to how to get it back to the light blue, so we will have to run with it this way."

The young lady stepped up to the cube and positioned herself by it and placed her hand on the cube and then placed the scope over the exact marking she had done before. Almost instantly the lighting changed to red. She slowly backed off and then stopped turned and walked to the back of the group.

It was several minutes later they got word of the man's death. They were not sure if their actions had anything to do with the incident, but they knew it probably was not a coincidence. They certified all their records and made sure the video tapes were pulled and sealed at that time.

Herman then stood there looking at the cube and turned to the team leader. "Okay, let's look at the tapes."

When they ran the tapes, they showed just what she had done before. There was no difference in her action except the lights were blue at the time and then went red.

Herman then walked over to the cube and placed his hand in the same position he had done before and the red light changed to amber instantly. Everyone looked around at one another.

Herman was the first to say anything. "It's an actuator, a switch. And, I would bet it's a security switch."

I couldn't help myself; this was just plain dumb. We were swimming in the dark and heading for a waterfall and I was beginning to think we would never see it in time. "But what the hell is it activating?"

Herman could tell I was more frustrated than curious. "Joe, it's activating a defensive mechanism. What happened to that man was a defensive reaction by the cube and its duty to the construction site or the object we are working toward."

I was finding it hard to believe anything by that time and for the sake of the argument and the team I cooled down. "All right, I can accept that, but Herman, as we play with this thing, what is happening in the area where the accident took place. Do the readings change out there and if so, how?"

Herman was standing there looking at the cube as I was asking the questions. "We will need to do these tests all over again while we're monitoring the area beyond the cube. We now know, well let me rephrase that, we think we know what the cube is doing and the markings on it are probably in regards to a warning system for anyone venturing beyond that point when the lights are red. This is a security system designed to protect the operation from outside influences. So, we start the test all over again after we set up our monitors."

I walked over and sat down on the edge of the roadway and watched the scientists carry out their testing. Everything went just as it did before, so I was sure we were on the right track as far as the purpose of the cube was concerned. What was eating away at the back of my brain was what else would set this thing off and how many more could die as a result of it.

The results of the test confirmed our belief about the cube, when activated it set the system into a defensive mode and the worker who died was the closest to the initiation and the first to die. We now knew the cube was an activity controller and we could not be in the area unless it was in the blue mode, but how to get it back to the blue mode? That was the question.

Herman was the one who came up with the solution. It was simple oh so simple. "Joe let's call it a day and set the cube's position as the boundary until tomorrow morning. No one is to enter the area beyond the cube until we have completed our study in the morning. Let's leave everything as is and see what happens over the next few hours."

That seemed reasonable to me so I gave the order and the area was secured. The cube was left as is and everyone returned to the main base for supper and then a sit down in order to take a long hard look at the data they had collected so far.

As I woke up the next morning, I thought about the two days before and the death of one of our people. At the end of the day, we had determined the cube was involved in the event and it had gone red light when the investigative team working on it tried to determine the type and source of the light the cube generated.

Dr. Blumfield accidentally changed the light from red to amber when he leaned over the cube and placed both of his hands on the top surface of the cube. We recreated these events and they repeated just as before. It appeared we had found the problem and had also come up with a way to continue the excavation of the road to the object.

Whether the cube was blue or amber this morning I had already decided we would resume the work on that part of the project. What still needed to be done was to try and determine what the field being produced did to cause someone to commit suicide and where was it being generated.

What kind of a discharge could cause a person to do what that man did? Obviously, the cube came from a far more advanced society than anything we had come to learn of. The feeling right then was this society was an Earth based society, but it had been here way before the dawn of time. That time recorded by the current occupants of the Earth. It was a puzzle needing to be solved before we got to the object. If we failed to do that, it could cost us dearly.

As I walked in to the dining hall, I spotted Dr. Blumfield, Herman, sitting at a table and headed for him. On the way I grabbed a cup of coffee and a doughnut and then moved on to the chair across the table from him.

He was working on a dish of scrambled eggs and bacon and reading a book, the title of which I could not see. "Hi, Herman, what goes?"

He set the book down and looked up at me. "Morning, Joe. Well not much, oh, I dropped by the cube on my way here this morning and the light when a shadow passes over it comes on blue."

He had said that so nonchalantly it almost got by me. "What?"

He continued to eat his breakfast and affirmed what he had said. "Yeah, it was blue this morning."

I was stunned and had no come back of any kind that would make sense. "Damn, that thing is driving me nuts."

Herman shrugged his shoulder. "Joe,

it's a traffic controller."

I was still out of it. For some reason what he was saying was not making it through my head. "What?"

He finally leaned toward me and looked me straight in the eyes. "I said it's a traffic controller, well not really, but that is the way it is working.

"Look, Joe, we don't want to make this too simplistic, but we know it is a defense system and now we know how. When it discerns a risk, it stops all activity and initiates the defense system." He was drawing his discussion out on the table top at the same time. "The thing that keyed it yesterday was the actions of the investigative team. I'm not blaming them, I'm simply stating as they conducted their investigation, their activity fired the defensive system up and it started generating the suicide effect. I have no idea why they chose that mode of protecting themselves, but it's what they did."

It was finally starting to penetrate my head and I was beginning to understand what Herman was trying so hard to tell me.

"Joe, we can now work the site as long as we do not set the defense system off again. My suggestion is we place a monitor on the cube twenty-four hours a day, seven days a week and if and when it changes colors, they warn every one of the events and everyone in turn would clear out of the area. My gut feeling is they chose this method in order to give people a chance to clear the area before the effects hit them. Clever, I would say."

All I could do was sit there and shake my head. I had several emotions going. First it was too simple and second, why play with fire. "Okay Herman, you're telling me you feel we can resume our excavation activities and we keep people on site at the cube to alert the work crews of any changes in its status."

By this time Herman could see I was finally getting it and he was nodding his head yes. "That's right. We know it has at least three capabilities, and I would venture to say there are others."

Where the hell did that come from, he kept coming up with these comments me had no foundation or rational behind them. "What are you saying?"

Like a well-organized teacher Herman kept pushing me in the direction he wanted me to go. "If this is a full range security system, what we saw yesterday and the day before was the low range response. I would not be surprised if it had a mid-range and a high range response as well. So, we resume our work, but pay close attention to the cube and move when it changes, no matter what the change is. Got me?"

I understood what Herman was saying it was just that it did not feel right. "I don't know, Herman. It sounds a little risky to me."

He was looking straight at me and nodding his head. "Joe, we need to get back to work on this project. Yes, there will be a risk, but we must take precautions. I believe they built into their systems time to react and withdraw from the area before serious events happen." He continued to eat his breakfast, letting what he had just said sink in.

It struck me he had been here before or in a situation similar to what we were facing.

"How about this?" He had just taken a bite and was swinging his fork around in front of him. "We ask for volunteers to resume the work on the site and if everything appears to be working out all right, then we can send the full crews back in."

I could see this man was on a mission and that mission was the project. He wasn't going to take no for an answer and I didn't blame him. "Herman, let me take your proposal to Stan and Bob and get their feedback. If they approve and we are satisfied with the procedure you're recommending then it's a go."

He went back to his breakfast and ended the conversation with. "That's good with me Joe."

I knew I had just been manipulated by an expert and yet I could not really disagree with him. As I walked across to Stan's office, there was this back of the mind feeling again. The plan was a good one and the precautions were reasonable, but something was pricking my mind and I did not like it, no not a bit.

As I walked into Stan's office, he was bent over studying a stack of papers before him. He did not hear me and when I started to talk, he almost came out of his shoes.

His whole body jumped and that in turn made me jump. "God, Joe, you scared the shit out of me."

I could feel my face flush as I regained my composure. "Sorry, Stan, I didn't realize you were that deep in thought. What's going on?"

Stan picked up several pieces of paper and held them up toward me. As I took them, he said. "I've been reading over the autopsy report on the man from the accident the other day."

I stood there looking at the first page of the autopsy and reading the young man's name. "And?"

He sat down in his chair and leaned back. There was a slight edge of rejection in his voice as he started to talk. "Joe, it's not good. That man had a third of his brain scrambled and not by the cat either."

I had been thinking about Herman's plan and not really anticipating this. It caught me off guard. "What the hell are you saying Stan?"

He settled back in his chair and turned to face me. The look on his face told it all. "That kid was chewed up from the inside out. Something got into his brain and turned it to mush."

As I watched his mouth while he talked, I felt myself start to flush. I looked for a chair and sat down and leaned forward and put my head in my hands.

"Was there any indication of other life forms in his brain or body?"

Stan was quiet for a few seconds; he could see I was shaken by what he had just said. "No, it was clear of any foreign matter just that the brain was damaged severely." He let that sink in before continuing. "The doctors speculate he was unconscious when he walked over to the cat and crawled under it."

When he said that I was ready to throw up, I sat upright and looked at him. "Unconscious? That I can't believe. How can that be?"

He was shaking his head as I reacted to what he was saying. "That's how I felt until they explained it to me and how it works. Some people who suffer severe brain damage such as this are still capable of being mobile and processing information. Their central nerve center is functioning just fine, but their rational center is gone. The brain can function and the person will know nothing about it. To all degrees and purposes, they are unconscious at that point in time. People in that state have been known to kill and not even realize what they were doing or what they had done."

How do you react to something like that? I was caught in a situation that demanded something be done, but what?

I looked back at Stan. "Man, this is unreal." I sat there a few seconds trying to figure out how to approach Herman's needs. So, I just went for it. "But we have a situation I need to talk over with you. The research team feels it is all right to resume the excavation toward the object at this time. They have determined the cube was the trigger that set this situation off. It was triggered by the investigative team who were working on the cube. At the time the death took place the team was trying to determine the light source and type of light the cube was generating when it went red. The man was killed at just about that time.

"Dr. Blumfield, Herman, feels the cube is a traffic controller in a way. It responds to levels of activity around it and, in this case, it went into a low-level security breach mode.

"He believes, as do the other scientists, there are probably mid and upper levels of security this thing controls. Just what those are, we do not know? They recommend we monitor the cube twenty-four hours a day, seven days a week and anytime the cube changes in any way we evacuate the excavation site until they can clear it for reentry."

Stan sat there looking at me, waiting till I finished. "How do you feel about that, Joe?"

I was still reacting to the information on the young man's death and finding it hard to concentrate. "I'm not sure." I sat back looking around the room trying to organize my thoughts. "We need to get things going again, but I have this feeling there is more to this than we understand, a whole lot more. I would hate to see another person die, but if we oversee this project as they suggested, I believe we can move in and out as events dictate. Right now, I would say let's go."

As I finished, he reached over and picked up his phone. He called Bob and Terry in and laid the situation out to them. As they listened, Bob appeared to be disturbed about something. Terry was all right with the plan.

I looked at Bob. "Bob, what's wrong?"

Bob looked at me and sat back in the chair. "I don't know. I keep getting this feeling in the back of my mind. I just don't know. I guess we need to get this thing moving, but I have reservations."

I felt a shiver run up my back. His reactions were just like mine.

I leaned toward Bob. "What is it, Bob? I think you know."

He was looking pale and uneasy and I was sure he had a bigger role in this entire situation than any of us thought. "Joe, this thing is a trap."

That one took the wind out of me. "A trap, what do you mean?"

He couldn't sit still and he was wringing his hand continuously. "Yeah, and we're being sucked right into it."

Stan leaned over his desk looking straight at Bob. "Come on Bob you can't be serious."

His eyes were having a hard time focusing and I was sure if we pushed him, he would have passed out. "I know this sounds crazy, but I can't help it." He was clearly having a problem with something. "My whole body is screaming trap, and I can't for the life of me figure out why."

Finally, I stood up. "Stan, I have been having the same feelings. Bobs are just a whole lot more advanced than mine. The term 'trap' may be a little too harsh, but there is something going on here. I agree we need to get things moving again, but I want to caution you we need to take care and be especially alert from here on out."

The four of us sat there letting the reality of the situation sink in. We had a major decision that needed to be made and if we made the wrong one it would come back and haunt us the rest of our lives.

Stan sat there looking at us. Of the four of us there he was the one with the clear head. "I agree and as for Bob's feeling I totally accept them. So, let's get the protocol down and get it out to everyone."

The decision had been made and we were now going to pursue our target and deal with any threats that may come from the cube.

After our meeting and completion of the new protocol I went on back to the cube location and found Melanie. "Melanie, we need to talk." I filled her in on the process and the protocol for the cube and any changes it may go through. I made it clear that safety came first "Do it safe, but do it hard." and that the monitors watching the cube were to act immediately when and if a change took place.

"Remember Melanie, act first and report second. Any decision you make will be supported by me. We are going to be working in a dangerous area so scale it up and no one, but no one, is going to be lost to negligence on anyone's part."

Next, we located the leader of the investigation team who had been working on the cube.

Melanie and I sat down with him. "Here is the protocol for the cube. No one is to touch that thing for any reason. You can observe, speculate, and dream, but do not touch it at any time or in any way. Sorry, but the excavation of the road to the object is the priority. The cube will have to wait until a later date for hands on analysis. If you have any questions, you can contact Melanie or me directly. Understood?"

The team leader looked at the papers and then to me and nodded his head.

The first crew moving back into the area was the two cat operators and their spotters. With them, went two engineers and two archeologists. Everyone else was ordered out of the area until further notice.

Now, the excavation started in earnest. The process went well and in just three days we were at the foot of the mountain where the object was buried. We finished prepping the area and then the excavation teams pulled out leaving the area ready for the archeological teams to move in and start their dig.

It was at this time when the second cat operator reported an object in the center of the valley following the ditch configuration and running in a straight line from the first cube and the foundation layout across the road from the first cube. He advised it appeared to be a second cube, but all he could see of it was one edge where he had scraped the soil away from the object.

I had him pull his rig back and clear the area. Next, we had the investigation unit come in and take over the excavation of this new cube. Within three hours they had the cube dug out without touching it. It was a twin of the one back at the main gate of the area. It appeared to have the same markings on all four vertical sides as well. When they blocked the sun, it too had the blue lighting of the markings on the sides.

By this time, I was sure they were connected and advised the team the same protocol we set up for Cube One was now to be applied to Cube Two, hands off until the main dig was over.

It was at this point I had a thought. I called Melanie and told her to meet me at the port of entry building across from the Cube One. When I arrived, she was already there?

"Do you have a map of this area with you?"

"Yes, I do."

"Okay, let's see it."

She walked over to her truck and pulled out her map case.

As we laid the map out on the hood of the truck, I located the two know cubes on the map. "Melanie, I want you to do something for me. We have two cubes now. The distance between the two cubes is about fifteen hundred meters or a Kilometer and a half. I have a strong feeling there is a third one and it will be fifteen hundred meters directly north of Cube two and if I was right, it would put cube three at the other side of the valley, in effect isolating the valley from the rest of the base area. I want you to take a team and go out into this area and find that third cube."

I pointed the location out on the map for her and she then took a red pencil and marked the spot where I felt the cube would be located.

Knock it down Melanie. Now this is important. Look for it, but take care that you don't stumble over it or touch it. Find that thing and then clear the area around it for twenty or thirty meters. If I am right, it will be exactly like the first cube in size, in markings, and with the lighting. Now find that thing and find it fast. Do it safe, but do it hard. Got me?"

She was looking at the map and getting her orientation right. "Will do, we'll get right on it."

By this time my mind was exploding with thoughts and random feelings. I had no idea what the hell was going on. All I knew I was having these feelings and I had never had them before. I remembered Bob was experiencing the same type of feelings and was sure it was not a physiological or psychological issue. This had to be cube influence, but just how it was being done and what effect it may eventually have, I was not sure.

I was becoming convinced the cubes were having some kind of an influence on me and I was not sure whether it was good or bad. Right then I thought it was bad, that is until I learned better.

I was sure by my feelings there was a third cube and I had a strong feeling there were more, a lot more. The cubes, the lights, these feelings, they were all connected somehow in some way. I hoped we'd find the answers to those questions soon.

Chapter Four

THE START OF THE STORM

Within hours, the archeological teams were moving into the area at the end of the road. The next part of the dig would be by hand and small machinery. So far, we had found a trove of artifacts of every size, shape, and color. I expected that to increase.

The same feeling was starting up again and this time they were intense. Just then I got a call from Bob and he sounded strange. "Joe, do you feel it?"

I could feel something. "Yeah, Bob, I do and you?"

I could hear the strain in his voice as he started to talk. "It's more intense than it ever has been. Joe, I got a bloody nose when it came on me. Also, my vision is going. I don't know what it is but whatever it is, it's killing me."

Just the sound of his voice alarmed me. "Bob, get your ass out of there and over to the medical tent right now, hear me?" I waited for a response and it finally came.

"Will do Joe." He didn't sound good at all.

I called the medical tent to alert them of what just happened. Someone answered. "Who is this?"

"This is Doctor Adams."

Doctor Adams, yes, I had met him and he was good man. "Doctor Adams, this is Joe Nash. Something is happening to Bob Hammer and I told him to get over to your tent as soon as he could. If he's not there in the next ten minutes you get over to his office and find him."

Adams was almost responding before I had finished. "He just came in Joe."

Damn that was good news to me. "How does he look Doctor?"

There was a pause. "Not good, he's bleeding from his nose, eyes and ears."

That grabbed me tight and I jumped to my feet. "Shit, I'm coming over."

Just then my radio came to life. "Joe, Melanie here."

"Yeah, Melanie."

"Joe, we found it."

I could hardly hear her. "Repeat, you found it?"

She came back but sounded subdued as well. "That's right and it was exactly where you said it would be. Joe it's identical to the other two and it's lit up in blue as well."

I was heading out my office door and going over to medical at this time. "Okay, Melanie, get the area cleared out so there is an area around it big enough to work our equipment around it."

She was ahead of me on that issue as well. "I have already started. We now have line of sight from here to the other two cubes."

Man, things were going crazy, but I found I loved every second of it. "Sweet, I'll be there in a few. I have to run and check on something and then I'll be there. Stand by for me there."

"Will do."

By this time, I had made it to the medical tent. The doctor met me outside the tent.

The look in Adam's eyes told it all. "Joe, he's bad."

That was the one thing I did not want to hear.

"Joe we can't get the bleeding stopped and he can't stop talking. I think you need to hear what he is saying."

He turned and opened the door and I went in. "Are you recording it?"

He showed me to Bob's room and opened the door. "Yes, we started that as soon as he came through the door."

When I walked through the door Bob looked at me and smiled. I walked around to the head of the table.

Bob was watching me as I came toward him. "Joe, their talking to me."

I quietly asked him. "Who are, Bob?"

His face was gray white and clammy. He looked like he was going to die. He looked right at me and motioned me closer. "Them Joe."

I reached out put my hand on his shoulder. "Bob, listen to me, who are you talking about?" I had a sick feeling coming over me and I was getting scared.

The look in his eyes was that of a crazy man. It scared the hell out of me. "Joe, it's them. It's the cubes."

The look on his face was even scarier than the way I felt. "Bob listens to me. How do you know it's the cubes?"

"I can see them and their talking to me." His eyes were wide open and there was blood in both corners of each eye.

I pulled my radio out and called Melanie. "Melanie Joe here, are you there?"

"Yes Joe, we're by Cube Three right now."

As I watched Bob. "Melanie, what is the cube doing right now?"

There was a pause. "Stand by."

I waited for her to come back on to me. "Joe!"

There was an edge to her voice this time. "Go ahead, Melanie."

"Joe, it's an orange color, a deep dark orange."

"Is it solid?"

She was quiet for a few seconds. "No, it's flashing but there is no pattern to it."

"How do you feel, Melanie?"

"I feel just fine."

I continued to check on her. "Any headaches?"

Her voice was firm when she replied.

"No, none, Joe, what is going on here?"

I needed to check the other cubes. "Stand by Melanie."

I checked the other two cube sites and they too had deep, dark orange lights on their respective cubes. I walked over and sat down beside Bob.

I got his attention. "Bob, listen to me."

"What?" His eyes were still wide open and looking everywhere.

I leaned in close to him. "Can you tell me what they're saying to you?"

He seemed to be a little more controlled by this time. "At first I could not, but now I'm beginning to understand what they're saying."

I continued to work with him. "Bob, this is important. You must keep providing us with what they're saying."

He continued to relate to me what the cubes were telling him. "Their telling us to back off. Do not attempt to get to the machine. They don't want to take action against us, but will if we refuse to back off."

Damn, that was not good. "Can you ask them a question?"

"Haven't tried, but will. What do you want me to ask them?"

"Ask them if there is any way we can

find out what this place was and when it was first built?"

I watched him as he made his first attempt to communicate with these things. I could tell that it was not easy. The expression on his face told me he was trying to approach them from a neutral position and not to show any sign of aggression.

He sat there looking at his hands and then at me. "I'll try. I'm new at this, you know." He closed his eyes for a few seconds and then opened them and looked straight at me. "Joe, they told me the facility has been active since 6510 and has been in operation continuously from then on."

He said 6510, that tells me nothing. What reference point do they use to mark their time and year sequences? "Do they know what year it is now?"

"They're confused about the time issue. I keep getting this stand by recalculating message. They just said they were unable to determine that."

This didn't help at all. Now we had a cube that had no idea what time it was and it could mean a whole lot of things. "Okay, ask them this. Are they a security system?"

Finally, we got a positive answer. "Yes,

125

they are. They are in charge of the security for this base."

I was trying to take logical steps in bringing up each question. "What organization is the base for?"

The returning reply through Bob was. "The Demion Empire."

What the hell, it suddenly dawned on me we had just developed a communications link between us and the cubes and they were here and functioning as a base of operations.

It then dawned on me something strange was going on between Bob and the cubes. "Bob, listen to me. How do they know English?"

Bob shook his head, and held his right hand up at the same time. "Joe, they don't, it's all thought or mental communications. No language issues are involved."

Damn, this was dynamite and I had no idea where to go from there. "Bob, how are you doing?"

He looked terrible. "Not too good. I think this process is going to kill me, but I can't stop it. Let's keep going for as long as I can make it."

I was running on shear adrenaline by this time and really had no idea just what I was doing or where I was trying to go. All I knew we had some kind of contact going and I wanted to keep it coming.

I then thought of the next question. "Bob, what is the name of this land we are on?"

It came back almost as fast as I asked it. "This is the Bandilan Range which is located in the upper part of the Sandlieon continent."

I was just grabbing for questions. I knew we had the link going and I wanted to keep it moving along. At least until someone else could come in and organize this dialog. "What is the name of this planet?"

Bob seemed to becoming more stressed with each question and exchange. "They call it Yearth."

Finally, Bob reached out and took hold of my arm. "Joe I can't go on I need to sleep."

He was starting to wilt right there in front of me. I had questions coming out my ears, but he was fading fast and needed a break. We had to stop. "All right, Bob, you relax and get some rest. I'll talk to you later on after you get over this thing."

I felt the sting of the pain he was having in the back of my head. It was not anywhere near his level, but it was there.

Just then my radio came to life. "Melanie here."

"Yeah, Melanie." I was trying to deal with Bob's situation and my own symptoms that had developed.

There was that stress level in her voice again. "Joe, I have two people down, both bleeding from the nose, eyes and ears. Get me some help here, now."

That brought me back to what was going on. There was one Hell of a situation developing here and I needed to get on top of it.

"Melanie, are they talking?"

Her stress level was huge. "Yes, but it's a bunch of gobbledygook. Nothing makes sense at all. Joe, I'm scared. What's going on?"

I could tell she was scared and I didn't blame her. "Can't say right now, Melanie, I've got people coming right now. They'll be with you in minutes."

There was a long pause and then I could hear her trying to talk. "Okay, I'll call you later."

Damn I was proud of her right then. She had more than her hands full and she hung in there. "Right, hang in there Melanie, we're getting a handle on this situation and it should be worked out before long."

Just then, Stan came running up. "What happened to Bob?"

Crap I had two major issues going and he wants to know about Bob, what the hell anyway. Cool it man, calm down and answer the guys' question. He needs to know. "Stan, he has finally stabilized and is resting. But we have two more people down out by Cube Three, they are being brought in now with the same symptoms as Bob's and mine."

"You? But you're standing and working just fine." There was a clear sense of surprise in his voice.

I tried to remain calm and explained it to him. "Yeah, I am, but I have the same feelings, just not as hard. Stan, the cubes are trying to communicate with us. So far, we have determined they are from the year 6510 and are part of the Demion Empire."

Stan stood there looking at me. His face was a little ashen and he was clearly in a mild state of shock. "Joe, what the hell are you talking about?"

I looked at him and realized I needed to take the time to fill him in on what was happening. This was not the time to let things get out of hand. "Stan they are from the far past, before our existence even started. They are from a time before, when the earth was younger. They are advanced way beyond us and these machines are their security system for this base.

"By the way, the base is located in the Bandilan Range on the Sandlieon continent. And, they want us to stop trying to get to the machine. They sounded rather firm on that one by the way."

Stan started to pace. He paced back and forth and shook his head. "This is impossible. This is stupid. This is out of the question. What the hell do we do now, Joe?"

All I could do was stand there and let him unwind a little. "I think we need to pull everyone back and away from their assigned duties and report back to the big tent. We need to get our heads together and talk this over. We also need to see if anyone else is having any odd reactions or experiences. I don't know what else to do right now."

He had stopped pacing and was now thinking about what was going on. "Yeah, I know what you mean. Okay, let's pull everyone in and get our heads together and see what we can come up with. I'll head back and get everything set up for the conference. Frankly, I'm not sure just what we should be doing or where we should even start."

In a little over an hour, we had notified everyone able to attend the meeting to assemble in the meeting tent as soon as possible. We were clearly at a point where we needed to slow things down and organize our response to the events that have been manifesting themselves.

Stan, Terry and I met in Stan's office to get organized before the meeting. Stan started the discussion. "All right, we need to determine where we're at right now and how we're going to run this meeting."

I sat there for a few minutes waiting for someone to start and finally took the initiative. I learned a long time ago when things become so complex and they're approaching lock up you needed to stop and get back to basics. That is what I proposed. "Stan, I would suggest we start from the beginning and then move forward to where we are now."

Stan immediately recognized the move and took that approach as well. "Agreed, Joe you go ahead and start the briefing."

What the hell, did he just drop the

meeting in my lap? A flash of anger charged through me and then settled back. He was right I was the person closest to this mess so it should be me.

Still, I wanted to make sure that is what he wanted and that he was not just confused. "Are you sure you want me to get this thing going?"

His sixth senses had told him he was outside this mess and he would only add to the confusion and really not take the meeting toward the direction needed. "Yes, you've been closer to everything that has been going on than I have and beside I want to be sure all the facts are presented accurately. We don't have time for mistakes or communications screw ups."

With that we started to brainstorm to come up with the agenda and data presentations. Once we were done working the agenda out, we headed for the meeting tent. When we got there everyone was present and waiting to get started.

I moved to the dais and kicked it off. "Okay everybody listen-up. We have had a number of significant things happen in the last three hours. They are serious and are the reason for the suspension of all activity concerning the dig. We need each and every one of you to get your computers out and online. If you have note pads, get those out as well and be prepared to enter this data or make a presentation about your data.

"What we do here in the next few hours will determine the success or failure of this entire project. Unless you are sick or completely incapable of dealing with this process, you are here for the duration."

I paused to give the first remarks time to sink in and see if any questions came from it. There were none.

"All right now we will give you a run down on what has happened. We have three more casualties on site. One is Bob Hammer and then two other workers who were working at a new discovery site."

It took an hour to bring everyone up to date on what had been taking place across the project site. People were making notes of all the details as they came out. I had just finished referring to the Cube Three discovery. Just then a hand went up. "What third cube?"

I stopped and looked over at Stan, we had missed that and I needed to back up and cover this issue. Stan nodded his head. "All right, let's start from the beginning. It's becoming obvious that we are not all on the same page. Please refer to your computers under project description. That will give you the preliminary information on this dig. Now we will fill in everything that has taken place over the last fourteen days."

I gave those present a complete and detailed rundown of our activities at Project Majestic, making sure we covered the cube discoveries and the hazards that are related to them. A number of questions were coming up that helped in my ensuring everything was covered and explained up to that moment.

"Now this brings me up to the discovery of Cube Three which was found while I was dealing with the emergency condition of Bob Hammer. In a short time from now you will hear a conversation I had with Bob, but first let me continue.

"I had sent Melanie and a crew out into the northern boundary of the valley to look for a third cube I was sure was located at a point about fifteen hundred meters due north of Cube Two Melanie and her crew found the cube right where we had thought it would be. By this time, I was into the process with Bob.

"Bob related to me what he was feeling

or sensing. The cubes were communicating with him, in his brain and it was damaging him. The thing was, we had now developed a line of communications with these cubes and they were covering a lot of material. It was about this time that Melanie called again and advised me she had two people down with the same symptoms as those found with Bob Hammer."

I was walking back and forth by the dais by this time and found I could not stand still. I don't know if it was just nerves, or the influence of the cube. "It was then when we closed the entire project down. In the last fourteen days we have now had four casualties, one death and three down with bleeding symptoms. What we need to know right now is whether anyone else is having the same symptoms. I for one am. Mine are mild compared to the other three people.

"So, if you have any pain or feelings of presence in your brain or the back of your head we need to know right now. If you recognize any of those feelings stand up."

Off to my left, I saw Jennifer stand. Just about that time a small trickle of blood started coming from her nose. One of the medical staff moved in quickly and escorted her out of the meeting room. Three more people reported the same symptoms and were taken away.

"All right, now you have seen what we are talking about as far as symptoms go, so pay attention to yourself and your fellow team members. Any signs are to be treated seriously and that person is to be taken to medical immediately.

"Now, the issue with Bob Hammer, as far as I know, Bob is the most severe of all those of us showing symptoms. What we are going to play for you right now is a recording we got when interviewing Bob during his crisis. Please stay quiet and listen to the entire tape before saying anything or reacting. We will play this tape as many times as you want, but it would help if you would control yourselves during the playing.

"What you are going to hear is a conversation between Bob and I and the cubes. That's right the cubes. Pay attention to what Bob is saying. He is in a lot of pain and trying to relate to me what was happening to him and what he was hearing.

"Now it is important you hear this tape. We at least need each team leader to hear this in total. If any member of any team can't listen then, please let your team leader know and then quietly get up and leave the room. We will call you back when we're done listening to the tape any questions?"

No questions came up and we started the tape. At first everyone stayed put but as the tape progressed a few simply could not remain and they left the room. The last thing we needed at that point in time was someone getting sick during this phase of the meeting.

After the playing of the tape several times and the return of several who could not listen to the tape, we were ready to continue the meeting.

"All right, everyone let's calm down now. Before we get into a full-fledged discussion mode, I need to relate a number of other items to you. Some you are aware of and others you may not be.

"We have determined within the valley proper there were no insects or animal life of any kind. That area is void of any life forms other than plant life. Even the soil is void of any living creatures of any kind. As we considered this issue, Professor Blumfield speculated the cubes were programmed to deal with biological life forms and they took their job seriously. As long as they have been here, they have eliminated any and all biological life forms from this area.

"Next, the cubes are in perfect synchronization. That is, they respond in exactly the same way all the time. If one goes blue, they all go blue, red all red, orange all orange. Their markings are all the same exactly and their size is perfect to within micro measurements. They appear to be made from the same material as the roadway.

"They are positioned in a perfect equal lateral triangle that is precisely fifteen hundred meters on each side. As far as we can tell there is no hard-wire connection between the three cubes and yet they communicate perfectly. We have tried to shield them from one another to no avail.

"As of right now that is where we are at. Currently everything is status quo. The cubes seem to be happy with our absence on the site. So, in order for us to continue we will need to figure out a way to overcome their abilities to stop us and keep us out of the project area."

Just then a hand went up. "Sir, question?"

I pointed at the man. "Go ahead."

"Have we tried to move any of the three

cubes?"

I then turned to the attendees and repeated the question and then addressed it. "At this point we have tried to move Cube One, but to no avail. We cannot find any anchor system or any hard-wire connections between the cubes or to some anchor point around or near them.

Those things are solid in place. We are not sure or have little idea as to what they are capable of in the event they need to protect themselves. So, we opted to not try to move them anymore. Personally, I don't believe we will be able to move them."

As soon as I finished answering the first question a second hand was raised. "Is there any idea as to how they are powered? That is, what their power source is?"

"Judy, it is Judy Right?" She nodded her head. "Right now, we have no idea. As best as we can determine there are no wires or hard connections running near or under any of the cubes. There is no internal power source that we can detect and whether in the light or shielded from the light the activity remains the same and the lighting effect remain the same."

Judy then asked a second question.

"Are they solid?"

As with each and every question I repeated it so all could hear. "I have no idea. So far, we have not been able to determine whether they are solid or not. We have tried ultrasound and that has resulted in nothing. X-ray resulted in nothing. They even went so far as to tap on the top and sides and still nothing. The material it is made of has resisted every attempt to penetrate it either by electronics or mechanically."

It was clear everyone was getting into this discussion and that was good. The interest level was high and aggressive by this time. Just then another hand went up.

"Sir, I'm Harper Williams with the west road excavation team."

I walked over to his side of the room and addressed him directly. "Yes Harper."

"Can you give us a listing of the artifacts and larger items that have been uncovered to date?"

Good question and one I could not handle directly. "Harper, that is in the data on your computer. However, I will say this. We have found a road runs east and west on the south side of the valley.

"At the mouth of the valley we have

found Cube One which sits just off the road to the south. Cube Three sits fifteen hundred meters to the north and Cube Two is located at the foot of the mountain in an equal lateral position to the other two cubes. To the north of the road, across from Cube One, we found the foundation of a small building made from the same material as the roadway. We believe is a port of entry or security gate house.

"During this process we have found a significant number of artifacts, the purposes of which we have no idea at this time. It appears we have lots of evidence, but no real understanding of what the evidence means. We have yet to locate a piece of evidence that will bring about the explanation of everything else we have found or will find."

I noted we were losing time and ended the questioning and then progressed to the next subject. "Anything else, if not, then we need to start looking at the data and get a brainstorming session going here. So, let's take a twenty minutes break and then we can all meet back here."

I looked over at Stan and he was nodding in agreement. He got up and walked over to me. "Good job, I think they are more than just a little interested and you seemed to have gotten them heated up."

Twenty minutes later everyone started to come back into the meeting. During this time, after talking to Stan, I had gone to the medical tent to check on Jennifer. She appeared to be all right, but was dealing with a headache. She was the second one who was hearing the cubes. I made sure there was an audio technician with her to ensure everything was recorded. The doctor felt she would be all right.

As we got the meeting going, I advised everyone on the condition and prognosis for those who had been removed from the meeting with symptoms. I then opened the floor for discussion.

Professor Blumfield was the first to rise. I invited him to the dais. He paused for a minute before starting his presentation.

"Ladies and gentlemen, I have been scanning the information accumulated over the life of this project. My first impression was we had moved too fast in this endeavor, but then I reconsidered the frequency and speed of each and every one of the discoveries and find, so far, this project preparation and progression is most commendable.

"We are now at a standstill and with no

plan for continuing on. Well, for those of you who know me, that does not sit well with me. I am a firm believer in continuing on, maybe in a different direction, but moving on none the less.

"I agree with the current situation. Until we can form some dialog and meaningful communications with these cubes, we best not venture into the project area. But there is nothing that indicates we cannot venture away from the area. I am primarily referencing the east bound road excavation. I think we should be pursuing that route now; with everything we have. Where it goes and how long it takes us to get there could well mean the difference between success and failure of this whole project.

"May I propose we assemble a blue-ribbon team to deal with the cubes and gaining access to the project area? At the same time, we shift all our resources to the excavation of the road to wherever it goes and I can assure you it is going someplace. That someplace may well be the key to our gaining access to the project area."

The place fell silent. No one made a sound. Not a cough, not a word, not a movement.

Finally, I stood up and walked up by the professor and leaned over. "I think you hit on something. Are there any more questions? If not, is everyone in agreement with Professor Bloomfield's ideas and recommendations."

With that everyone raised their hands in agreement and the meeting was over.

The next morning, we moved in on the east bound road with vengeance. A blue-ribbon team, headed up by Professor Blumfield, went to work on the access issue with the cubes. Everything else was dedicated to the east bound excavation. Herman had decided the team would work with Jennifer and Bob to see if they could gain more data from the cubes and their reason for not wanting any more excavation of the base area.

In the beginning, there was some grumbling. A lot of people felt we had been conned and the cube thing was not that big an issue. But their attitude would change drastically in just a few short days. What was about to happen would change everything.

Excavation of the east bound road was going well. One thing we noted was there were insects and other animals in the area of this excavation. The biologists felt the population was within the norm for that region of the country. There was nothing unusual.

Within short order, we had three cats working the road area, one on the road and one on either side of the road. I wanted a thirty-meter open space along the road.

It was around two o'clock in the afternoon when the north side cat came to a crashing stop. He had hit something and that something was formidable. You simply do not stop a D-9 caterpillar like that.

The operator moved the cat back and got down and walked over to the spot where he had hit the object. At first, he saw nothing and then he saw a red glow in the underbrush. The first thing he thought of was a cube and turned and started to run. Melanie had seen the cat stop and was walking over that way when she saw the operator turning away from the area in front of the cat.

He didn't get far before the shock wave hit him and knocked him flat. When it hit Melanie, she was thrown back in the direction she came from. Almost everyone within a fifty-meter radius was hit by the wave. Everything fell silent except for the idle of the big machinery. Several men from the south side of the excavation ran over to Melanie and helped her up. She was bleeding from the nose and also the left ear. A call was put in for medical.

I received my alert shortly thereafter and raced to the scene. They had Melanie on a stretcher and they were preparing her for the ambulance when I got there.

I ran over to her and dropped to my knees beside her. "Melanie, what happened?"

She was in a lot of pain and was finding it hard to breathe and talk. Her breath had been knocked out of her and she had not recovered completely. "Not sure, Joe, but I think the cat hit something over there in the overgrowth. I saw the operator walk over there and then he turned and run back toward the cat when something went off. The shock wave hit him and then me and anyone else within about a 50 meters area of that site. How's the operator?"

I put my hand on her shoulder. "We lost him, he's dead."

She lay there quietly as tears started to flow from her eyes and run back under her ear. "God, how can that be? This route was supposed to be safe. What's going on here, anyway?"

"I don't know honey, but we're going to find out." I was holding her hand and could see the pain of both the blow she took and learning of the operator's death.

Just then Stan and Professor Blumfield pulled up.

Stan walked over to Melanie and I. "What the hell is going on here Joe?"

I let go of Melanie's hand and stood up facing Stan. "I'm not sure. That cat operator hit something over there in the undergrowth and now he's dead. I don't know if it was a land mine or something else. Whatever it was it killed him and hit Melanie hard enough that she will need medical attention."

Melanie reached out and grabbed my arm. "Joe."

I leaned over toward her. "Yes, Melanie."

She was holding on to me as tight as she could. "Joe, there was no sound."

I didn't get what she had said and asked. "What did you say?"

Her face was contorted with pain as she said. "There was no sound, nothing. I heard the cat and then I heard it hit something. It was like a deep thud. When it went off there was no sound, but I saw the shock wave

147

coming. It was like looking at a transparent balloon. It expanded out from that spot over there in the brush."

Professor Blumfield stood there looking at the spot where the cat hit the object. He turned toward Stan and me. I think I'll take a walk down there and see what there is to see. "Joe, you want to go with me?"

I was standing there looking at the technicians working on Melanie. "Yeah, I think so."

Stan stepped over to Herman and took hold of his arm. "Wait a minute guy, that's not a smart move."

Herman was looking in the direction where the driver had died; he slowly turned facing both Stan and me. "Stan, sooner or later we are going to have to go over there and see what the hell is going on. It might as well be now. You coming?"

The three of us walked over to the spot of the object and as we approached, I could see the amber light through the undergrowth. I heard myself say "Another cube" before we even got there.

Sure, enough it was a fourth cube. Only this was a small one, maybe half a meter on all sides. It had similar markings on it and the glowing light. What really stood out was that it had no sign of damage. I mean a D-9 cat had hit it at maybe twenty-two kilometers an hour and it did not budge it or damage it in any way that I could see.

I immediately signaled a stop of all excavation activity. I looked across the road at the cat on the south side and it was just approaching the same relative location that this operator had. I found myself literally running across the area and the road to the south side. The cat had stopped and I ran past it to a point matching the north side. Sure, enough there it was, Cube Five.

Herman had run after me figuring the same thing that sent me across the road. "Herman, how far are we from Cube One?

He looked off toward Cube One. "We're about three hundred meters."

"OKAY, get a crew out here from archeology and start the clearing of these two cubes. Next, I want a team of surveyors to shoot a line along the road way to the three-hundred-meter position and mark it. I'll bet hard money we will find Cubes Six and Seven there."

I then directed the cat on the road to go out ahead of the north and south side cats. We

149

can mark the probable location of the rest of the cubes as we come upon them.

The next thing I needed to get done was to get Melanie back on the job. It was vital she get right back into the fight. I wanted her to continue to oversee the rest of this project if she is cleared by medical.

I can tell you I was not the least bit happy with this situation. We had lost another man and that was not acceptable. I turned to Stan. "Stan, we got careless again and it cost us another man. When are we going to learn each step and each movement needs to be calculated and prepped before we move on?"

Stan was still looking the scene over and shaking his head. "I know, Joe, but this seemed so safe."

I guess I was being a little blunt but felt we had made a terrible error. "Well from here on out nothing is safe. What bothers me is where those cubes were placed. They are exactly thirty meters out from the edge of the road." I was pointing out the locations and their relationship.

Stan was walking beside me and looking at each point of concern as I related them. He then looked at me. "Joe, do you think they were placed there deliberately?"

"Yes, I do Stan, but not for us. Their engineers designed this project and built this road and they set the guidelines for placement of those cubes. We come by so many millions of years later and stumble onto the exact measurements they used in the first place. No, this was not meant for us, it was meant for whomever they were afraid of those millions of years ago."

About an hour later I received word of two more cubes exactly where we thought they would be. Stan, Herman and I had retreated to Stan's office when the word came to us. "Stan, I think we're in a war zone of some kind. I have an idea. Where are we keeping all the archival finds?"

Stan seemed to get a shot of interest as I asked that question. "Well, they're all stored in the logging hut Joe, and then boxed and sent into storage."

"Okay, let's get over there. I want to see some of that stuff." The fact was we all wanted to see what had been coming into the storage area. I had a deep down feeling the answer was there all the time.

At the main storage hut, we had them bring out several boxes of items and lay them out on a table. They were an odd assortment of items. Nothing even so much as resembled a tool of any kind I was familiar with. I sat there and looked at them waiting for something to click.

I picked up a cylinder. It was about a half inch in diameter and maybe four inches long. The metal it was made from was not familiar to me, but the feel was. I looked around and saw a second one and then a third. Each one the same size and weight and each one hollow. With one end closed off.

As I set them on edge, I asked Herman what he thought they could be. He sat there looking at them and then his eye brows went up. "Yeah, you got it don't you?"

"Damn well better believe I do, they're cartridges."

Stan leaned forward. "What the Hell. Aw damn it to Hell, anyway. Why didn't we see this earlier? Pete!

Pete leaned around the end of a row of shelves. "Yeah Stan?"

"Start bringing those boxes out here one at a time. I want everything out on tables for us and I want them now."

"Okay, but it may take some time."

"Pete, we've got a lot of time. Just get things rolling, all right."

Pete turned and nodded his head and headed back into the storage area. "Will do."

The reality of the situation was finally making sense to me. "This explains a hell of a lot. Those cubes are defensive all right, but they are military. That explains the levels of force they have built into them. This must have been a rather important location to have this kind of a buildup of defensive strength. Now I'm really questioning what the object is at the base of the mountain. Maybe it's not a tunneling machine, but something more formidable."

Two hours later all the items were on display and a layout map was on the wall showing the location of each item as it was collected. As we identified each cartridge and its location when found, we saw a definite pattern developing. They were found along the perimeter of the facility between Cubes One and Three. A second string of them was identified running along the road going east.

As the conflict came to the site it spread out along the defensive line of Cubes One and Three. Or, was the conflict moving away from the defensive line starting at Cubes One and Three and then moving down the road eastward as if they were in pursuit of the other side? All the cartridges were the same make and design. You would think there would be cartridges from the other side mixed in along the road.

Stan reached out and started sifting through the items on the table. "Let's take a closer look at the rest of the items."

Sure, enough we found a second design that was common in the pile of items. These were a flat case like item. These were half an inch wide, four inches long and three and a half inches deep. The cases had channel lines on the side just three eights of an inch from the closed off back of the case.

These were found running along the road and were intermingled with the other cartridges, but were on both sides of the road and not just the one side as the others were.

There had been one hell of a battle going on here. I don't know, nor do I care about what their weapons looked like, but they were there and in abundance.

Herman sat back and looked over at me. "All right, what else do we have here? Joe, look at these objects carefully. When I first saw them, I thought to myself they were some kind of a nail or pinning spike. But, when you hold them next to these flat cases, they look like they would fit into the case almost perfectly, just like this."

Herman slipped one of the items into the case and it went in to the point of the channel on the back of the case and stopped. It fit perfectly.

We had the casing for a weapon and the projectile the weapon fired sitting right before us. I wondered if there was any kind of a projectile that would fit the round cartridges. I reached over and picked up a box and opened it and sure enough there they were. Bullets and they fit the cartridges perfectly. We had a story going on here and it explained a lot of what was happening at this site.

By this time, I was more confused than enlightened. So, if one side had the cubes then why a hand-to-hand battle between the two forces? Why were the cubes not used? It was obvious they had not been, or at least not at the time this battle was going on. We had cued the cubes two times by simply touching them, while here there was a massive battle going on and it didn't appear the cubes got involved.

On the other hand, they may well have been involved, but we just could not see that action in the artifacts currently before us. It would take a considerable amount of digging and rationalizing to come up with an acceptable theory. All right, that didn't make sense, but we were making progress.

Herman came up with the most insightful comment of all. "Joe, as I sit here, I realize they were advanced beyond anything we could dream of and yet they were not capable of living peacefully among themselves. What chance do we have of achieving that goal ourselves?"

I couldn't argue his point with him. He was being sincere in his observations and remarks. "Herman, I don't have an answer for you, but I do know we are faced with a number of machines designed and built for war and they are still active. The question is how we deal with them. We can't destroy them, that I'm afraid is obvious. When a D-9 cat hits one half the size of Cube One and it does nothing to it, there is little chance we can overcome them by force."

"But, is it force that we need for them? Joe, here we have a battle going on. From all the evidence it must have been one hell of a fight and yet the cubes just sat there waiting."

"Waiting for what?"

"Wait Joe, we assume they were

156

waiting, we don't know that. Maybe they were occupied by some other situation or necessity. There are any numbers of reasons why they were not active, or did not appear to be active.

"No there is more to this than we are looking at. There must be a way to overcome their status. Obviously, it can't be done by force, and we don't have a key or a combination to use to shut them down.

"So, I guess the answer is we overcome them by using our heads and figuring this thing out. Gentlemen, I'm even more curious about the object in the mountain and I'm going to find it and find out what it is. There is some way to overcome these things and we're going to do it and do it now. Get the investigative teams in here now."

Right now, all I had was a bunch of artifacts, several actions by the cubes, that have cost lives, and we were no further along than the day when I stepped out of the helicopter. I'm a patient man, but there are times when being patient does absolutely nothing for the situation at hand. If Herman's plan is to bring all the investigative teams in on this issue and target them on one point then I was for it and ready to go.

Chapter Five

MIND OVER MIGHT

Within an hour everyone had assembled at the meeting tent again. I immediately advised them this meeting would be concentrating on the cubes and nothing else. If anyone had a different agenda they wanted to address, this was not the place or time for it. Our purpose was the cubes.

With that, we got started. Stan laid out what had taken place over the past twenty-four hours and we were going to address the ways and means of overcoming the cubes. We would not be leaving this place until we had an answer and that was final. Food and drinks would be brought in.

Again, Stan deferred to me to head up the meeting. I checked to make sure everyone was present that we felt needed to be here and then started the meeting. "All right, let's get started. Now we have completed the overview, we need to know if there are others who should be here and we will have them here stat."

Several other names were brought up and we sent units out to find those individuals and return them to our location. Within forty-five minutes everyone was present.

I called the meeting to order. "I am going to turn this meeting over to Professor Blumfield. He will be directing our efforts in this matter, Professor."

Herman got up and walked to the dais looked the group over and then started. "Ladies and Gentlemen, I'm going to give this to you with no frills. The cubes are from a time, maybe millions of years ago, when there was another civilization living here on Earth." You could hear the reaction to Herman's first statement as it moved across the room. "The time of this conflict was 6510, their time. This place was known as the Bandilan Range and the continent it is located on was called Sandlieon. These cubes were brought here by a military branch of the Demion Empire. The planet at that time was called Yearth."

Before the Professor had finished the first part of his presentation those present were reacting to his comments. Several wanted to ask questions, but were put off until he had finished the briefing.

"Please understand all of our current communications with the cubes have been mental and the language is not an issue. Second, please note the close match between their planet Yearth and our planet Earth. We have no explanation for that at this time."

The Professor paused as he took a drink of water and gave the group a chance to let his comment sink in.

"Now, the earth is about four and a half billion years old. We know for at least the first one billion years it was not habitable by anything. But after that things started to happen. There is nothing that says there could not have been other civilizations existing on this planet sometime in the past.

"In order for that to happen there would have had to be a catastrophic happening that would have literally stripped the surface of the earth of everything recognizable. What we have here is an anomaly. Something strange happened way back then which left this place standing and now we have it and we're going to solve the puzzle it has become."

The room had fallen quiet by this time and everyone was listening intently to what was being said

"To date, we have a total of seven cubes. Cubes One, Two and Three are located in the valley. We have four cubes that are exactly half the size of the first three and they are located along the road going east out of the base area. As you know these units are dangerous and will remain classified as such until further notice."

Again, the Professor paused and let things sink in. On the big screen the location of all the cubes had been posted and each one given its obvious name. Again, Cubes One, Two, and Three were in the Main Base area. Cubes Four, Five, Six, and Seven were shown along the main road going east away from the base. Though several people wanted to ask questions at that time he would not recognize them. He wanted everyone fully briefed before they ventured into a question-and-answer process.

"Now, let's get to it. We know this. We cannot gain entry into these cubes. Second, they are indestructible by our standards. That is, we have not been able to even make a mark on them. Third, they can communicate with us. Though it is hard on the individual who is the go between, we can talk to them and that appears to be our best access point at this time.

"We are sure there are several more cubes out there, probably around the size of the smaller ones. It appears the smaller ones are the more dangerous and the larger ones are the key to our access to the dig area.

"So, I think it is safe to say we avoid the small cubes and concentrate our efforts on the bigger ones. Having said that, we now must put together a protocol for carrying out conversations with them and what we should avoid and should follow up on. We also need to determine whether we could link them with another computer and then work an online conversation. If we can do that, we remove the people who have been used as the link and give them some relief."

He finally had finished the briefing phase of the meeting and then moved on into task and support processes. He stepped around in front of dais. "Who here are our computer wizards?"

Three hands went up.

"Would the three of you please step

over here to this side of the room?" He pointed at a table located in the corner. He then spoke to the three individuals.

"All right, you three will start the computer developmental phase of this project. Don't hold back. Let your minds go wild and build us a machine that is capable of extensive data processing and analyzing."

Herman then turned back to the others. "Now, who has an in-depth knowledge of social structures and their progression?"

Two hands went up.

As he had with the prior team, he directed these two to another table and set them to work. "All right, your job is to study the conversations between the cubes and our personnel. What we want is an understanding of the minds that put these things together. Get detailed in your analysis and I need you to dig and dig deep. Don't let the slightest period go unnoticed."

For the third time he turned back to the main group. "Who have a background in military applications by civilizations?"

Three more hands went up.

This group was directed to another table on the other side of the room. "We have a number of weapons application items you

163

will be given to analyze. Put together anything and everything you can on the society that made these items and its knowledge in the art of warfare."

Once he had finished assigning the tasks to the first three teams he returned to the rest of the group. "The rest of you will apply yourselves to analyzing everything this organization has done over the several months we have been on site. What I want is a complete understanding of our protocol and areas where we may have been in error in trying to achieve our goals. Be critical, please. We need to know where we blew it so we can, if possible, go back and correct it."

Like the accomplished instructor he was he had worked the whole of the group into a working organization that was designed to address specifics.

"We eat in two hours. Make sure you break for that and no playing around. I want you sharp and well fed. Do not, I repeat, do not push yourselves to a point where you set aside proper personal care. If you need a nap, take one. If you need a shower, take one. If you need a snack, call for one and it will be brought to you.

"After the meal you will have another

three hours to finish your preliminary observations and actions. Be back here at that time prepared to give your presentations and recommendations are there any questions at this time?"

A hand went up at the back of the meeting room. "Yes, professor."

"Yes."

The person stood up and then asked. "Will you be grading on a curve?"

The place fell quiet and people started looking toward the person who had asked the question. It was one of those uncomfortable moments when one is not sure as to whether they should have done that or not.

But Herman went along with it. "Young man I never grade on a curve. I grade based on the degree of effort and knowledge and skill one puts into the task. I expect your best that is the reward for an instructor when those he labors with bring forth results that force me to expand my knowledge base. No curve, just good works."

With that everyone broke with their respective teams and Stan, Herman and I went to Stan's office to go over the coming meetings and process.

"Herman, I think they're in good humor

right now. Hope it stays that way."

Herman walked over to a chair and sat down and leaned back putting his hands behind his head. "Well Stan I think they're all good people and if anyone can come up with anything these people can and will."

Stan nodded his head and turned to me. "Joe, what do you think? Should we continue this thing or just call it quits and clear out of here?"

I had been thinking about what Herman had just said and looked up. "Stan, we're already in the pan and if we abandon this project now, we'll end up in the fire. No, we have to keep going, there is no other choice. This thing is solvable, we need to knock it down, find the right key and use it."

"Herman, are we on the right track?"

He looked at me. "Actually, Joe, the question is, are we on any track? This is one hell of a complex situation we have gotten ourselves into and we are going to have to find a way out of it. We have activated these things; these cubes and we must find a way to deactivate them and make them harmless. God only knows what they could do if left unattended."

Almost as an afterthought, "Joe, how's

166

Jennifer doing?"

"I checked on her about an hour ago and she was doing fine. They plan on releasing her tomorrow, but she will be on light duty for a while."

"What about Melanie?"

"Damn, Melanie. I forgot all about her. Hey, fellas, do you mind if I break away for a few and check on her?"

Stan nodded his head. "Not a problem, Joe. Go find her and make sure everything is going right."

I left the office and headed out to the port of entry gate to find Melanie. When I got there, she was standing by her rig and directing several people as to what she wanted done next in finding the rest of the cubes. I walked over to her. "Melanie, how's it going?"

She looked a little frazzled and had an ace bandage on her left wrist. "Hi, boss. Well, we found two more cubes, the small ones, and they're active. We have pushed another hundred meters out and the road is starting to break up."

She said that so calmly I almost missed it. "What, say that again?"

She leaned back against her rig. "Yeah,

it's starting to break up. At first all we saw were a few cracks and then chunks of the edge were missing and then whole sections.

"The terrain in front of us is now closing in with trees, which tells me the road is no longer there."

I stood there looking down at the ground. That was not something I wanted to hear right now. "Damn, I was hoping it was going someplace."

Melanie stood up. "Well boss, it was. Come with me and I'll show you something interesting."

We got in her rig and started down the road.

"How far out does the road run right now?"

"About one and a quarter kilometer, but that is not the thing I want to show you. It's just ahead of us."

As we approached two cats sitting by the road, I noticed that it was an intersection. "You're telling me there are more roads?"

She looked over at me and smiled. "That's right, one going each direction north and south."

It was almost like getting a present when she said that. "Great, have you started the excavation?"

She nodded and pointed out the window. "Just getting ready to, this intersection is just beyond the second set of cubes and so I believe there will be additional cubes about three hundred meters in both directions from here. We are preparing everyone for that issue now. Note the cubes on both sides of the main road are thirty meters in from the road and they are also thirty meters in from the two new roads. There should be more cubes both north and south of us."

The thought then hit me. "Melanie, has anyone ventured out into the forest beyond these cubes in this area?"

She turned and looked at me. "Funny you should ask that. I set up a team to do just that. They will be leaving in about ten minutes. It will be dark in about two hours so they are limiting themselves to one hour in and one hour back out."

I was more than happy with her initiative and decision making. She was turning out to be a great assistant. "Great, let me know what comes of this, Melanie. I'm sorry for not getting back to you sooner and more often. Things have just been nuts back at the base. You knew that Jennifer went down?"

She stopped dead in her tracks and continued to look straight ahead. "God, no I did not know that. Is she all right?"

I reached out and put my hand on her shoulder. She and Jennifer had become close friends over the couple of months they have worked together and I could tell the news had hurt. "Yeah, she is, but she'll be on light duty for a few days. They plan on releasing her tomorrow. It was scary as hell for a while there. Melanie, you take care. Don't take any chances. This job is not worth getting yourself killed over. Okay?"

She was still looking away from me and had shifted her view toward the top of the forest. She then turned to me and reached up and wiped a tear off her cheek. "Okay boss. I'll be careful and will watch out for our people as well."

This was one tough woman and she was becoming indispensable to me. I looked her in the eyes. "Melanie, you're doing a great job here, keep it up. Talk later."

She gave me that half smile she had. "Will do boss."

I returned to the meeting hall and got

there in time for dinner and then went to my room for a much-needed nap.

My phone rang later on. I'm not sure how long I had been out. When I answered it, I could hear Melanie talking, at first, I could not understand and then realized I had the phone upside down. "Hold on Melanie, let me get awake before you continue. All right, what's up?"

She was excited and talking twice her normal speed. "Boss we found the additional cubes except."

Her phone was in and out and garbled somewhat. "Melanie you're breaking up, except what?"

Finally, she started to come through and I heard her say. "Boss they're large cubes."

If I heard her right, I had not expected that. "What? You said large cubes?"

She came back and confirmed what she had said. "That's right, they're large cubes and they're active."

I was up and heading for the door by this time. "Which road are they on?"

The reception was getting much better as I approached my truck. I heard her saying something. "The north road about three hundred meters in."

Parts of her response were not coming in yet, but it was getting better. "Where are you, Melanie?"

Finally, things cleared up and she came back. "I'm at the intersection. My phone would not work near these cubes so I had to get back to the intersection before my phone would work right."

"All right, I'm on my way."

I called Stan and advised him of the find. He and Herman decided they wanted to come along with me so we all met at my truck and headed out. When we got to the intersection, Melanie was sitting on the ground by her rig.

The three of us got out of the truck and ran over to her. "Melanie, are you, all right?"

She was sitting on the ground with her legs spread and her arms back with her hands on the ground holding her up. "I don't know. There was a large strong shock wave released from the direction of the new cubes and it knocked everyone flat. Boss I've never experienced anything like it. It was even bigger than the small cube on the east road.

"I've seen blasts caused by explosives and the shock wave they create, but this one was so strong it smacked clear into my core. It was different and it's got me real scared. There was no sound with it, just the shock wave. I have no idea what set it off. We were all back here at the intersection when it went. You should see what it did to the forests across the road and east of it."

I turned and looked over across the road to the east and the forest was laid flat. "What about the exploratory teams working into the forest area?"

"Joe, I have no idea. They don't answer and they should be heading back by now. If they are on time, they should be coming out right there in about fifteen minutes."

I looked where she had pointed and then turned back to her. By this time, she was standing up again. "Have all the other crew members called in? Is anyone missing?"

"No Joe, everyone called in and reported their position and condition. The only thing we do not have is the location of the exploratory team."

There was an eerie quietness around us. Nothing, not a sound of any kind, "Melanie we want to go down to the cube and take a look."

I got a feeling by her reaction to my request she would prefer not to go back into that area. In just one day this woman had been knocked down two times by these cubes and she has survived. She looked at me and then nodded. "All right Joe, we can take my rig."

We headed to the location of the new cube and as we approached the area, I could see the forest across the road from the cube, to the east was laid flat. The shock wave had gone out in a one hundred eighty degrees arch starting at the south side of the cube on around to the north side. Everything behind the cube toward the base was still up and intact.

Just then Melanie got a call. The exploratory team had returned and they need to talk to her as soon as possible. It was important.

We all scrambled back to the rig and back to the intersection. The team was resting along the road when we pulled up. As we got out of the rig the team leader walked over to us and what he said would change everything.

Melanie looked at him. "What's up, Troy?"

He stopped and took another drink from his water bottle. "Melanie, we found a building."

I immediately responded "You mean

you found a foundation of a building?"

He turned toward me. "No Sir, I mean we found a whole intact building."
Melanie then interrupted.

"Troy, this is my boss, Joe Nash." We shook hands and I continued. "How far in?"

"All the way to our limit for this search, one-hour in."

I couldn't help it; this was just too important "How big?"

He took another drink and then started to lay things out for us. "It was a single-story structure and appeared to be about two hundred meters by five hundred meters, Sir. The walls look new, like they had been built yesterday. It is made of the same metal concrete material the roads are made from."

No way, this was unbelievable. We now have a building in the forest two hundred by five hundred meters in size and it had never been seen from the air. That just did not seem right. "You're telling me there is a large building out there and yet with all the incoming helicopters, we have never seen it?"

He was nodding his head. "Sir I had the same reaction until I looked up toward the roof and there are trees growing on top of the structure. They provide a perfect canopy over the building."

That seemed reasonable at the time and I continued to question him "Could you see into it?"

He was shaking his head. "No Sir, there were no windows, but we did find a door."

I continued to push the issue. "Could you open it?"

He took another drink. "No Sir, it felt solid and thick. There were no handles or any means of pulling or pushing it open. Yet, I'm positive that it is a door."

This was crazy, and I knew instantly everything had just changed. We were now looking at an actual structure, an actual facility that had to have been occupied and if we could penetrate it who knows what we would find.

I then turned to Melanie. "All right, Melanie, I want all your resources working on a road back to the building first thing in the morning. Be sure and pick a good route back into the area and by all means avoid any small or large cubes. Got it?"

She was already writing notes and making plans for the approach to the building. "We'll start at sun up, boss."

It was then I realized I had forgot about

Stan and Herman and then turned to them. "Sorry guys, do you have any questions?" They both shook their heads no.

I was still in the 'go-for-it' mode. "Okay, Stan and Herman, we need to get back to the meeting room. Everyone will be gathering there in a few minutes and we need to be there. It's all in your hands for the time being, Melanie, do it right."

As I said that I turned back to her and got my first real look at her since we came on scene. Her clothes were covered with dust and her face was all smudged with dirt. Her hair was a mass of tangle. The kid looked like she had just come out from under a pile of Rugby players. Yet, she still was focused and ready to go.

"Will do, boss."

As I walked back to my truck, I couldn't help but think that this kid was probably the best in-your-face assistant I had ever had. I made a mental note I would not be letting her slip off to work for anyone else. Whatever it took that kid, that young woman, was going to be a permanent part of my organization.

We got back to the meeting tent on time and got back to work. At the meeting, the teams presented their preliminary concepts and ideas. It's a wonder what people can do under pressure and this held true in this situation.

The computer team had developed a concept that would take less than twenty-four hours to gather the parts and build the system. They would be ready for a direct link up with the cube in about thirty hours. Their only question was how the link was going to be made?

The anthropologists were ready. Based on what they were provided with, they felt the social structure of the Demion's was that of a military based civilization. They were well advanced and probably had at least twenty-five thousand years of history behind their civilization.

The team leader presented their preliminary findings. "We have no idea as to their types of transportation, but based on the design and makeup of the artifacts we can expect just about anything.

"Based on what we have recovered so far, they had a technology that is way beyond our own. Their craftsmanship was exemplary and elegant. This speaks to a well-educated base population. They were exceptional in their social make up and hardworking overall. Naturally, everything we have put down in the report is subject to revision. Right now, this is the best gut feelings we can come up with."

The military experts wanted to get going.

I was probably most interested in what this team had to say in that they would be working directly off the items we had located in the artifact storage area. "All right, what do you have?"

The team leader, a younger man, stood up and brought an arm full of papers and data chips to the front. "We have a lot," the team leader responded. "First of all, they were advanced so far beyond us in weaponry we can hardly begin to address it here."

There was just so much evidence at this point they had to cut their presentation back some. So, they concentrated on the big stuff. "Let's start with the cubes. These devices are basically fire bases. By that we mean they were both defensive and aggressive or offensive. They have the ability to select weaponry and apply it in a highly selected field of fire. Not only that, but they are capable of attacking the opposition either physiologically or psychologically. This was demonstrated in the death of the first member of our project. It was again demonstrated in the shock wave attack that took another life.

"We do not know the extent of these units' firepower or capabilities, but right now they are extensive based just on what we have seen so far.

"Next are the cartridge cases that were found." He picked up several of the items and started to show them around. "There are two specific types along with their projectiles. We have to tell you we are looking at two different technologies here, one the Demion's and the other an unknown society or military power. We believe once we finish an in-depth study of these artifacts." He then paused before continuing. "We will find one of these military sides is Earth based and the other off Earth based."

That stopped the room dead in its tracks. People were going through papers, computer systems, talking between each other, and taking notes. What he said brought all to a dead stop.

I stood up. "How can you say that?"

The team leader took a deep breath. "Joe, it's the projectiles. He held both types up so everyone could see them.

180

As I sat back down, "What about the projectiles?"

He continued with his presentation. I for one was interested in what he was about to say and hoped to hell it was believable. "It's the projectiles, these rectangle ones, they are so different and so odd they would never have been made within the limits of our planet. The process needed to produce them is beyond the scope of this planet."

I turned and looked at Herman and then back to the team leader. It didn't fit from my perspective. "No, you're not getting through to us. That explanation simply will not carry."

I guess I sounded frustrated or something, but he turned to me and smiled. "Yeah, that's exactly the way I took it at first."

I could see the frustration building in his face. "Joe, let me put it to you this way. The projectile on the left could not be produced within the Earth's gravitational field. Nor could it be produced within an atmosphere as we know it. It's impossible."

It still was not getting through to me. "You're telling us there was a battle here between Earth based and alien-based armies?"

The team leader seemed to show a

sense of relief. "That is correct."

The room fell dead silent at that moment. A tension had developed throughout the room as people were trying to come to grips with the idea that one of these items was not of earth origin.

He continued. "If we speculate, we think the Demion's were fighting for their very existence here. This may well have been the final battle of that existence.

"As you look at the two different types of cartridges, one is round and elongated and the other is rectangular or boxlike in shape. The boxlike cartridge is the alien cartridge."

I guess I still wasn't getting it or else I simply did not want to. "How do you know?"

He was feeling the pressure but remained calm as he explained. "There are some simple tests we can do to help determine the metals make up. We did a couple of those test and some of the components of those cartridges were not of this Earth. In fact, we don't know what they are."

I felt a little sorry for the guy, but their assessment of what the artifacts meant did not make sense to me. "All this in just two hours?"

By this time the team leader could feel

the attitude of everyone in the room being against them. "Well, we had some help there. Several of our team members know some of the metallurgists who were working on these items, so we called them and got the scoop on this stuff. They were reluctant to give it to us at first until we filled them in on what we were up to. By the way, two of them want in on this project. Is that all right?"

All I could do was to shrug my shoulders. "Sure, it is, the more the better."

"We'll call them."

He turned back to his presentation and continued. He knew he had stirred up a real controversy and he was not done yet. "Now back to our findings. It appears some of the artifacts are in fact parts of weapons. We do not know if they were broken down by explosions or were extra parts that were available for repair purposes. Or, they could be part of weapons that were being maintained at the time something happened. The fact is every item of this nature found around this area is weapons parts. The puzzle is why are all of them disassembled? Why is not one fully assembled weapon around?"

He again paused to let that statement sink in. It was like he was trying to draw us into a mystery and he thought he had the answers as well. "We think the other two reports fit in well with our findings. We also think we need to be more diligent in our processing of the lands in the area. In our desire to get to the object in the mountain, we have charged across the ground oblivious to the possibility, no, probability there are remains of members of those two armies there in the ground."

Another silence passed over the meeting room. Everyone was looking around to see what the reactions were of everyone else. It was probably the most uncomfortable moment of the evening.

I turned and looked at Stan and Herman. "Okay, everything has changed. Get everyone in here now. I want every person involved in the project here now. Damn, I hate it when someone is right and I'm totally wrong."

Herman walked over by me. "Joe, take it easy. We're making great strides. I am totally pleased with what is taking place and how this thing is going. In fact, I am more than pleased. I think we have finally found the key to getting past those cubes. If we do this right, we have it made. Joe, the key is our minds. The cubes have the capability to be a real problem, but we have our minds and they will overcome the cubes in time. And right now, I think that time is getting shorter."

Chapter Six

THE BATTLE FOR YEARTH

The meeting started late, but everyone was there. That included the scientists, the machine operators, the support teams, the maintenance teams, medical, logistics, everyone. The meeting room was packed, but we were able to get them all in.

It was my job to start. I stepped up to the dais and tapped the microphone, it was on, and that got everyone's attention. "Listen up, people. We have a lot to do and a short time to do it in. Right off the bat everything has changed. So, the following things will take place stat. Get me, that means fast. Pay attention for your part in this. We don't have time to repeat everything two and three times.

186

A few people came in late and scurried to their seats. "First, all machinery including cars, trucks, graders, cats, anything on wheels will be brought to the staging area just outside the base line set up by the cubes. Those machines will be parked and held in that location until further orders.

"Your maintenance and operations people will spend your time carrying out all the maintenance needs for each and every piece of equipment in the staging area. When we call for them, we will need them right then, not in two or three hours when you finish servicing them."

I stopped and waited for the reaction to die down and to check for any questions being raised.

During our staff meetings it had been decided we needed to move back to ground zero in our working the dig and that meant laying down some hard and fast directives. This would change everything we had been doing prior to this moment.

"Listen to me, people. It is vital you do this and do it as fast as you can move. Don't kill anyone doing it, but get those machines moved and do it first thing this evening. We want the majority of those machines serviced and ready by morning, any questions?"

Again, I paused and waited. The room was dead silent by this time and people were making notes and looking around to see what others were doing. There was silence.

"Second, and this is vital, anyone who has had even the slightest headache, vision problem, bleeding from anywhere on the face, anything that is not normal for you. Please report to the medical facilities first thing tomorrow morning. You will not be permitted to return to the work site until you have received a clearance from the medical staff."

I noticed a number of people getting together and talking by this time.

"Hear me again. This is important. It is directly related to your life, but even more so to the lives of your team members. So, be there and do not delay. Are there any questions?"

Again, there was silence. I gave those in their mini conferences a moment to respond if they had any questions.

"Third, medical people, sorry, but this is going to hit you the hardest. You will be prepared and ready at eight hundred hours for those responding to the last order. You know what you're looking for. Give these people a complete examination and if you're satisfied then give them a clearance and send them back to work. Do you have any questions?"

Again, there were none. It appeared the tone and demeanor of every one had changed. There was an air of concern in place of the normal state of everyone. Clearly, we had their attention.

"Fourth, all scientists, we have two objectives at this time. One is the main base inside the perimeters set down by the cubes. Second, there has been a building found in the forest area north of the main road outside the base line. We want two groups with all disciplines included to address these two locations."

That announcement set them off. There was a clamor of people trying to get their teams together and ready to try and gain assignment to the new building. The level of excitement had just gone off the charts.

I found myself having to try and overcome the noise of everyone reacting to the announcement of the new duty assignments. "Here are the working parameters. For the main base region, which includes all the valley west of the line set down by the cubes and includes the cubes.

You will conduct a complete and total archeological study of that area." They were finally starting to slow down and listen to me. "Now, it's big, about one and a half kilometer by one and a half kilometer in size. You will need to do your layouts and search every centimeter."

Hands shot up all across the room as people were vying for a selection as to where they would be assigned.

I selected the closest person with his hand up. "What are we searching for?"

This was the first time we had seen this level of excitement among those working the project. "All right everybody, calm down, we have a question being asked. He asked. 'What are we searching for?'"

I continued to speak but in a louder voice. "You're archeologists. Do what archeologists are supposed to do. However, the most important target is bones. We are looking for the remains of those who were here."

I finally had their attention again and was ready to hit them with the rest of the target news. "Now, prepare yourselves for this. Primarily we are looking for bones of occupants that have been in a military conflict. We need to know the locations, depth found, condition of the bodies, and violent damage done to them.

"Next you need to try and discern between those that are human and those that are not."

The room fell silent. A hand went up from the middle of the room. "Joe, are we talking aliens?"

It was almost as if everyone was waiting for the last shoe to drop. "Yeah, Mike, that's exactly what we are talking about. Our military team has determined the weaponry we have found so far is of two different technologies. They are certain one is not Earth based. So, do what you do. Make this the finest dig anyone has ever witnessed before.

"Now, listen up. The base team must work within the established controls of the cubes. Pay attention to one another. We are going to assign medical people to your teams to watch over you. If anything develops, do not play the hero game. Move your ass out of there immediately. Got me?

"All right, you know what you have to do. There are a couple of other concerns I have for you. When working around any of the cubes, please be careful. Do not touch the cubes in any way. We are not at that point yet.

"Next, do not point anything at the cubes. I don't care how harmless it is, just don't do it and that means your fingers too.

"The cubes will be monitored. As long as they are blue or amber, we feel fairly safe they will not be a threat. If they go red or orange, then get out of there fast. Run for your ever-loving lives, because that is just what you'll be doing. Got me?"

"Now, the building east of the base boundary line, that building is located north of the main road and west of the secondary north bound road. Do not, I repeat, do not bring any machinery into the area until all preliminary preparations have been done. By that I mean you will personally walk every square inch of area to ensure there are no small cubes or other unknowns.

"Once you have accomplished that, you can then call for the machinery you will need to clear the route to the building and clear an area around the building. Remember, the small cubes are the more deadly of the two types we have found. They will react and it will not be pleasant. We have already lost at least one person to their shock wave and several people have been injured, I don't want any others."

By this time the place was in a controlled state of riot. I was already worn out and decided to let things calm down on their own before continuing on. So far, I had covered a lot of ground and everyone needed a few minutes to work through it.

I walked over to Stan and Herman and looked at both of them. "Have we unleashed a monster here?"

Stan laughed, probably the first laugh I have seen out of him in weeks. "Joe, I think we have unleashed a group of people who have been waiting for this moment to really go after this place and learn a few things."

I nodded and turned and walked back over to the dais and start to get everyone's attention. "All right people, let's get back to work." I stood there waiting for the place to quiet down, which it eventually did. "Once you have the area cleared to your liking, your main target will be the penetration of the building. Our best intelligence about this structure is that it is around two hundred by five hundred meters and single story. We do not know if it has an underground element to it at this time.

"Next, there are no windows in this structure, just one door. Which means it is a fortified facility, so handle it as such."

I was trying to emphasis the necessity of our being careful and cautious as we moved in on the building and the area around it.

"People, take your time. There was one hell of a battle here and we don't know the extent of the armament used so if you find anything you cannot identify, mark it and back off. We'll get the weapons experts in there. Also, you are looking for remains.

"The teams working these two projects will be headed up as follows. Lloyd Stapleton will head up the Valley Team. Those wanting to work that area will report to Lloyd. Those who have been working that area and who want to remain with Lloyd will stay with him.

"The second team will be headed up by Herman Blumfield and they will be working the Building Project. Those not assigned to the Valley Team will now be assigned to the Building Team. Right after this meeting both teams need to form up with Lloyd and Herman.

"All right, everyone, listen up." It was like trying to stand in front of a herd of hungry elephants, they just kept pushing ahead and pinning me against the gate. "These two teams we have just identified are priority. The rest of us are here to support them, period. If the phone rings and one of these team leaders says jump, your job is to jump as high as they tell you, got that. Anyone starts playing games and you'll answer to me.

"Now, everyone has their assignment. DO YOU HAVE ANY QUESTIONS? If not get to bed and get a good night's sleep, I want everyone up and on line at eight hundred hours. Remember, do it safe, but do it hard. Get going."

I turned to Stan. "Stan, let's see what time it is? All right, it's ten o'clock. Let's go see Bob. We need to talk to him."

Stan had just picked up his papers and walked over to me. He could see I was agitated about something. "Joe, what's bothering you?"

He could see I had a lot on my mind, but his intuition told him there was something else, something I was not communicating to him and the other leaders. I was inclined not to address it at that time, but thought better of it. "Well, there is a whole list, but right now I need to talk to Bob about his experience with the cubes.

"Something is eating at me about this whole situation and I need to get a few things clear. I need you there so you can be aware of what I am feeling and what is actually bothering me."

"Bob is in his tent. He was released by the medical staff this afternoon, but ordered to take it easy for a day or two."

I stepped down off the stage and started walking toward the main entrance with Stan following me. "That's fine I just need to talk to him."

We walked across the compound to Bob's tent. As we entered the tent he was sitting at his desk.

I walked over to the chair next to his desk as he was turning toward me. "How's it going, Bob?"

He turned in his chair and looked at both of us. "Right now, Joe, I feel fine."

Stan continued over to the other side of his desk and sat down facing Bob.

"Any more contacts with the cubes?"

He leaned back in his chair. "No, but they're there I can feel them."

"Is it threatening?"

"No, as a matter of fact it's rather

comforting." He was sitting back in his chair with his elbows on the arm rests and his hands clasped together.

I guess I had a look of doubt on my face. "Really?" I was not expecting that response and it surprised me a little.

It was obvious he had seen it on my face and he smiled. "Yeah, they are sending out a low soft vibration that seems to calm every part of me."

I was listening to him closely and he did sound comfortable. "Does it scare you?"

There was this look of patience on his face that gave me a sense of comfort. "No not really. Joe, at first, I was concerned, but the cube assured me it meant no harm to me. Then it said we were one."

As I listened to him, I could see in his eyes he was relaxed and comfortable, especially when I compare it to the last time, I saw him. No this was a man who was clearly not in pain and was functioning just fine. "Bob, the reason we are here is that things have been happening all over the area. We have pulled all our machinery into the staging area and have assigned two teams to start detailed archeological digs in both the base area and the area east of the base and north of the road. We found a building out there and it's a big one.

"We have also found a smaller sized cube which has turned out to be more deadly and reactive than the bigger cubes. Can you tell if there is any contact with those smaller cubes through the bigger ones?"

Bob started to nod his head. "Strange, Joe, I had that feeling earlier today. I noted there was a communication taking place between the three cubes on the base and something else. It had to have been the smaller cubes."

It made both Stan and I sit up a little straighter. That was what I wanted to hear. "Do you know what the communications were?"

Bob leaned forward and put his elbow on the desk top. "Yeah, the larger cubes ordered the smaller ones to stand down."

I might as well have been slapped in the face when he said that. It was totally unexpected and exactly the opposite of what I was expecting. "What?" That caught me by surprise, a real surprise. I had figured the smaller cubes would be left in their normal functioning state and we would have to tread lightly around them.

A slight smile came across Bobs face as he watched my reactions to what he had just said. "That's right they ordered the smaller cubes to stand down."

I looked at Stan and he looked at me and then Bob and then I looked at Bob. I mean, this was not what I had expected and as a result I was somewhat confused and a little frustrated.

Finally, I just said what I was feeling. "What the hell does that mean?"

Bob sat back and shrugged his shoulders. "I guess it meant to stand down or stop whatever they were doing.

"Look, Joe, Stan, as best as I can tell, the people who were killed or injured were from reactionary responses of the cubes. Once they realized the people were not a real threat they stood down. They are restraining themselves. As long as we are not a direct threat to them, they will leave us to our business."

I sat up. "You have no idea, wait a minute." It was then when it hit me. You know the simplest most obvious thing is probably the most reasonable answer, it was the obvious response.

Stan knew almost immediately I had hit

on something. "Joe, what are you thinking?"

I actually became light headed when he said that. I then started a train of thought. "It just hit me. These cubes are military right? That means they are designed to respond to aggression or aggressive acts, right?"

Both Bob and Stan were nodding their heads as I spoke. "And, if there are no weapons, then those around them are non-combatants." Frustration washed over me. It was that simple and direct. The issue was threat and not anything more complex. They perceived a threat and reacted. Once the threat was gone, they stood down.

Stan's voice sounded breathless as he spoke. "Holy crap, Joe, you've got it!"

I almost wanted to cry it was so simple. "Stan, I think we do."

It had taken us all this time and the death of two of our people to finally see it and it was so simple, so obvious, I was stunned.

I turned back to Bob. "Bob."

He sat there and quietly responded to me. "Yeah, Joe."

I was exhausted and this whole event had drained me. "Bob, I need you to stay in continuous contact with myself and Stan. Got that?"

"I do. Joe, I understand."

Yes, I knew full well he did and now we did too and it made little difference right then. "Look, you're the key to this project right now. You are the only one who is on talking terms with the cubes and you're gaining an in depth understanding of them. Anything you deem to be of importance or a concern you need to relay to the two of us. We have decided to give the cubes all the space they want and work as if they were not among us."

Bob smiled, "Joe that fits in perfect with what I'm receiving from them."

I felt a surge of air rush out of my body and semi-collapsed back in my chair. "That's great. Now let's go find out about Battle Yearth."

The next morning everyone was told about their non-combatant status, before I let them head out to their assigned areas, I advised them. "We are worker bee's people, not soldier ants. As long as we maintain that attitude, the cubes are not concerned with us."

Everyone seemed to relax. All the teams and support groups seemed to take on the same attitude. After hearing the non-combatant status everyone headed for their assigned tasks and duties.

It was not long after they started, we learned we were on the right track. The walking teams in the forest came across what appeared to be bunkers. Because of the years involved, they were hard to see, but they were there. The earth around them had moved and aged over the millenniums, but the hardware they used lasted. The locations were marked and they moved on.

As the teams worked their way back into the forest area, the terrain started to flatten out. It was clear this area had been artificially re-conformed. It appeared more like a tree farm, yet the trees were of different types and sizes. Still the land was laid flat and clearly indicated activity in this area.

As the teams moved on, the building started to come into view. When first seen, it appeared as a dark mass in the thickness of the trees. From that distance it would not have been recognized as a building, just a dark area in the forest. When closer in it was noted, the trees had grown right up against the walls of the building, some literally pressed against the wall as they grew.

No other structural activity was found in the area and so they moved in and started the clearing process. It would require a road coming in from the north road coming off of the main east to west road. It was estimated they were around five hundred meters in from the road much closer than trying to run a road back to the main east to west road.

As they built the new road in from the north road, it appeared as though this area had been excavated before. It was not long before we figured out an old road had been in this place before, but it had not been made up of the usual metalcrete they used on the other roads. This road was similar to the one we were building and the indication of its presence was just a difference in the layering of the soil in the area.

Once the road was in, a number of crews came into the area and started the tree falling part of the project. The sheer size of the building meant an area, at least twice the size of the building's footprint would be required and it would involve a lot of logging. The good side of it was, the land was flat and the logging progressed well. Still, it would take several days to do the job.

Meanwhile, over in the main base area, the first body was located on the base proper. It was found about two thirds of a meter down in the soil and was lying face down, the body was stretched out and arms and legs spread. There was a massive area in the back, just below where the heart would be, blown out. It was a fast and cataclysmic death.

In actuality it was a fossil and not actual bone. The only things remaining from the original were all the metal items. Their metals were strong and resisted anything and everything that tried to attack them.

We learned why we could find no fully assembled weapons. This person's weapon was lying at his right hand on its side. The stock was gone, probably made of wood, plastic or some other secondary material. The rest of the weapon was there. It looked much like many of our current day weapons except for the ammunition it used and the size of the barrel.

As we stood there, Professor Blumfield walked up. "Interesting isn't it, Joe?"

"Yeah, it is Herman. What do you make of it?"

He walked around the open pit and stopped on the opposite side from me. "Well, it brings up a huge number of questions and the first one is. How could any of these artifacts have been preserved over the hundreds of thousands to hundreds of millions of years they have been here? The skeptics are going to have a field day with this one."

I was halfway nodding and shaking my head after he had said that. Frankly right then and there I cared not a single iota about any damn critics. "I don't know Herman. We have the roads and the new building and the materials they are made from. Everything we have found or worked on tells us this place is old and the information from the cubes verifies that clearly. No, the skeptics may try, but they will surely fail in any attempt to minimize this finding."

Herman turned and looked at the layout of the dig before us. "Well, anyway, we have one individual found and we did it in less than eight hours. I have a feeling they're strewn all over the place and we will be hard pressed to find places to store them once we start the collection process."

I understood his concern and nodded my head. "Well, Herman, in that case we'll just have to be innovative."

We had no sooner finished our conversation when Jennifer came running up. "God Joe, we found one."

I had hardly shifted my attention to her

as she came running up to us. "Found one what, Jennifer?"

She paused and got herself composed. "Joe, it's an alien."

The words as she spoke them smashed into me. It almost staggered me. I looked at Stan and his face were paste white. Herman had already started to move when I felt myself surge into motion.

We covered the distance in record time. As I walked up to the site there were numerous people standing around. I managed to push my way through them and to the edge of the dig.

As I approached the team leader was telling Herman what had taken place. "We have been using a ground radar unit and have located and marked numerous places where anomalies were showing up. When we got here, we got the reading, but it was different. The anomaly appeared to be larger and denser. So, we decided to dig here, and there it is."

Laying there in the center of the dig was a fossil of a being. It appeared to be lying on its back, legs and arms spread. The upper half of its skull was gone with the separation area a jagged mess of bone. As I looked down on this individual, I was wondering out loud. "What makes them so sure it's alien?"

I then looked closer and I could see it. The skull was larger than a man's and elongated. The jaw bone was massive and it appeared to have considerably more teeth than a human. Its chest cavity was extended and was larger than an average human. Both the arms and legs were longer and more heavily built. No, this was alien for sure.

I looked over at Lloyd. "Weapons; what about weapons?"

"We have not found any tools or weapons on or near this one, Joe."

I nodded my head and looked at Herman. "All right, at least this confirms our theory this was a war between Earth (Yearth) and aliens. Keep going everyone, we are on the right track."

Over the course of the next two weeks numerous fossils of both Earth and alien beings were found and recovered. It was a massive project, but it was building a story for us that would rock the world once it became known. Not only did this present the facts there were prior civilizations on Earth before any history of man started and there were in fact beings who lived somewhere other than on Earth.

By this time the building project was really taking shape. The forest around the building and a road into it had been done and we had this huge monolith of a structure sitting there. There was nothing like a parking lot, which we would have anticipated based on our civilization. In fact, there was no metalcrete at all. The forest just came up to the building and stopped against it.

As I walked up to the building, the side of the structure where the door was, I again noted it was made from the same combination of metal and concrete, we had come to call, metalcrete.

A team had walked the entire perimeter of the structure looking for hidden windows or entry points and none were found. The place was solid as steel and almost impregnable. The point here is, nothing is impregnable and as long as there is a door present there is a way in, all we had to do was figure it out.

I walked up to Herman. "Herman, remember when the first worker was killed? At this time one of the archeologists was just placing her hands-on Cube One."

Herman was busy looking the building

over and then turned to me. "You're right, Joe, do you think maybe the same method could open this door?"

"Well, there is a good chance there's some kind of a combination involved which actually uses that process. The worry I have is when we touched the cube someone died. Is that possible here?"

Herman continued looking at the building. He had a way of kind of going away into his mind as he was observing or thinking about something. The greater the puzzle the deeper he went into himself. "The key is we have to eliminate the term impossible and keep in mind anything is possible in this place."

I turned to Stan. "Well, I guess we are going to have to try something. How about this? Is Bob Hammer available yet?"

"Well, yes he is, as long as he does not overdo it."

"Stan what if we brought Bob out here so he could walk around the grounds and building and then take a look at the door itself? No questions, just observing and walk around it. There may be a chance the cube could give him some insight as to how to gain entry to the building."

Stan mulled the idea over a few seconds. "All right Joe, let's try it."

The next morning, we brought Bob over to the building. As we pulled up in front of the structure, he was impressed by its size and condition.

I then told him. "Now, Bob, we are going to try an experiment and you're the catalyst in this experiment. We need to have you get out and walk around in front of the building. You will note there is a door right in the middle of this wall." I paused long enough so he could take a good look at the area of the door. "After you walk around in front of the place, we want you to walk up to the door and stand there in front of it."

He looked over at me. "What is supposed to happen?"

I smiled. "We have no idea. What we hope will happen is it will open or at the least the cube will communicate with you and either tell you to go away or tell you how to gain entry. I guess what I want you to do is try to get that damn door open for us.

"Kind of like a puzzle game, we know it will open, we just don't know how to open it. Do you have anything coming in from the cubes?"

"Yeah, it's got that low vibration going, has been for days now."

Bob sat there looking out the truck window at the building. He seemed to become calmer the longer he looked at the place. As soon as he opened the door and got out of the truck, he felt the vibration move up several octaves. He stood there with the truck door open looking at the place where the door was.

I noticed his action, it was like he was experiencing something, what I was not sure. "What is it, Bob?"

He looked back in the truck at us and then turned back facing the building. "The vibration changed. No message or anything like that just a change in the vibration. It went up two octaves I've never experience this before."

I leaned over toward the passenger door. "Go ahead Bob, continue."

As Bob walked away from the truck and started walking parallel with the building the cubes started a tapping vibration in his head. It was a strange description but there was no other way to put it. "Now it's tapping. You know, like someone tapping the lead end of a pencil on a desk top, yet it's still vibrating."

211

The tap increased in speed as he approached the building and when he was within ten steps of the door it stopped.

By this time Stan, Herman and I had gotten out of the truck and were walking up behind Bob. "What's up, Bob?"

"I'm not sure what to do next."

"Is the vibration still there?"

"Yes, and it hasn't changed at all."

He then took the next step and stopped again. We couldn't hear what was going on in his head, but we could see there was something going on.

Bob reached out behind him with his right hand, as if he was reaching for something to hold on to. "Now there is a tone in my head. It's a "C" tone."

He stood there watching the door and concentrating on whatever was going on in his head. He took a second step and the tone went up one octave. The next step and it upped another octave. When he got to about three steps from the door, the tone stopped and even the vibration, which had been there all along, stopped.

He took the next step and raised his right hand and placed it in the center of the door palm down. A blue glow appeared

212

around his hand and the door slid in-ward and then started sliding to the right revealing a long dark hallway. We then entry.

Bob looked back at me and I gave him the sign to go on in. As he stepped into the hallway it suddenly lit up. The entire surface of the upper walls and ceiling lit up. It was a solid mass of soft white light.

Herman's immediate response was, "How could that still be operational after nearly a billion years of just sitting here and doing nothing?"

Stan, Herman and I followed Bob in to the hallway and we started down it. The walls on both side of the hall were completely flat. No doors or insets of any kind were visible. It was a strange looking place.

The first thing that hit my mind was, "What a waste of space." As we continued down the hall, we first heard a quiet whisper of a sound and then we saw the first indication of a door appear on our right.

An indentation just appeared on the wall and another one appeared on the other side of the hall as well. It was a strange effect in that they did not open they just slid inward about four centimeters and then stopped. Markings of the same language we saw on the cubes appeared beside each door as each indentation appeared. The effect was spooky and unsettling.

After we had gone a short distance, maybe fifteen meters, the outside door started to close. Bob stopped and stepped back two paces and the door reversed again and opened.

Herman raised both hands. "All right, let's stop right here. We're going to have to figure out a way to keep this door open. We don't want you standing here all the time making sure we have access.

"There has got to be a method to block the door open or set it up to open automatically for anyone who comes along.

Well let's try it. Bob, go ahead and walk down the hall."

As he did the door closed. Herman then turned and walked toward the door and when he got to within five or six meters, it opened. He went on outside and then turned and the door closed. As he walked back to the door, it again opened. It was on automatic.

We were all trying to understand how it went to auto and then stayed there. Just then Bob raised his hand. "As long as there is a living being inside the building the door will be on auto mode. The only way it cannot be in auto mode is if one of the occupants locks out access."

I stood there listening to Bob and it came to me. "During the battle someone inside the facility put it on lock down and when the last one of them died inside the structure it went from lock down to closed. It was no longer on auto open because there was no one alive inside the structure."

Herman stood there listening to me and then nodded in agreement with my assessment of what had happened.

With that, the research teams flooded into the building and went everywhere. We quickly found all doors were accessible as a result of Bob's opening of the main entry door. When the first inner room door opened there was an air transfer which had not taken place in God knows how many thousands or millions of years. As we entered the office, we were amazed and shocked at what we saw.

The room lit up like the hall had. Sitting at a desk located at the midpoint of the back wall was a female. It was obvious she had been dead a long time. She was mummified and most of her clothes and content of the desk top were intact. The building was a treasure trove and it would take years to complete an in-depth study and evaluation of this place. We were not only looking back in time, but back to a time that was way before the human race re-initiated itself on Earth.

I stood there looking at this woman sitting behind the desk. She looked like she was sleeping. Both of her eyes were closed and she was sitting with both arms on the desk and her mouth was closed. She actually looked peaceful sitting there.

I couldn't help but wonder about what had happened, and whether she had left any one, any family behind when she passed. She had been locked away in this room for God knows how many millions of years and still she looked to be at peace. A strange and lonely feeling came over me and I felt I needed to leave her and respect her last moments alive.

We had scored big with the building, but the buried object was still our goal. We still had much to do before we could even begin to approach it. Hopefully, they would find evidence here that would help explain the object we were working toward.

Right now, we had two vital actions taking place, the main base search and the building search. The building search was turning out to be the more important and we set up a search control system in order to better manage the discoveries as we came upon them.

As each inner door was opened, a team would enter and make a determination as to its level of priority. If a body was present, the room had top priority. Rooms without bodies, but with furniture and equipment, such as what was found in any office, were classified second priority.

Common rooms, such as meeting, dining, communications, and so on were third priority. Empty rooms were the lowest level of priority.

Our hope was to set up a system that would bring the most important results the fastest. We needed information, as much as we could get. The battle that took place here must be understood if we ever hoped to approach the object and make any sense out of it.

The search had been going on for maybe three hours when one of the technicians walked up to us. "We have found something we think you should see."

We followed her to the inner areas of the building. As we turned a corner into another hallway, we entered a much larger hallway. It was probably three times wider than the first one we entered and was easily one to one and a half meters higher.

At the end of the hall, we saw two massive doors that were standing open. Inside the doors we found a large room. At the far end of the room was a dais located in the center with two large screens on the left and the right.

I stood there looking the room over. "Stan, Herman, do you see the screens? They have media here, guys. That means there must be a storage system for all the media activity."

"Yeah, Joe, and by the looks of the rest of the room it's a command center. There has to be an untold amount of data and other strategically important information they needed and used during the battle."

"You're right Stan there must have been, but it probably does not exist to this day. If it was electronically maintained, the passage of time would probably destroy everything. I doubt if any of this equipment in here will function."

I turned toward Herman. "Why do you say that? Everything else that would depend on electronics has functioned so far. Why not this area as well? It is possible and probable that all the media and data records or storage is gone, but there is no reason why the hardware should not work."

My mind was scrambling to try and make sense out of everything we were seeing. It was then it dawned on me I was not seeing the obvious. I was not seeing what should be there.

"Guys, there is a problem?"

"Yeah, what is that, Joe?"

"Herman this building is sitting right in the middle of a war zone, right?"

"Well, so far that is true."

"Then why is there no damage or signs of assault outside or inside this structure?"

I sat down at one of the consoles at the back of the room and looked at the surface of the desk and the panel of switches and screens in front of me. I turned the chair to face square on and, (*bang,*) the panel lit up.

I jumped up and backed away from the desk as Stan and Herman stood there. As I moved away, the desk went dark and looked as it did before. I stepped over and sat down again and turned to face the console and it lit up again. Stan and Herman moved in closer and leaned over the desk on both sides of me.

Herman's face had gone almost white as he looked at the console. "Joe, what did you do to start that and what is it?"

"Don't know guys. But it's running."

At the same time, several other people were doing the same thing and reacting in the same manner. Desk consoles were lighting up all over the room. Sometime during the process, the big screens at the front of the room activated.

Stan hadn't said a word and then suddenly asked. "Joe, where the hell is the power for this place coming from?"

"Hell, I don't know. But let's hope it lasts for a few minutes, I'm into this thing now."

People were looking over the consoles and wondering what all the markings meant. Finally, someone reached out and touched a green button. As I looked around, I noticed every console had a green button on it in the exact same place. These buttons were triangular in shape and had a circle in the middle with a blue dot inside the circle. We all sat there waiting for something to happen, but nothing apparently happened anywhere.

Finally, Stan became aware of what was going on and got control of the situation.

"Hey people, pay attention. Don't push anymore buttons until we have some idea as to what we're doing."

Someone else called out. "Look at the main screens."

Everyone's attention was drawn to the front of the room and the main screen. A line of symbols was running across the top of the screen assembly. The symbols ran from the right to the left. This told me that their written language was written from left to right and was read the same, just like ours.

Bob walked up to the front of the room and stood there in the middle looking up at the main screens.

I went up by him. "What are you doing, Bob."

"I may be able to translate all this for you."

Just the way he said it surprised me. "How?" No sooner had I asked when it dawned on me. He could communicate directly with the cubes and they could tell him what was being said.

"Right, got ya. Go ahead and ask."

"Get me a recording unit."

Someone reached over and passed him a mic. "All right I'll start at the beginning of

221

the next message. Here it comes. 'Tactical unit blue pulling back from quadrant four, under heavy assault by Vandions, current strength cut by two thirds, will not be able to sustain this quadrant much longer.

"Tactical unit red in quadrant three we're under heavy attack. We have been able to plug holes between us and quadrant seven, tactical unit green almost wiped out. Need additional reinforcement this region."

Bob's face was ashen as he continued to translate the images going across the upper screen. "Notify base perimeter they will break through within the next two to three hours. There are too many of them and our ammo is running low."

"All units from command, these facilities are now locked down. You no longer have access here. We will maintain control of forces from this position for as long as possible.

"All units, when given the order you will break and pull back to static position eight. All reinforcements have been positioned on that line. That is the no return line."

"Joe, what the hell is 'no return line?'"

I was transfixed by what Bob was

reading. "I have no idea, Stan, but it appears to be a significant order."

I turned back to Bob. "Bob, Bob, can you break away for a few minutes."

Bob turned facing Stan and I. "Their getting the shit kicked out of them."

I could see Bob was getting drawn into the event personally. "Bob, remember this is history. It happened tens of thousands to hundreds of millions of years ago. It's all done and over. Don't get tied up in it. There is nothing to be done."

He looked down and then straightened back up. "Right, I know, but it's hard not to."

I was looking him square in the eyes by this time. "I know Bob, but we have to keep everything in perspective. Now, can you check with the cubes and find out if there was video or a similar media available, we may view?"

Bob turned and walked over to the console again and stood there looking down at all the buttons and switches. His hand reached out and pushed a gold button.

Meanwhile, over in the base proper dig the scientists were finding more and more body fossils. In some places they were stacked one or two on top of one another. In

223

some piles they found Yearth and aliens piled together, right where they fought and died.

As the dig moved closer to the mountain, the numbers of fossils increased. They were everywhere. It had to have been a mass orgy of death. The scientists could not even imagine what it must have been like. The aliens appeared to just keep coming and they simply outnumbered and overran the defenders.

They continued to dig and find and identify the fossils of a battle long passed in a time which the Earth of this time knew nothing about. Finally, about halfway to the base of the mountain they found a huge number of fossils. They were stacked one on top of the other all over the area. In this situation, they were almost all alien. There were few Yearth bodies anywhere in this mess.

Twenty meters in they started to find the line of Yearth forces laying in every conceivable way and manner. As the scientists stepped back and looked at the overall picture it was clear that there had been a separation of the two opposing forces and they all died within their own lines. It was the strangest picture they had ever seen.

At the building, Bob was continuing in his translation. "They're coming at us from every direction. They just keep coming. There's no end to them. The left flank of the line is in hand to hand fighting now. We'll be there shortly. Command, we may have to activate Dehaven. Got me? We may have to activate Dehaven. We've got you. We can't do that until the line is totally lost."

Bob turned and walked away from the screen. "I need a rest and get me something to drink."

Stan called to the team leader. "Get some food and drink in here now."

Within five minutes, the food and drink were on the desk by Bob. He picked up a bottle and drank it down in seconds. He was clearly under a heavy level of stress and I was questioning him about going on. But he wanted to.

Bob continued. "Command we're losing it. Fire Dehaven now or we'll have a total catastrophe."

"Team leader, you know what that means don't you?"

"Yes, we do, but there is no other way to stop them. Either do it now or they gain control of the system. Do it now."

225

"Command to all units, Dehaven to come on line in ten, Dehaven fired, countdown started."

With that Bob sat down. I stepped over and put my hand on his shoulder. "What is it, Bob?"

"Dehaven."

I was puzzled by his response. "Bob what is Dehaven?"

"Dehaven, Joe, Dehaven is the cubes. They set the cubes off and they raked the entire battle field killing every living creature within their range. Everything died, Aliens, Yearth people, animals, insects, everything, even those here inside the structure. They all died right where they were. The entire battlefield, all of it, is sitting here just as it happened nine hundred thirty-three million years ago.

"It was the last battle on the face of the Yearth. By this time every city, town, village, road, bridge, track, whatever were destroyed and gone. Joe, there was nothing left, even the aliens were gone. All that is left is this area here in Brazil. Why it survived, I don't know, but it did and we're here now to learn of their existence. Oh, and the object? Yes! That is the System, whatever that means."

226

By this time the dig had come to a complete stop on the base proper. No one was doing anything. There were so many data and artifacts people were overwhelmed.

Jennifer called in just then and related the situation to me.

After hearing her report. "Okay, Jen, let's call it a day and have everyone return to the meeting room. Have them take their time. We won't be doing anything before eight o'clock this evening. Tell them to get cleaned up, get something to eat, and relax until we call everyone together."

Meanwhile, several language specialists in the structure had been taking the recordings of Bob's translation and putting them into a computerized translator. They were building a system to translate all the markings and data systems we had found. In just a matter of days, we would have access to just about anything this past society had been able to accomplish.

Just then, Melanie came up to me. "Joe."

I looked around toward her. "Yeah, what?"

She had this worried look on her face. "Joe, I found something I think you need to see."

I was still busy watching Bob as he calmed down. "Where?"

She remained quiet and slowly said. "It's here in the structure."

I looked at her and realized something was going on. "Okay. Stan, I'm going with Melanie for a few. I'll talk to you when I get back."

Stan turned and nodded at Melanie. "All right, Joe, we'll wait here."

We left the main room and went down the wide hallway and then turned away from the door. We went probably twenty-six meters when she turned and pushed her way through a door. As I entered the room, I found myself standing in a stair-well and the stairs were going down.

I guess my mouth dropped open as I looked at her. "A basement?"

She started shaking her head. "No Joe, something much more intriguing and thought provoking."

We went down ten levels before coming to a small room with one door in it. At none of the landings above were there any doors. She opened the door and as it swung open, the lights came on and I was looking down a long square tunnel. It ran off to the west, due west.

I looked at Melanie. "Don't tell me it goes to where I think it goes."

"Yap, no more digging. It's there."

I knew she had been there, to the object. "Did you go inside?"

She shook her head. "No, I felt we should do that orderly and properly. I wanted to, but knew better. Right now, all I can tell you is there is one hell of a massive object down there at the end of this tunnel. When you get there, you will not believe what you are looking at. Boss, it's so far out there I have no way of telling you just what to expect."

I think I was leaning against the wall when I turned to her. "Melanie, was anyone else with you?"

"No, boss, just me."

I knew this girl had a head on her shoulder and right now she had earned her pay this time around for sure. "Okay, let's get back to Stan and Herman."

As I walked back into the command center, they had the main media screens functioning. I froze in my tracks as I watched the fighting going on between the two sides. For the first time we were seeing alien beings walking and dying here on earth. And, of course we were seeing citizens of a prior civilization in close and deadly combat with the aliens.

It dawned on me what we were seeing was something that took place hundreds of millions of years ago and it was as clear and clean as if it was just now happening. I walked on over to Stan and Herman and just stood there.

"Herman, when did they get it on line?"

"About ten minutes ago, Joe. Bob got it from the cubes and has been able to locate a complete library of media files that appear to cover the entire conflict and in addition extensive files on the normal everyday lives of those back then."

"I wonder?"

"What Herman, what do you wonder?"

"Well, I was just thinking are we looking at our future?"

"You mean you're wondering if we will make the same mistakes and have the same conflicts as they did." I said as I watched the screen.

"No, I said I was wondering if what we are seeing is actually our future."

"Herman, I don't understand what you're saying?"

Finally, he turned to me. "Look, we have assumed this location is the result of a civilization that existed over nine hundred million years ago and this may be true, but is it also possible we are seeing what we will eventually become and what will happen to us at that time." Herman was clearly concerned as he talked.

I stood there in a state of mild disbelief. "Herman, if that is our future it was 6510 and we are in 2035, which is only three thousand nine hundred eight years from now and we know this was happening over nine hundred million years ago."

He was nodding his head but was more than just a little serious. "I know, it seems like that, but time can do strange things. Could it be possible this happened nine hundred million years ago and is only three thousand nine hundred eighty years from now?"

"Herman, if that is true, then time is running in a circle. I don't think that is possible."

"Joe, I think it is absolutely possible. And I think we are about to prove it." He was serious as hell.

This was an argument I really did not want to have and especially at this time and this place. I still had to say something. "That just does not make sense at all."

Herman shrugged his shoulders. "Well, it's just an idea right now, but it's one we will need to consider."

Finally, I nodded. "All right, I'll go along with that, but it's disturbing as hell."

I then dropped the bomb shell on the three of them. "By the way, just in case you guys want to know, Melanie found a way to the object."

Everyone stopped talking and Stan turned and looked at me. I'll tell you right here and now as I watch them react it was the most fun, I have been involved with in a long time.

"That's right, she found the object. So, would you gentlemen like to accompany me? Bob, that includes you."

Chapter Seven

ALIEN HERITAGE

Twenty minutes later we found ourselves at the door to the tunnel. Melanie opened the door and stepped inside. As soon as she entered the tunnel the lights went on the length of it. It was a large structure with walls around ten meters high and it was all of twenty meters wide. We started down the tunnel. Melanie estimated the distance was around one and a half to two kilometers. It would take us around half an hour to get there, taking into consideration our conditioning.

As we walked down the tunnel, we started to notice different items and indentations on the walls. Some places looked like display shelves and other appeared to be for hanging things. They were about every ten meters. The floor had several lines running parallel to the wall and every so often there was a line across the tunnel floor perpendicular to the lines running the length.

None of it made any sense to me. In any military organization I was familiar with every building, vehicle, and tool was designed and built for a purpose. There were no frills. "Herman does these design elements suggest anything to you? These lines and indentations did not suggest a military or governmental purpose."

Herman stopped and looked around at the lines and wall features, "No, I can't say that it does. Remember, we're in an alien environment here and what we think really doesn't apply."

At about the half way mark, the tunnel changed in its size. The ceiling dropped down and the floor stepped up. The new floor to ceiling measurement was now around six meters and the width was now ten meters. The distance from the old floor to the floor of the new level had three steps that were the width of the new tunnel or hallway. We could not determine a reason for such a radical change in the shape of the tunnel.

We also noticed the light changed. It was now a lower luminous light. Before it had been bright and washed the floor and walls with a clean white appearance. Now it was a yellowish color and much lower intensity. The sound changed as well, the echo was gone and everything sounded flat.

Melanie pushed on down the tunnel. "We're about half way there."

From that point on, there were no more wall fixtures, if I can use that term. The rest of the way was simply a depressing environment.

Finally, as we approached the end of the tunnel, the walls on both sides started to angle in. By the time we got to the end they had reduced the space between the walls to just one meter, just wide enough for one individual to step through at a time.

We stopped at that point and were looking at one another. I guess we were trying to determine who would go first. Finally, Melanie said she would go ahead. I guess it was a situation where we knew someone should go first if for no other reason than for respect of the ranks, but no one seemed to want to take the lead at that time. Anyway, she found it and she should have the first step into it.

As Melanie step through the gap, another set of lights went on, but this time it was in a huge cavern of a space. The roof of the cavern arched up from the floor and over to the other side from us. I would estimate the highest point of the arch was around fourteen meters and the distance across was close to twenty-eight meters That matched the width of the object predicted by the sounding data.

The walls were of the same metalcrete and were smooth as glass. The lighting was much different though. There were two parallel runs of lighting panels that were an equal distance up the walls and down from the center of the arch. In addition, every nine meters there was a lighting strip that ran about two meters from the floor up and over the arch and down the other side to a point about two meters from the floor on the other side. It was a bright clean light, much like that in the largest part of the tunnel.

When I looked left and right, the ends of the chamber were probably around one hundred thirty-five meters in both directions. That would be the two hundred seventy meters the machine was thought to be. There were no partitions or cabins or internal buildings. It was one huge cylinder from one end to the other and with a flat floor. It wasn't a tunneling machine after all.

That was the curious thing about this place. It was a made object, maybe not a tunneling machine but a machine nonetheless. I was at a loss as to what it was for and where it came from.

Right then I looked down and I saw a circle around where I was standing. It was lit up by a dull bluish light. I looked over at Stan's feet and then Bob's and then Melanie's and each one of us had a circle around our feet, but a different color. I looked at the others and they then looked down.

Bob was the first to move and when he did, the circle moved with him. Whichever way he moved the circle was with him. I bent down and realized the circle was in the floor, not projected on top of it.

"That has to be a tracking system of some kind."

Stan was looking around. "Well, where do we go from here?"

I suggested we pick a direction and go. So, we decided to go right and headed for the end of the machine. As we walked, we noted the circle kept perfect contact with us and every so often a flash of light would charge up the wall and streak across the ceiling to the center of the arch and then disappear.

"What was that, Joe?"

"Stan, I have no idea, but make a note so we can address it later on."

About this time, we heard it. It was a low muffled sound which seemed to fill the air. It came from nowhere in particular and everywhere all at once. It was not loud or uncomfortable. It was just there. As we moved closer to the end of the machine, the noise grew louder. Based on its current level, I would estimate when we got to the end of the machine the noise would be around that of a normal adult male talking at a normal level. It was not uncomfortable and would probably not become uncomfortable.

When we got to the end of the machine, the wall was straight up, but this time it was not a solid surface. At the midpoint across the machine there was an indentation. We angled toward that spot and as we approached, we found a set of stairs going down. Well, there wasn't much around here to see so we went down.

As we came to the bottom, we found a

door and when we tried to open it, nothing. Bob walked over to the door. He looked at me. "If this and the building structure are part of each other then it is only reasonable the access through this door is the same as the access through the other door."

He put his hand on the center of the door with the palm down. Immediately, a blue light appeared around his hand and the door slid inward and then slid to the side.

He stepped through the door and, as we have become accustomed to, the lights went on. The ceiling in this area was around three meters high. I looked to my right and saw another indentation in the wall and another set of stairs. If I figured it right the upper open space above us was fourteen meters or so high. There must have been around that much space below the upper deck. This meant there could be as many as four floors in the lower half of this machine.

Melanie then started down the stairs toward the next level down. As she moved down the lights came on. We all moved down the stairs to the next level. As we approached the next level, we found another door, the stairs continued on down. Melanie opened the door as Bob did and we entered the second landing.

I then looked around the area we were standing in and noted a hallway went right down the center of that level and seemed to go on as far as the other end of the machine. I assumed if I stepped over into that hallway it would light up just as all the others had.

Stan did just that and as he entered the hallway it lit up as was expected and then we noted for as far as we could see there were doors, staggered about ten meters apart for as far as we could see. This place was going to be a challenge to search and inventory.

We decided not to continue down the hall and left that job for the coming research teams who would be working in this machine.

We started down the stairs and as we moved down, the lights went on in a progressive manner. When the last person passed the last light, it would then go off. It was strange watching the lights moved down the stairs with us. As we came to the third landing, I noted the stairs continued on down from that landing. On the first landing we found one single door and it opened in the usual fashion. The same was true for each landing thereafter.

This floor was all partitioned off. In

front of us was a hallway about three meters wide. To our left and right we could see two other hallways set at equal distances, each appeared to be three meters wide. The central hallway went probably seventy-five meters before it dead ended. There appeared to be a hallway teeing off of the central one. This place was a labyrinth. A maze of hallways and places used for whatever all those millions of years ago.

We all stood there looking down the hall and realizing what we were looking at was a treasure of incalculable value but we could also see a task so big we knew we did not have anywhere near the number of people needed.

"What do you think Joe?"

What the hell was I to think any way? We were standing at the entrance to a lower floor of a machine I had though had been a tunneling machine. I just couldn't think at this point.

Finally, I turned and looked at Stan. "Listen this is too complex and involved for us to venture any further. May I suggest we return to the main building and plan our procedure for this place? It's going to take an army to go through and make any sense out of it."

Everyone agreed and we headed back to the main building. Just the sheer size of this machine was mind busting. As we walked back the way we came everyone was silent as we tried to deal with the magnitude of the job this place had in store for us.

About forty minutes later, we reentered the command center. As we entered the facility one of the military specialists approached us.

"Something has happened here you need to know about. We have found a meeting room over here to the left. If you would come with me Jennifer will be able to fill you in."

I was quickly reaching a point of overload and really didn't need anything more. "Now what the hell have they stumbled on to anyway? I don't know if I can take many more surprises this day."

We walked into the room and I went directly to Jennifer. "Hi Jennifer, how you doing?"

She turned toward me and I could see she was tired and a little pale. "All right, Joe, but we have found a number of things out. When you left, we were viewing some of the media files we had been finding around here."

She pointed out the piles of records they already had reviewed. "The computer whiz kids came in with their machine and set it up and turned it on. Everything hit the fan. Not bad, but there was so much of it we had to shut everything down and start over."

She reached over and threw a switch. "Finally, we restarted the computer and it made a direct link with Cube One. The interchange between the two of them took maybe five minutes. That's when the flood gates really opened."

Jennifer then swung around and pointed at the main monitor. "We started seeing massive amounts of Demion media files and their everyday life. They were a military unit as we had thought. We also found media files on the Vandions and what they looked like. There is so much here I'm going to cut right to the chase and leave the rest for later." She then punched several keys and brought up a whole new set of files.

She turned to us. "We were wrong on our assumptions about Earth based civilization and aliens being at war. Oh, they were at war it's just we identified them wrong. The aliens were not the ones we thought.

Those that looked like grotesque creatures from space were in fact the earth species at that time, the Vandions. Those we took as Earth based and looking just like us were in fact the aliens, the Demion's. This structure was theirs, as was the object and the base and the cubes and most everything else tied to this base."

She sat there a few seconds and then shrugged her shoulders. "We are them and they were the Demion's. They, we, invaded this Earth, which the true inhabitants of this planet called Yearth, and destroyed the entire population, except for this one military unit that had been assigned to attack and destroy this base the aliens had built in this area of what is now known as Brazil.

The end result being what we have found here now. They annihilated each other and in doing that left this base and all with it behind. Right now, sirs, it appears to be the basics of the story and what happened here almost a billion years ago.

"We don't know why this area survived the past nine hundred million years, but it did, and, in doing that, will rewrite our entire history." She was pushing buttons and running files across the screen as she spoke.

"The original inhabitants of Yearth were destroyed. For how long the world remained empty of the human race is recorded in the archeological record across this world.

"Now, the question is how did humanity as we know it come back? Clearly, we are not of the Vandions race, but are from the Demion's race. That is what we now know, but we need to trace this much deeper."

She paused as if she needed to prepare herself for what was to come. "I can tell you this, the amount and type of records recorded in this place rival anything I have ever heard of. It is massive and it covers every conceivable science there is."

As Jennifer presented the information, my mind began to bring together all the issues we had been working on and facing over these past several months. As I sat there it became clear to me the Demion's had not populated the world and if they did not, why did they come and invade in the first place?

That stuck in my mind. Why did they come here and invade in the first place if they did not occupy the planet after destroying the Vandions? Why? There had to be a reason.

Right then Jennifer got my attention. "Joe, Joe, are you, all right?"

245

I sat there looking at her, just staring.

"Joe, what's wrong?" Stan reached over and took my left hand. "Joe, are you sick, guy?"

Then it hit me. "God, the object!"

Stan was looking me square in the face. "What about the object, Joe?"

I found myself repeating. "Stan, the object!"

Stan was now nodding his head. "Joe, what about the object?"

I turned in my chair. "Herman?"

"Yes, Joe." Herman stepped forward and bent over by me.

I then point at the monitor and asked. "When you look at all this facility has and the depth of the records and data that is stored here what does it remind you of?"

Herman thought. "Well, let's see. As I look around it was obviously a combat command center, but the size, expanse in subject matter, and levels of technology is not normal for a facility such as this, unless."

"Yeah, unless what?"

Herman stood up and turned toward the screen on the wall. "Unless it was a research center as well, that's it. We have a facility here with a huge number of offices and

246

technology. It's advanced in every conceivable science we have checked on so far and then you have the object." Herman was clearly becoming more excited as each second passed. "Instead of building them as one, they are separated and one is buried and they are connected by a tunnel.

"When you look at the design of the tunnel, it brings up a number of questions as to why they built it that way. Joe, it's a research institution with a detached experiment center."

I slapped my hand on the table top. "You've got it Herman. This place was built as a center for the re-population of the Earth. The only trouble is the Vandions attacked it and in the process of defending it and all the valued technology, they set off the Dehaven device.

"That device killed everyone in this entire area. Not one being was left alive. In fact, not one biological life form was left alive." I was seeing it all and it was monumental. "And, the base within the cubes was sterilized of all biological life of any kind. The Demion's were not going to occupy this world they were going to re-populate it through genetic manipulation."

I stood up and grabbed the papers that were in front of me and turned toward the door. "We need to get back to the object and start a full-blown scientific study of the facility and this one as well."

"Stan?"

"Yeah, Joe."

I stopped at the door and looked back at him. "Get everyone back to the base and close this place up. Tomorrow morning at nine hundred hours, I want all scientists in the meeting room ready to work. Terry needs to be there as well. We're going to need additional scientific assistance in this thing. I would guess another fifty to seventy-five scientists."

I then looked over at Herman. "Herman, I'm going to depend on you to help organize this process. Up till now it's been basically an engineering process with scientific backup." Herman was already up and moving. "That needs to be reversed. Now it must become a scientific methodology with engineering support.

"So, by the morning you and I will have to get the framework of this system set up and ready to plug people into. What we are about to find out and learn will change everything."

By this time everyone in the room was standing and picking up their paperwork.

"Oh, by the way, did I mention we can expect a visit from the Demion's before we are done."

That stopped everyone in the room. I could feel the reaction to my comment as it ran through those present.

"Wait just a minute Joe. Are you saying that as a result of our activity here, the Demion's will be returning?"

I leaned on the table looking right at him. "Herman, I'm not only saying that, I can prove it. In fact, they are already on their way. This was not just an accidental find. This was deliberate." I started picking up papers and files and waving them. "This was set up those many millions of years ago by the Demion's for the express purpose to return and see what their handy work has produced."

Herman was standing across from me. "Joe, how did you come up with this anyway?"

At this point I knew without the slightest doubt what I was saying was in fact the truth, they were coming. "In actuality it was not me, but Bob and I. You see from the day Bob was tapped by the cube I have been wondering why. Why him? What was it that caused the cubes to select Bob over everyone else here? I felt the touch of them, as did others, but we did not have that one genetic marker that the cube was looking for. Bob has that marker and they zeroed in on him."

Herman's face just lit up and I could see his entire demeanor change and shift right there in front of me. He now realized I was right on it, and we had pushed the button just like any curious animal as it ventures into the trap.

"Their reaction to our first contacts was to ensure their primary objective was not damaged or sidelined. Once we activated them, and they determined we were non-combatants they started looking for the marker." I had never felt this excited in my life. "Remember their last order received was to implement Dehaven, which they did. That was the cubes last contact before going to sleep. I believe they had timed out and it triggered their going into hibernation.

"When we arrived, we woke them up and they reacted. But, as soon as they determined our status, they stopped and then started their search. Once they located Bob, they found the marker and that triggered their automated system and they started sending their information and data home. Bob kept telling us about the low vibration he could feel and hear and then as we moved in on the structure, he reported hearing tapping sounds and then tones, each one a communications element to the Demion's."

Everything was suddenly happening at once. It was as clear as it could be for me. They were coming back and we were the ones who had invited them. They played us just like a well-oiled machine and we had done everything they wanted us to do.

"It's the cubes, guys. Not only did they start a dialog with some of us, they notified their creators as to what was taking place. This entire facility is a test to determine the level of progress we have made since they planted us here. People, our parents are coming to see how we made out."

Chapter Eight

THE RACE IS ON

Herman stood there with this sly smile on his face as if he was watching one of his students suddenly connect with all he had been teaching. "All right Joe, say you're right in all of this. What does that mean to us?"

We had finished our preliminary tour of the building and were finishing up our preparations for the next morning's meeting. It was my hope Herman would be running the session as we worked up the procedures for moving into the alien machine and continuing the process in the main building.

Basically, we were speculating on my comment about the aliens returning here to Earth to determine what we had accomplished after all those years.

I had turned toward Herman. "I don't know, Herman. What if they are not satisfied with our progress? Does it mean they will terminate us? Their actions are wide open and we have little or no way to determine that, except for what is in these facilities."

"Then what you're saying is, what is to come will be found somewhere in all this?"

"That's right Herman. Here or in the object." He was listening closely now. "So, Herman, we need you to take over and organize this search in a scientific manner. However, it must be fast. I know in order to do it right, it is normally slow and easy, but we don't have that luxury at this time. This must be done fast and dirty, but in detail."

"Joe, that's a contradiction." He was shaking his head and pushing his chair back at the same time.

I could hear the exasperation in his voice. "I know, but I'm trying to emphasize the fact we do not have a lot of time and we had better be ready when they get here."

Herman then leaned forward looking right at me. "One question."

"What?"

"How long will it take them to get

here?" It was a serious question and it held the key to everything we were trying to do.

I shrugged my shoulders. "That, my friend, is the most important question of all. Remember, this event took place almost a billion years ago. That means this civilization, the Demion's, have been progressing for the past one billion years while we have been going through our creation and advancement. We don't have any idea as to how long they had existed before they came here and we don't know if they still exist now."

Herman leaned forward. "You have a point Joe, but I still think we need to instill some order and control in this project and speed never helps in that process."

"All right, I see what you're getting at. The best way to handle this is to set up priorities." I was not sure just where to start and hoped he did. "Our problem will be determining what those priorities are. What the keys are?"

Herman stood up and walked over to the writing board. We had discovered most of the conference rooms in the building had sections of walls that one could literally write on with their hands and fingers.

He started to lay out the organizational

needs for the project and the points of difficulty we were faced with.

I held up my hand. "Hold it, Herman. May I suggest the keys are here, right here in these facilities."

Herman looked over at me. "I don't doubt that, but what are they?"

I had gotten up and walked to the writing board. "How about this, we put together teams of five or six scientists in varied fields and then assign them to sectors of the facility and the object." I had taken over the board now and laid my idea out. "For example, at the object we could assign teams to a floor and each team would be assigned one of the hallways and then when all the hallways are assigned, we move down to the next floor and do the same."

As we discussed our plan Herman also drew the layout of the object and areas within the object teams would be assigned to. The fact was we were developing a map of our assault on this project and it was going to be a big one.

Herman was clearly satisfied with our progress. "That will work. Now, what do we do to key them to the targets of interest?"

Herman continued by answering his

own question. "That's not going to be to significant Joe. I suggest we target anything that appears to address genetics, technology, facilities design, weaponry, and space travel. If there are any others, we can add them as we need to."

He had now moved to the next board and started laying out lists of the wants and needs in targeting the keys we were looking for. After almost an hour we had a fairly well detailed layout of our process for the object. It was rough, but over the next few hours we would clean it up.

"Then let's set this up and get the teams put together. Then we need a place where everything that is portable can be taken to and staff there to deal with each item as it comes in.

I felt myself smiling as he said that. "Herman, I have the perfect place."

He was still looking at me. "Where?"

I stepped back from the boards and spread my arms. "The main floor of the object. We have an area there that is twenty-eight meters across and two hundred seventy meters long, all the room in the world for our needs."

He smiled and sat back onto the table

and looked at the boards. "That is perfect. We'll set it up that way."

After about four hours of organizing and assigning people to areas we had a system going. It was a little haphazard, but it was working.

Then it dawned on me we were missing one important element of this whole project. Bob.

"Herman, what would you think of putting Bob back in touch with the cubes?"

Herman stopped and walked over to the table and placed both hands on the top and leaned toward me. He was shaking his head and had a worried look on his face.

"Well, let me rephrase that. We need to get Bob back into an active dialog with the cube and start inquiring about the Demion's and our relationship to them."

By this time Herman was looking down at the table top. "Joe, there is a danger there, we may push a button which could bring a wrong result from them."

I stood up and walked around the table to the writing boards and looked at him. "I don't think so. If we are on the right path, the cubes have actually become our protectors. We are of the Demion society and they were created by and work for."

We left the conference room and walked over to the small office Bob had moved into. When we entered, he was writing something down on a pad in front of him.

As it turned out, Bob was already in a dialog with them and had been for some time. As I walked up to him, he looked up and smiled. "Hi, Joe."

"Bob, how you doing?"

He was still smiling. "Joe this is getting more and more interesting minute by minute."

"How's that Bob?"

He leaned back looking up at Herman and I. "As you know, the initial contact with the cubes was painful and hazardous to our health. Once we got past the initial stage, the pain started to subside and it became more comfortable and clearer. Right now, I have no pain and there is no fatigue whatsoever. It's almost like I am receiving energy from the cubes. I don't know how, but that is how it feels."

He reached out and picked the pad up and seemed to concentrate on it and then wrote something down. He then looked back up at me.

That prompted me to ask. "Bob, have

258

you had any significant conversations with the cubes?"

He was holding the pad and nodding his head. "It's nothing like a normal conversation, the information is there, as your mind addresses it. In other words, if I think weapons, the first thing that comes to my mind is the type of weapon I want to consider. Then a menu appears and it lists all the types tactical, personal, antipersonnel, etc. Then I just think the one and it moves to the next menu."

I was trying to visualize just what he was saying. "Bob, are you seeing this menu?"

He paused while trying to come up with a better and more descriptive answer for me. "Well in a sense yes and no. I can't explain it to you. All I can tell you is as fast as I think the cubes provide the data I want. It even provides video files, which strangely enough I can see. Joe, I'm comfortable with the process now and have no fear of working with it for you."

He had put the pad down while explaining this process to me and when he finished his sentence he stopped, picked the pad back up and started writing again.

As he was writing and listening to me, I

was still talking. "Great. What we need is for you to start to delve into the history of this place with the cubes. Where they came from and what they came here for. Do you think you can do that?"

He again started writing on the pad. "Yeah, that should not be a problem. The cubes are actually trying to educate me and we're progressing quite well."

He then tore several pages off the pad and handed them to me.

I took the pages and started to look at them and then remembered to ask. "Oh, one other thing, is it possible to find out how long we have before the Demion's get here?"

"I'll do my best."

"That's all I ask Bob."

I took the pages from him and started to look them over. They were covered with references to the facility and it purpose. At the bottom of the last page, he had written. "They're on their way."

It then came to me to ask him. "Can you tell if the cubes are a threat to us any longer?"

He turned toward me and smiled. "I would say they are not. If anything, they are our protectors at this time. The real hazard is if an outside force tries to come in or intervene, then there's going to be hell to pay."

When he said that he looked right at me, his face was hard and it gave me the impression things were just starting to develop.

I reached out and put my hand on his shoulder, "You really think so?"

He sat forward and up from his desk and placed both forearms on the desk top. The look on his face told me he was more than serious about what he was saying. "Joe, not only do I think so, they have said so. Right now, this area, inclusive of all the cubes and these facilities, are off limits to anyone other than us. The Sentry Cubes are set to address any intrusion into this area."

That was a new term and it sounded foreboding to say the least. It was something I didn't want to hear. "Sentry Cubes?"

"Those are the smaller of the cubes and they can be real nasty. What they did when we first discovered them was nothing compared to what they are capable of. What they are capable of is beyond anything we could imagine. Those babies are pure violence and when they start, they usually don't stop

261

until all signs of oncoming life cease to exist."

His demeanor had changed radically this time. The look on his face was even harder, but there was a fear presence as well. It was a fear which defies defining. It was deep and uncompromising.

That could be a problem for us. "Well, what happens if we try to bring additional personnel into this area? Will they let us do that?"

"Joe, as long as the people we bring are here by our own desires, they will not interfere, as long as they're unarmed. That means unarmed, non-combatant, personnel and that is the key for people coming onto the locked down base."

I guess I was pushing the limits on this but I needed to know. "So, if we tried to bring a military unit into this facility, they would not let that happen?"

He was nodding his head and settled back in his chair. "That's right. Even unto killing everyone involved."

Right, I got my answer "Got ya."

The answer he gave me was straight and to the point and needed no further explanation or details. I got the message.

That was it for the day. We had the

organizational meeting that night and all assignments had been given and people's questions answered. We had sent everyone off for the night and had finished our final review of our plan. We then retired for the night.

The following morning, we met again for breakfast and talked over the plan again and then reviewed all assignments. People had already been reporting to their area of assignments and had started the search process of both the main facility and the machine.

As we left the mess tent we went by Bob's office in the main facility and checked in with him. He advised us everything was moving smoothly and the cubes were satisfied with our activity and progress.

Herman and I left Bob and headed back to the object. I wanted to be in the area where everything was to be accumulated so I could see our progress. It was not long after I got there a stream of things started to appear. There were boxes of small items, most of which had no meaning to us.

Then the larger items started to show up. They had actually found and then transported them to the collection area by elevators located in the walls just over from the stairs at both ends of the object and that was really speeding things up.

It was not hard to tell most of these were of a scientific nature. As they landed on the tables they were cataloged and then a team would take the item away to start their in-depth analysis of it. With Herman at the helm, everything was running smoothly. Our only problem was we had no idea how long we had and how much we could learn in the time we did have.

I was pondering our next move when, Stan walked up. "Joe, we need a sit down." He had a funny look on his face and I had a feeling this was not just a simple sit down.

"Now?"

"Yes, right now." The warning flags were flying high.

I asked him directly. "Are you mad about something?"

He stood there a second. "No, but I have some questions and reservations I need to address with you." I think he was holding back.

I nodded and agreed. "Then let's find a place where we can have some privacy. How about the meeting room off the command center? We can have Bob sit in with us. I think we need Terry there as well."

He was nodding his head. "That would be great, Joe. See you there in say an hour?"

"I'll be there, Stan."

What was his problem? I guess I should have felt a little worried as well. Things had been going so fast and everything seemed so mixed up. It was near impossible to get it all straight right then. Now that I think about it, we were fast approaching overload. There was just so much going on and so much needed to be done and so little time to do it in.

An hour later, I was walking into the meeting room. Stan, Bob and Terry were already there and waiting.

"Am I late?"

Stan looked up. "No, you're right on time, have a seat."

I looked at the three of them. "All right where do we start?"

Stan leaned forward in his chair. "I might as well get this thing going. Joe, in the last week or two we have been in a virtual mental storm. So much has been happening I for one am almost lost. I don't know who is doing what or who should be doing what. On top of that, we have been running back and forth between areas and projects like there was no tomorrow. Joe. I'm confused and frankly worried to hell about everything. I guess what I'm saying is we, the four of us, need to slow down and determine just where the hell we are."

I looked at Terry. "Where are you with this?"

"Joe, I'm nowhere. I have been so busy getting all the logistics set up and coming in I have no idea what the right is doing in relationship to the left. Now, my job is to organize and coordinate the logistical needs of this project, but it has moved so fast and taken so many twists and turns I am at a total loss as to where we are and where we should be."

"Terry, let me ask you this." I was getting rather nervous by this time. "When we bring equipment or new people in here how is that managed?"

He stopped and thought for a few seconds. "One hundred percent of our resources come in at the Normandia airport. From there they come north to us and enter the area from the south on the road coming off the national highway twenty kilometers to the east. We built this road first thing when we first started the project. It crosses the facility metalcrete road just east of the defensive line set up by the cubes.

At the time we did not see the metalcrete road because it was covered by forest floor. Our road then continues to the staging area where everything is off loaded and then cataloged and placed into storage.

"Often, we bring personnel in from the same airport via helicopter which land at the staging area just as you did when you first arrived here. We have never had a problem with the cubes or anything that would indicate the cubes were apposing us."

"How about the past two weeks?"

"No, not a problem."

"Are the helicopters civilian or military?"

He finished by saying. "Civilian, no weapons. Clearly that remains the key for us. Our primary goal with the cubes is to stay non-combatants."

"Stan, where do you stand on this?"

"Joe I'm being pulled from both directions. I'm ready to shut things down and turn it over to someone else, but I still have the desire to find the end of this thing and see what comes of it."

It looked like we had a problem and I was going to have to pull everything out of them. This was not good. "How do you feel about Herman?"

Stan seemed to perk up a little at the mention of Herman's name. "He has been a wonder for me Joe. No, Herman is not a problem. If there are any problems with him it's that he is so easy going and willing to be flexible. It simply drives me nuts!

"As a top scientist, I would expect him to be more demanding and more particular about who is involved and what they are doing. He is nothing like that. He has a target and simply moves toward it, darned if it doesn't make me want to get up and take off, I don't know where, I just want to get away from him."

Now the big question. "All right then what about me?"

I watched Terry and Stan look at each other and then over to Bob. Everyone remained quiet for a few seconds and then Bob spoke up. "Guys before anyone says anything they will regret, let me say this."

That got my attention and also, I felt my face flush. This whole thing was about me.

"Each of you has his own special abilities. So far you have all worked wonders together. This has not been an easy dig. In fact, it's been a butt kicker. Yet, I have been able to watch the three of you and marvel at your ability to work with and around each other. I am sure each of you has had your times when you could have well done without the other two, but overall, you've proved yourselves in this venture."

He looked at all three of us individually and then continued. "Right now, I get the feeling you have some strong hidden feeling starting to come to the surface and I caution you. Do not let your emotion bring about a problem at this time."

He let that settle in and then continued. "I am sitting here completely invaded by the thoughts of the cubes. I would love to get back to my old self and not have to know all that is coming into my mind, but the cubes have found me to be receptive to their communication and with that I am stuck with my lot in this project."

He paused to let what he had said sink in. "I depend on each of you in your own special abilities to help me deal with the reality of this situation. Without any of you I am sure I would have died sometime back. Yet, not one of you is perfect.

"Terry, you tend to become totally engrossed in your own world, that being the logistics of this base, and as a result you are not able to keep up with all that is happening. When you think about it you become angry and want to lash out at someone just as you're feeling right now. Terry, cool it. In time you will know everything everyone else knows.

"Stan, you too have been angry lately over all that has been happening. You feel you're in charge here, but at times feel Joe has taken that away from you. Well, let me tell you, you are still in charge and always have been." At this time Bob was looking straight at Stan and driving home his point.

"Joe has done nothing to counter your position. He has targeted every task you have given him and has done it with every ounce of energy he has. Joe is a target-oriented person and when working he will go for it with all he has. But he has never usurped your position or authority. So, relax and do your job."

He stopped as abrupt as he started and sat there looking at the desk top and giving us time to let what he had just said to us be absorbed.

We all sat there looking at Bob like he had just stepped on each one of us. I looked over at Stan and Terry and they were looking around as well.

Bob continued. "Come on, guys. I have been sitting here with the cubes talking to me 24/7 and I have come to know each of you from their perspective. The reason you three have total free run of this place and everything tied to it is because the cubes have recognized you as the key to everything that is coming.

He again paused and waited. He was trying to get us to understand the severity of what was happening to us during this meeting. He then continued. "You came in here ready to cut loose on Joe and he, in turn, would have retaliated. Here is a message for you from the cubes. Don't do it!

"They have determined you three are the key to everything right now and they will not tolerate you fouling the whole thing up. I personally do not understand what is going on here, but the cubes have your numbers and they are not going to sit by and let you queer this situation now. You are responsible for this operation and you will complete it."

When he stopped, the place was so quiet you couldn't even hear anything going on outside the tent. The air was heavy with his words and we knew he was serious and so were the Cubes.

I had to say something. "Wait a minute, Bob."

"Yeah Joe."

"You're talking as if the cubes have a real interest in this venture. What's going on here?"

He looked down at his lap and then up at the ceiling. "Right, well maybe I should have phrased it differently, but I didn't, so, the cats out of the bag."

"What the hell are you talking about?" I was starting to get really worried. There was something much bigger going on here.

He cleared his throat. "Joe, I was not supposed to say anything that would relate the cubes to this project, but I screwed that up just now. The cubes now feel you need to know more about this whole thing and you need it now.

He repositioned himself and then started in. "Once the cubes knew and clearly understood what we were doing here, they were in support of our activities. They have advised me when the incoming task force gets here, they will want to know what has been done. A clear account of what happened here is vital to them and they are willing to assist us in any way possible. However, if they think we are failing to achieve a usable end result, they will take that as a negative sign to them and that they will not like.

"Now you can take that as a threat or as a sign of trust, whatever, but you will not throw this opportunity out without paying dearly for it. What they mean by that, I don't know. All I know is they are serious and you had better listen to what I have said here. Do you understand?"

I found myself speechless for the first time in a long time. All I could do was sit back and accept what had just been said. He was right. Whether it was Bob speaking or the cubes, he, they, hit it right on the head.

Finally, Stan managed to speak. "Right, well I guess that put us in our places. As for me, it's over. Joe, you have my trust and support. I apologize for my thoughts and attitude, all right." He offered me his hand and I reached out and took it. I knew he was sincere and the issue was now dead and buried.

It was now my turn. "We all need to lay it down and move on. I trust you and also apologize for my feelings and thoughts and the same goes to you Terry. We get so tied up in our own little worlds we failed to see the other guy's side of the situation. For that I am deeply sorry and promise you it will not happen again. All I want is to successfully solve this mystery and then return to my normal life, whatever that is now."

Stan was looking directly at me and agreeing with everything I said. "I have one thing to ask of Bob." He then turned to Bob. "Bob, what made you say what you just said?"

Bob was still looking down at the floor. He was a tortured man with all that was going on in his head. "Stan, as I watched the three of you my mind sent a mental note to the cubes and they are the ones who said that. I was just the go between.

"Believe me when I say I personally trust each of you and have with my life over the past few weeks. But, right now, I am linked to the cubes on this situation and have decided not to fight it or resist it. This is happening for a reason and far be it for me to question it. Now, can we get back to work?"

As we left the meeting room Herman walked up. "I guess you guys have not heard the latest?"

Stan and I looked at one another. "Latest what?"

Herman continued. "Well, one of the teams in the object, while working the second floor down, found a biological laboratory, a big one."

"And?"

"Well, I guess it would be best if all four of you would come with me. Bob, we'll really need you for this."

We all headed for the object. It took us about forty-five minutes to get to the second floor of the object. As we entered the newly found laboratory, I noted how much it was like any you would find across the world.

Next, I noted the pristine condition of a place that had been buried for the last nine hundred million years or so. If I did not know better, I would say the occupants had just stepped out for lunch or something and they could be expected back any moment now.

I turned to Herman. "Herman what do we have here?"

Herman stepped over by one of the counters. "Well, guys, when we first walked into this place, we felt it was just a run of the mill laboratory. We quickly changed our minds when we found this."

He then reached over and lifted a vial from the counter top. In it was a solution, light green in color. In the solution was the body of a creature.

"What is that thing?"

"Gentlemen that is a human embryo."

Jaws hit the floor in unison.

"No way!"

"Gentlemen." Herman always became formal when pressing a point. "I can assure you this is a human embryo and nothing else. We have checked the documentation in the computer and it is a perfect DNA match for the human race.

"This is not a genetics laboratory; it is a medical laboratory. Do you understand? This is an embryo of one of the Demion's. It is not a hybrid or genetic upgrade of the human race. Everything we have found in this laboratory supports our findings so far. What we are saying is the Demion's are a genetic, DNA match with us. We are one in the same. Now, come with me."

He walked past us and we turned and followed. He had us completely unprepared and we had no place else to go, we had to follow. We crossed the hall into a second laboratory. This one was not unlike the other one, clean and everything in its place. We walked around to the back of the lab and to a desk. On that desk were photographs of what we were soon to learn were of an autopsy. What we were looking at were the pre-autopsy and post-autopsy picture of one of the Vandions.

This one had obviously been shot in the chest. As I looked at him, I noted there were striking differences between him and me. He had a large head, but my eyes were drawn to his six-digit hands and feet. I also noticed his eyes were like cat's eyes except the iris was horizontal not vertical like a cat.

Next to those pictures were another set, but this time they were of a Demion. Every aspect of his makeup matched ours to the letter. We were clearly one in the same and there was no doubt about it.

So, it was true. Our ancestors invaded this world and destroyed the population and then re-colonized the world with their own species. I had a strange feeling deep down inside. A whole civilization had been destroyed just for the sake of our ancestors to be able to colonize another planet.

I stood there shaking my head.

Herman finally spoke up. "I see you're

all reacting to the pictures here and I can guess you're feeling a little guilty over the fact the Demion's had wiped out a whole race of people just to take over this planet. Yeah, I felt the same way. But, hold on a minute. Come with me."

We left the second laboratory and walked down the hall and into what appeared to be a library. In the middle of the room was a large table and on the table were a number of other pictures. They appeared to be of general pictures of people doing any number of things. The pile on the right could have been from any town or city in the world. The pile on the left clearly did not match those criteria.

"Those are not photos of us are they, Herman?"

"No, Stan, they are not. These are photos of the Demion civilization." He waved his hand over one of the piles of photos. "And, clearly these are not photos of anyone who has or is living on this world." He waved his hands over the other pile of photos. "No, Stan, those are photos of the Vandions and clearly they are not on the world as well."

"As well?"

"That's what I said. Neither race is from

this planet. That explains why we never found any remains of a civilization in any way shape or form, no matter how long ago it was. Gentlemen, both the Vandions and Demion's are alien to Earth."

It took several minutes for that to sink in.

My head was swimming. I had thought I had this thing figured out and now they're telling me I had it all wrong. "Both are alien?"

"That's right Joe, both."

I was shaking my head. "Herman, do you know what you're saying?"

Herman was smiling. "Yes, I do. I'll even take it one step further. The Demion's were the first to set up a base on Earth, this base right here. They had time to build the main building and set up the defenses for the area. When they arrived here, they did so in the object. That is not a machine they built here; it is the machine they came here in. They landed here and had fully occupied this area and were carrying out in depth scientific research when trouble in the form of the Vandions showed up.

"The Vandions were the ones who came later and they tried to take control of the Demion's, facility, which resulted in a huge battle by the two outpost units. The Vandions came in force, while the Demion's were here for scientific purposes and so they had less military presence to protect their facilities. They fought a valiant battle, but were subsequently over run by the Vandions and in the process they ordered the Dehaven strike, knowing full well every living creature within the base would die and it would literally sterilize the land to future occupation.

"I am not here to justify either side. I do not have that much information to form any kind of an opinion. However, I can tell you who was here first and who came second and who started the conflict. Clearly the Demion's were here first. This was their facility and their base."

Herman was paging through some of the photos and then sat on the edge of the table and continued.

"That was almost a billion years ago and we have no idea as to what happened to either race. We assume the Demion's will be coming back at this time, but we do not know. We assume the cubes are Demion creations, but we have no way of proving that as yet. No, someone is coming, but we have no real idea which of the two it will be.

"So much could have happened over the reach of those nearly billion years. We don't know which of the two races still exist or not. My concern is when we learn the answer to that question, will it be too late for us if it's the wrong side.

"Besides, there is absolutely nothing we can do about who is coming and what their purpose is when they get here." He was clearly worried and concerned about what was happening. He looked like a man who has found himself in a trap with no way out.

"By their age alone their level of technology will be vastly beyond ours and beyond our understanding. So, Bob, it all comes down to you and your ability to communicate with the cubes. The cubes, gentlemen, it's the cubes. That is our last hope and we must address it now."

He then shifted himself. "One last point, when the Vandions came here it is obvious they came in some type of a space traveling vehicle. My question is where are those vehicles? Are they still on Earth or did they leave them in space someplace or did they return to their home planet? That will become more important to us as these coming events take place.

281

By now Herman had our complete and undivided attention and commitment to what he was relating to us. He then shifted his attention to Bob. "Bob, it's time to start asking some point-blank question of the cubes. It may well be dangerous and difficult to carry out, but we need you to do this for us."

Bob stood there looking at the photos and God knows what was going through his mind. He was tied into this thing deeper than anyone else and that could be the greatest of burdens. "Herman, I really don't think they will mind any kind of inquiry. Where do you want to start?"

Herman then got to work setting up the process of the questioning. "I think we need to confirm some of our thoughts and concepts first. We can explore other things later on. So, let's start with this question. What is the name of this base?"

"Sector 19-42." Bob responded as the Cubes provided the information.

Herman was set back by the speed of the response. He lost his orientation for a second and then was ready to continue. Bob had seen his reaction. "Herman when you speak to me now, it is like the cubes can hear you directly. They are linked to me and they hear what I hear and see what I see, understand."

"Yes, I understand and that helps a lot, Bob."

Herman re-oriented himself. "All right, let's continue on with this inquiry.

"Bob please define what that is specifically, Sector 19-42?"

"Sector 19-42 is a preliminary research base in the preparation for occupations of an uninhabited planet."

"Are there any other bases on this planet?"

"No."

"What is the name of this planet?"

"Yearth."

"How many Demion's were present on this base?"

"The total including military, science, labor, administrative, cultural, engineering, medical came to four thousand seventy-one personnel."

"How many space ships?"

"Just one. It is currently buried at the foot of the mountains."

"That object in the ground is a space ship?"

"Yes, this particular type is designed as

a housing unit as well as a transporter of equipment and supplies. The amount of personnel and equipment was the equivalent of about a seventy-five percent capacity load."

"How long was this unit present at this base before being attacked?"

"In your years it came to six years."

"During that time what was the primary objectives of this unit?"

"The objective of this unit was research, research to determine the planet's ability to sustain life and to provide the basic materials needed for a technological society to grow and advance."

"Was any genetic or DNA based activity carried out?"

"No."

"How was the populating of this planet to take place?"

"At a designated time, a seed contingency of male and female explorers would be brought to the planet and left as the start of the new occupation."

Herman continued to fire questions at the Cubes. "How soon after the initial exploration was that to take place?"

Bob continued to provide their

response. "It could be just a few years or several millennia before any seeding would take place."

Herman continued firing the questions and Bob continued to relate the answers coming from the Cubes.

"How many explorers would be involved?"

"That varies and could be anywhere from a few hundred to as many as a hundred thousand."

"What was the structure outside the base in the forest for?"

"When built, there was no forest in these regions. It was an administrative and command control center."

"Who are the Vandions?"

"They are a competing society that comes from a region of space that is populated by damaged planets."

"What does that mean?"

"Due to extensive nova activity in that area of space, a high level of Gamma discharge took place. This has been devastating on the inhabitants of those planets in that area. They also became extremely aggressive and we have to defend against them continuously."

"Are the Demion's coming now?"

"Yes, they were notified as soon as we determined your purpose and your level of technological capabilities."

"What will be their purpose in coming at this time?"

"To evaluate your growth over the course of the years after this planet was seeded."

"If we have not progressed as they would determine we should have, what will happen?"

"They will determine the level of assistance you will need to achieve their ultimate goal for you."

"And, that would be what?"

"Your technological growth and expansion into space so that you may join those who have overseen your growth and brought you to this point in time.

"They do not intend to cull us in the event they feel we have not progressed fast enough?"

"Never, the Demion's are beings who wish to expand across the universe. They do not carry out executions of other beings unless there is no way for them to avoid it."

"Such as what took place here?"

286

"That was unavoidable. The technology that was present on this base could not be lost to the Vandions. That would have been devastating."

"How long do we have before the Demion's arrive?"

"That depends on where they are coming from. Their domain is vast and they could come from any one of hundreds of planets which are relatively close to Earth. It could be as little as six months.

Bob looked at Herman. "Herman."

"Yes, Bob."

"May I interject something here?"

"Of course, you can."

Bob had turned and was now looking at all of us and concentrating on what he wanted to say. He took several seconds to come to a point where he was ready to start. "I think you are concentrating too much on the actions of the Demion's and not enough on this facility. You have been searching through the objects and structure for specifics yet you have not asked the cubes one question about those specifics."

That paused all of us. We had become fixated on the Demion's and not once on our goals for the base.

"He's right, guys."

"Yeah, I agree Stan."

Herman then repositioned himself and returned his attention to Bob. "All right Bob, let's start over and get to the facts."

Herman again repositioned himself and then continued. "First of all, what is the overall size of this base?"

"In your kilometers it is approximately eight by eight kilometers in physical size."

"Why are the cubes set in the triangular fashion?"

"Prior to the growth of the forests in this area, it had been open ground and the placement of the cubes set the boundary for a landing zone. That configuration gives us control over the zone and if any uninvited ships come in, we can take whatever action is appropriate at the time."

"Have ships from the Demion's visited the Earth in the past, other than when this base was built?"

"Yes, they make periodic trips to view the progress of the populations."

"Why, have they not carried out direct contact during those trips?"

"Because at that time you had not found this base yet, the time of contact was all dependent on when and if you discovered this base."

"Why is the space ship buried in the mountain?"

"That is the design of the unit. It comes in and digs its own trench and then settles into it. Over time the mountains covered the ship just as you found it."

"Do you have any means of helping us translate your language for us?"

"Yes. Until you asked, I was not allowed to intervene. I will start the program now and it will appear on the screens in the command center."

"Do you have a schematic layout of the base and its building with labeling of what the purpose of each are?"

"Yes, again I could not provide that until asked."

"Are there any other buildings or facilities we have not discovered as yet on this base?"

"Yes, there are. The schematic of the base will now show those buildings location, depth and access points."

"Weapons, what about their weapons? Where are their weapons stored?"

"That, you will not be privileged with.

Your history has been too targeted on weapons and not enough on growth and relational development. With the loss of the base, all weapons were destroyed by us. Those pieces of weapons you have found will be of no use to you in the development of new ones.

"You as a race are about to become educated in living without the use of weapons other than for absolute defense. Anything beyond self-defense will not be permitted. The annihilation of the two forces that took place here was a necessity and meant the sacrifice of all those manning this base before any weapons of war could be obtained by the Vandions.

"That was a conscious decision by the defenders of this base. They chose to sacrifice their lives in order to keep the Vandions from obtaining our weapons. That has happened before and will happen again. But, in the end, we will not provide you with any means of destruction, either to yourselves or others."

That stopped Herman short and Joe leaned over to him. "Go on Herman keep going."

Herman continued. "Is there anything we have failed to ask you that will be vital in our preparations at this time?"

"Yes, you are a young society with little experience compared to the rest of the universe. You have spent much of your time vying for positions of dominance and control, one over another. You have become a violent race that has given greater dependence on force and less on reason.

"I can assure you are not uncommon. But, once you progress and enter into the worlds beyond yours here, things will change. Violence is a tool that is reserved for those times when all else, and we mean all else, has failed. Violence is not considered a lifestyle, but is a weapon that is only initiated when and if all other paths have failed.

"Much of your violence can be attributed to your primitive state at this time. If the Demion's determine you are ready to graduate to an upper level of existence, then you will be schooled in the use of violence and your control over it. This will not be a simple or easy task and with that, you will be given assistance. It will be an assistance you will not like at first, but it is necessary."

"What do you mean?" Herman could sense a change in the Cubes presentation to them.

291

"Once the Demion's arrive and make their determinations as to how you have been progressing and what your social structure is, they may implement the guard cubes system across your world."

That stopped us cold. Now my worst fears were coming to the surface. The cubes had pushed the right button this time and I was having a difficult time dealing with my emotions.

"What do you mean by guard cubes?"

"You called them security cubes; we call them guard cubes. They are designed to respond to violence with a superior level of violence. Once installed, you will live without violence or you will die by violence."

Stan jumped out of his chair. "Stop this and stop it now!"

"Stan, what are you doing?"

"Herman, we need to talk to Bob and talk right now. Did you understand what that thing is saying?"

"Yes, I do, Stan, and I'm just as confused and concerned as you are."

"Joe, what about you?"

"Damned if I know Stan. I could think of a few places around the world those little buggers could be placed, but I don't think I want one in my backyard."

"Bob."

"Yeah Joe."

"Would it be possible for me to ask a question or two?"

Bob shifted his attention to me. "Of course, it is what do you want to ask?"

I thought for a moment trying to formulate the question as best as I could. "What would happen if we said we did not want any interference from the outside, nor do we want any of those security units placed anywhere else on Earth?"

They all sat there waiting. Finally, after several minutes Bob then turned and shrugged his shoulders.

"What does that mean?"

"Stan, it means I don't know what to say. They would not answer me."

"Ask them again."

"I just did Stan and they're silent."

Stan was looking at the others. "Silent?"

"Yeah, not a thing, it's just like they shut down or something. My mind is not feeling them anymore."

I leaned forward toward Stan. "I don't like this, Stan."

"Joe neither do I, but what the hell can we do?"

"Not a damn thing Stan, we can just sit and wait."

And, we did. It must have been two hours or so when Bob sat up. "Guys, the vibration is back."

"All right, are they talking to you?"

"No not yet Stan. Hold it. Oh boy. Ah shit." Bob was looking around like a man trying to find a hole or place to hide. That sure as hell got our attention.

"What's going on?"

"Wait Joe, it's laying out a list of issues we must correct before we can reject anything from the Prime Command. First time I heard that term."

"Ask them who the Prime Command is?"

"I did Joe; they told me I didn't need to know that right now."

That pissed me off. "Yeah, we do. Tell them that."

"I did."

I was on my feet by this time. "And?"

"No answer. Where is it." Bob was almost in panic mode by this time.

"What?"

"The list. They're going to set it up on the big screen in the command center and on the wall screen here."

We sat there as the screen came alive and then the listing started. I wasn't too sure about the others, but the presentation of this list was something I had serious doubts about. In a word, things did not look good at this time.

1. You have to demonstrate worldwide that you can all live with one another without resorting to violence. That includes nations, states, town, and individuals. When your crime rate is zero then you may speak for yourselves.

2. You must demonstrate you have a one world government. That all nations have an equal access to the formulating and writing of laws of conduct for nations and individuals.

3. All standards of living are equal across the world for each and every individual regardless of nation, race, or cultural beliefs.

4. No cultural beliefs, including

295

religion, are forced or demanded of anyone by anyone else regardless of their social position.

5. All your weapons are specifically designed and built as a defense for the whole of the world and not individual nations.

It was like reading a letter of condemnation. There was little if any chance of those rules being fulfilled anytime soon anywhere on this earth.

Bob then continued on. "What their telling us is unless we can demonstrate each and every one of those five issues as they laid them out, we have no say as to whether the security cubes placement are carried out or not. If we resist then the Prime Command is prepared to take whatever steps are necessary to place the cubes as they desire.

"Guys, I don't think they're going to back down on this. And, I don't think there is anything you or the United Nations can do about it."

We sat there watching Bob and he waited for any further information. Bob then turned. "Actually, none of the five issues are that bad, other than being pretty much impossible to achieve."

I felt myself snort a short laugh and started shaking my head. "Bob, I agree. The problem is I don't like being told what to do. And, I believe that is true for most of the Earth."

Bob was shaking his head and looking at each of us. "I think this time, just maybe, we're going to have to keep our mouths shut and go along with them." He then pointed at the screen. "You've seen the power of those little things and to have them sitting wherever around the world is something I can hardly grasp. But it appears it's going to happen no matter what we say."

I have to admit my hackles were up and I was not about to settle for this kind of a bullying game. "Has anyone at the UN seen this?"

Bob was still sitting there looking at the list and he turned then and addressed me specifically. "Joe as a matter of fact they have. This same screen was sent there as well. Somehow, the UN was brought into this process several hours ago.

"Their damn near in a state of riot there right now. Leveler heads there are sitting down and going over these demands. They'll get back to us once they have some semblance of control and preparedness achieved."

By now I was beside myself over the listing and pretty much everything else. I threw my hands up in the air and lay back in the chair. "Guys this is just hunky dory, we have a bunch of politicians looking at a list of issues brought before them by an alien power so far advanced over us it's ridiculous. And, they expect to come back with an answer. There is a better chance of a pack of monkeys working up an answer than that bunch."

As I looked at the others, they were all trying to deal with what had just happened. Herman was shaking his head and gripping the arms of his chair.

Terry was, I don't know what he was doing. He was just sitting there and looking straight at Bob.

Stan looked over at me and held both of his hands up with the palms facing me. "Easy, Joe, you don't want to anger that side now, just when we're getting into the meat of this thing."

I sat there looking at him for several seconds. "You're right I'll pull my horns in."

I was not totally sure of the others, but I was mad as hell and if I had had any sense I would have gotten up and left the building, the base and Brazil behind me. Things never work out that easy though.

My mind was swirling with thoughts and emotions. Several weeks ago, I had come to this location to carry out an excavation of an object the United Nations desired to unearth and take a look at. From the day I arrived I have seen a carefully planned and executed plan take shape that had been developed and put into motion almost a billion years ago.

The part that really pisses me off is that this whole thing depended on us walking into this place and springing the trap and we did a great job of it. Damn, I hate being played like a sucker.

Chapter Nine

PREPARATIONS AND PROTOCOL

"OKAY, people, here is where we are. We have been in a dialog with the Cubes for several hours now. We finally got into a question-and-answer format and, while carrying that format along, we got to asking specific questions." I paused before dropping the big one on them. "We eventually got around to what the Demion's may or may not do when they get here. The answer has everyone from here to New York on sticks.

"They are planning on placing security they call them Guard Cubes, around the world to address our tendencies for violence."

That got the meeting going all right. People were looking around and shaking their heads. It was clear what was being related to them was not welcome and was in fact accepted as a threat and not assistance. In a word, they were mad.

"Yeah, your right, those nasty little things that tends to kill people. That is their intent unless we can demonstrate we live by those five standards they listed. We don't now and I doubt if we ever could.

"Anyway, it's out of our hands now. The UN is taking over the issue of those five conditions and we are not going to be involved in it. So, we have only one avenue left and that is to complete our research into the two facilities here at this base."

Everyone was still dealing with the threat they felt was being directed toward us. The place was losing its order and some of those present were heading for the door.

"People, Stan Davenport, Herman Blumfield, Bob Hammer, Terry Huntington, and I have been in conference and we feel we need to continue with our work. No matter how this works out, we need to get our act together so when they arrive, we can demonstrate a well-run research and archeological protocol.

"Everyone, go back to your seats and

let's get back to doing what we do best. We informed you of the current situation because we feel you should know about it, but that does not change our purpose. Please, sit down and let's get back to work."

Damn, it was like talking to the wind. For the most part they were mad as hell. I realized we needed to let them vent for a few minutes and so I sat back and let things boil for a while.

Finally, they stopped and started to return to their seats. They were clearly unhappy with what they had heard, but they also knew what we were doing here was something that needed to be done. Whatever the Demion's are planning we still had a purpose and we were going to continue on.

Once they had calmed, I got back up and continued with the briefing. "So, set all that aside and let's get back to what we do best, our work. We have anywhere from six months to a year to get prepared for their arrival. So, we have decided we are going to put our best face forward and impress the hell out of them. Are there any questions?"

That was the wrong thing to ask. The place went mad again with everyone raising their hands and wanting recognitions. We finally gave several team leaders the opportunity to ask their questions and then one of us responded. It turned out to be the right thing at the right time.

After another hour of question and answers we were able to work our way back to the organizational meeting we were there for, so I continued on. "Okay, Herman has set up the battle plans and you can contact him for your assignment. Get with-it folks, and if you need anything let us know and we will see you get it."

There we were, an unknown future, in regards to the security cubes, and the UN working on the five conditions the Demion's had listed. We could control our own situation, but leaving the other to the UN was like giving the crooks the keys to your house, cars, bank accounts, and retirement system.

In other words, there was no chance in hell the UN would come up with anything other than proof the Demion's were right and should install the cubes. Just to think of it was sickening.

For the next couple of hours, we spent giving the assignment to the teams and finishing up the protocol needs. Once that was done, we then headed back over to the building and went to the conference room we had been using for our talks with the Cubes.

Finally, the others took their seats, I turned to them. "Do you really want to try and do something about the cubes thing?" There was a plan boiling up in my head and the more I thought on it the more I knew it was what we needed to do.

Stan stood up and walked over by me and then looked back at the other. "Well, of course we do, Joe. That is if we can." That opened the door and boy did I run through it.

I got up and walked around to the door to the room and closed it and locked it. Everyone else was starting to look at each other. They were clearly uneasy with my actions. "I think we can. So, if you're ready to listen I'm ready to lay it out."

Again, Stan looked at the others and then turned back to me. "If you have something let's, get it out."

I nodded at Stan and then turned to the others. "First of all, Bob. As we are in discussion, can the cubes hear or discern what we are saying?"

"To repeat what I said before yes they can hear everything I hear and they know everything that I say."

I thought on that a few seconds and then asked. "All right, would you have any problem with being out of this discussion?"

He smiled at me. "Not one bit, Joe. I'll just go on into the command center and find a quiet place to sit down and relax. You need me for anything let me know."

"Thanks Bob."

Bob got up and walked out of the room. Once he was clear, I made sure the door was locked and started to lay things out.

I walked to the front of the room by the viewing screen and started. "From now on, we discuss nothing of this around Bob. We must keep this between ourselves. Next, nothing from this meeting goes into any computer. Third, nothing but nothing will be left lying around. We move and everything on paper goes with us. Do we all agree?" The three of them nodded their heads. "All right here we go.

"First off, we will never be able to compete with the Demion's at any level. They are so far advanced over us it would be a useless attempt to try and beat them.

"Second, it appears violence is a key for them. The number of times they reference violence tells us something. They do not accept violence as an alternative unless fighting for their life. Then they will choose annihilation of both the enemy and themselves.

"Third, the thing that really keyed their returning here at this time was our process in excavating this base and searching out what happened and what caused it. Once they determined we were non-combatants, everything changed. The Cubes became our benefactors and the Security Cubes went on standby.

"My proposal is, we must demonstrate to them the vast majority of our world is peaceful in nature and also abhor violence, there is a segment of the world who uses violence to carry out terrorist attacks, to invade other nations, and to subjugate their own nations. It has been this way for centuries and we still achieve technological progress in spite of them."

"Joe, are you trying to target the problem children on Earth?"

I stood there and thought about his question. Was it my place to determine who were the problem people or was I just trying to cast a light on our problem and let the Demion's make the decision? "Herman, you bet I am. I see here an opportunity to get everything we need and clean up the world in the process. I am not talking about forcing our national political system on everyone else. Each nation can run itself as it wishes. What I am targeting are the radicals, the greedy, the hate mongers, those who live on the weakness of others. If we can direct the Demion's at that element of mankind, we will achieve something never been seen on Earth in all its five billion years of existence."

"Joe, you are one devious individual and I love it. But, how do we go about it?"

"Herman, we do what the magicians do. We redirect their attention away from a world-wide solution to our violence, to a regional view. Just imagine what it would be like to have a few dozen guard cubes placed in those places on Earth that have and are a terrorist haven. Just imagine having the cubes in those countries in Southeast Asia or Africa or South America where their leaders are using the nation's natural wealth to benefit themselves and no one else."

I had not seen Herman like this before, but right now he was grabbing hold of my idea and liking it. "That's it. That is the way to go. Great, but how are we going to do that?

307

Joe. How are we going to get the Demion's to do just that?"

I smiled at the perfect timing of his question. "Herman we are going to stir the pot."

"What?" that got everyone's attention.

"That's what I said. We're going to stir the pot by getting those problem areas to stand out for the Demion's and show them the true nature of many on this Earth."

You could see the puzzled expressions crossing their faces. "Joe, I hope this does not mean we are going to create violence?"

"No Herman, we're going to highlight the violence already there and where and by whom it is being carried out.

"Over the years, the many militant factions who have come and gone have one thing in common, they want attention for their cause and are willing to hurt, maim, and kill to get it. Well, we're going to give them what they want. All the attention they in the world."

They remained quiet and I could see the doubt in their faces as well as the puzzlement. "And just how are we going to do that?"

"Files Herman, lots and lots of files, we are going to import every file including, documents, pictures, and videos, we can find and then feed those files to the Demion's with the necessary explanation of the problems we have been dealing with." I paused to give them a chance to catch up with me. "That, for the most part, the world is in search of peace, but for these few who find peace to be a determent to their way of thinking."

Stan had been sitting there quietly listening to the dialog between Herman and myself when he asked. "But don't you think that concentrating on these issues could back-fire in that they could assume this was the way it is all across the world?"

"No Stan, if we do it right, we can show them just what has been going on for all this time. I would suggest we go back to the beginning of the twentieth century and cover the two world wars, especially the second. Then the Korean War and then the Vietnam War. From then on, we can cover all the areas where they continue to war and export their terror outside to other regions of the world.

"At the same time, we show the peaceful life styles of most of the world's population and how they have suffered as a result of these few power seekers."

It was starting to register on them what

it was I was trying to do. Herman finally said. "Now I think you've got something there."

"Herman, if we work it right, we can clearly demonstrate we are a peaceful world and we have suffered a lot in our pursuit of peace."

I turned to Stan. "Stan, what do you think?"

He was still thinking and sizing things up. "I think, Bob is going to be up to his ears in this thing."

I nodded and smiled. "You're right. Bob is the key and he will be the one feeding this to the Cubes. When we're ready we will have Bob in and get things going."

Stan then raised another question. "Without asking him if it's all right with him?"

I shook my head. "Stan, we can't do that because it will go straight to the Cubes and then they will know what we're up to. Bob has already told us he will help in anyway necessary."

"Right, I didn't think of it that way. All right, I'm with you."

I sat there a minute thinking. "We're going to need help on this and I know just the right people for it."

"Who's that?"

I smiled at Stan. "Jennifer and Melanie of course, they both have extensive computer experience and knowledge and they are just the right ones in the right place at the right time."

"Where are they right now?"

I looked around at the rest and then realized they were my people so I should have known. "I'm not sure Herman. Things have been so crazy lately they could be just about anywhere. Give me a few to find them and we will get going on this."

It took almost an hour to find them and then another hour to get them to the meeting. Melanie was in the Object that is the space ship, digging around with her team and had left her radio sitting on a table in one of the meeting rooms on the floor above them. Someone finally stated they knew where she was and they went to find her.

We learned that Jennifer was back in the medical tent. She had started bleeding again and they could not figure out why.

I called over to the medical tent with my portable. "Doctor, this is Joe Nash, I understand you have Jennifer there, is she able to leave there and come to a meeting at the facility building?"

"Yes, but we cannot guarantee she will be able to stay or even work Joe."

I agreed. "All right, have her come on over and we'll evaluate her situation at that time."

"Do you want us to send a medic with her?"

"Yeah, you better."

Doc then advised. "She'll be on her way in twenty minutes."

"Fine Doc we'll talk later."

When both had arrived, I brought them into the meeting room. Melanie was clearly tired, but you could see she was wired and wanting to continue with her work. On the other hand, Jennifer did not look good at all. She was pale and having a hard time keeping her energy levels up.

Once we had Melanie and Jennifer together, I laid out the plan. They were to go onto the internet and find all the information including photos and videos on terrorist activities, military aggression, and crimes against humanity they could put together. The point was to show the extent of the activities by those who cannot live in peace and how they victimize the majority of the world's population.

"What about those times when the innocent of both sides was targeted or accidentally hit during an exchange? You know what I mean, what about collateral damage?"

"Melanie, I would prefer we not include those issues and events. However, we should be ready to address those issues, if it comes up. Prepare a response to those issues and be sure to lay it out in relation to the actions of the terrorist who brought those events up and caused the collateral damage. You know, using the innocent as shields and so on."

"Got it."

Everything was set and ready to go. It was our goal to give the Demion's a total picture of the worlds attempts to deal with these issues and in doing that keeping the issue of violence as low as possible. When we did try to resist, we wanted to demonstrate the level and extent we went to in order to avoid harming the innocent. We had to concentrate on those of violence, but we also needed to emphasis the level of restraint shown when we did act.

I was sure we had put together a good plan and it would give us our bests shot at getting the Demion's to understand our situation. Now it all depended on Bob and his tie to the Cubes.

I felt we were ready and that meant I needed to see Bob. "Guy's, I need to go talk with Bob."

As I walked to the command center, I saw Bob sitting at one of the consoles off in a corner of the command center. As I walked up to Bob he turned and looked right at me. "They'll be here in two months." He spoke.

It stopped me short. It just seemed like he was always dropping something on me. "Two damn months! Are you sure?"

"Yeah Joe, there's no doubt about it. The main ship is in continual contact with the Cubes and they are clear on their arrival times."

"Main ship? What does that mean?"

Bob stopped and turned toward the console again and then back to me. "The Cubes advise they come with a number of ships to ensure their own security."

"Who from?" This was starting to bother me a lot.

Bob, in a matter-of-fact voice said. "From anyone or anything."

"How big are these ships?"

Bob waited again and then responded. "As they arrive and position themselves around the world they will appear about the size of the moon, although they will be much closer than the moon."

All right "In measurement size, how big?"

"As much as thirty-five kilometers across Joe."

"You have got to be kidding me." Man, this guy keeps hitting me with these things. That means one of their ships would be as big as the greater Las Vegas area.

"Yes, that is an accurate description of the size of these ships and they're not even the biggest they have."

After that exchange I knew we needed to get our plan going and going now. "Bob, we need you in the meeting room when you're ready."

"I'm ready now, Joe. Let's get this thing going."

As Bob entered the room Melanie and Jennifer had the computers up and were pulling the files and documents we wanted into their memories.

I walked over to Jennifer. "Jennifer how are you doing, are you feeling better?"

She looked up and smiled. "I'm fine. As soon as we came into this building, the pressure fell off and I am feeling fine now."

I sat down at the table with them and went over what the plan was. "All right, Stan has filled you in on what we want?"

"Yes, and we have maybe a quarter of them already on line and ready for your presentation to the Cubes."

I knew they would be the best for this job. As with any young person today, they grew up with computers and they were second nature to them.

I motioned to Bob to come over and take a seat facing the wall screen. "Bob, you can sit at the head of the table facing the main screen. Please concentrate on everything we show you. We want the Cubes to receive it all clear and uninterrupted." He nodded his head and took his place and the show started.

As the process started Bob concentrated on the screens, he would indicate with his hand when a new image was needed. Within just a few minutes they were flashing images across the screen faster than I could see and recognize them.

As the process continued, I pulled Melanie aside. "How much data were we planning on feeding the Cubes?"

She stood there a few seconds. "That's was up to Bob. We will keep the data flowing until he indicates he is ready to end it. I felt that was the most logical route to go."

She was confirming my plan in having her and Jennifer coordinate the job. "Fine, please let us know when you're done."

"Will do, boss."

I then turned to Stan and Herman. "Would you please come with me?"

I turned away from the screening and headed for the door.

As we left the meeting room Stan reached out and took my arm. "What's up, Joe?"

I waited until we were out of the room and the door was closed and then turned to them. "I think we need a little insurance in this situation."

Stan leaned back against the wall "Insurance?"

"Yes. Listen, if this fails, we will need to have a fall-back plan we can implement."

Stan was clearly not tracking with me. "And, just what do you think that should be?"

I shrugged and stood there looking at him. "Well, I'm not totally sure yet."

"You think we need a backup plan, yet you're not sure what it should be."

All I could do was grin at Stan. "That's right and that's why I need you two with me now."

So, it started the quest for the final answer to the Demion's in the event our first plan failed. As we walked along the hall and stopped at the many doors along the way, we saw the numerous offices and rooms where the bodies of those who worked here met their final moment.

As we walked the halls of this alien complex, one could feel the forces and drama that took place here all those many years ago. Herman was particularly quiet at this time and finally mentioned. "As I look at all this, I can't help but wonder about the families and friends who didn't know why they never came back."

It struck me he was sincere in his feelings and then it hit me. MIA. These were the Missing in Actions of the Demion's. If they were truly a peace-loving people and non-violent then they must have feelings toward those they have lost."

It was then I knew. "Guys, I think I've got it."

Stan looked at me. "Got what?"

"The secondary plan, Stan."

"What is that?"

I felt the idea charge through my head. "MIA!"

That stopped us right there in the middle of the main hallway. Stan turned to me. "Are you thinking what I think you're thinking?"

"What's that Stan?"

"The finding of their dead and the protocol they desire we follow in caring for their remains."

I guess I had an evil smile on my face because Herman seemed to back off for a second. "You've got it."

Stan smiled. "Joe, that is simply brilliant. You think it may work?"

"There's nothing wrong with trying it Stan, nothing at all."

There is one thing that has been true throughout history and it is the formality a society follows in caring for those who have passed away. It is a process vital to any society and one that really demonstrates a society's attitude toward its dead and their final disposition.

In taking this route, we were playing a

dangerous game. We had no idea if the Demion's had any traditions concerning death, or even cared or believed in a traditional method in body disposal. But we also felt as with any social structure, death was a difficult situation for those close to a lost loved one. That's assuming they loved one another in a manner in which we love others both as mates and friends.

Yet, I was fairly sure I had touched a meaningful issue with them. As an advanced civilization, they would care about one another. They cared enough to oppose violence unless it was the absolute last option and then any violent action would probably include those making the decision. So, death of a relation, friend, and loved one would have an impact on them. I was ready to bet on it.

We know death has a significant impact on family and friends in any social structure on planet Earth. Within the United States we clearly respond to one's death with a fairly clear and traditional process. The care of the deceased is fairly standard. The body is removed from the location and either taken to a mortuary or a government facility to determine cause of death.

The care that goes into the final release of a loved one is true no matter what the beliefs of the particular cultures are. It's the rituals which become important for those who have lost a loved one. My purpose here was to relate the fact civilized beings, even those of advanced cultures have a traditional methodology in dealing with those who have passed. So, it is reasonable to believe this is true for the Demion's as well.

That would be the key to our activity concerning their dead. As we progressed through the structure and the spaceship, we found additional casualties from the battle way back when. These in turn were removed and placed in a special holding area for further study and then disposal. All of the bodies were still in storage and as we found more, the numbers increased.

It was almost time to address the issue with the Cubes.

Every detail concerning every body found was gathered and placed with each body. We were able to determine they did have personal possessions, at least it appeared so. Some of the bodies had jewelry on their hands and around their necks. We found items we had never seen before, but assumed they were time pieces of some type they wore around their wrists. Each and every item within close proximity to a body was taken and placed with the body.

It took us almost two days to gather everything together and prepare the bodies for presentation to the Demion's. It was then, I went to the meeting room. Bob had just returned from a break.

"Bob, how is the transfer of data going?"

"We've been done for a day now and there has been nothing back from the Cubes about any of it."

"That would seem reasonable. We sent them a lot of data and it may take time for them to convert and review it."

"I guess you're right Joe. So, it's a wait and see situation then."

I then brought up the new issue. "Bob, I would say that is right. However, we have a second job for you, I want you to go to the Cubes and request information and assistance on what to do with the deceased we have found in the structure and buried ship. We have located six hundred seventy-three bodies. We want to know how the Demion's would want them cared for and prepared for when they get here.

"In addition, we have a mountain of fossil bodies in the base area which need to be cared for, but we have no idea as to how they would want this handled. There must be around twelve hundred to fifteen hundred fossilized bodies on the excavated base area."

Bob sat back and related the situation to the Cubes. He became quiet and said nothing and showed no signs of anything significant taking place. I started to leave when he raised his hand to have me stay. After several minutes he turned to me. "Joe, we have something important here." He waited and sat there still. "They are asking the conditions of the fossil bodies in the base area."

That was what I was waiting for. I told Bob. "Advise them they are in varied states of severe to little or no physical damage, but they are piled and intertwined with the fossil remains of the Vandions."

"Those found in the structure and buried ship was generally mummified and none of them showed any physical damage."

There was a significant pause in their response to us. And then it came.

Bob was sitting there, intent on whatever it was he was getting. He then turned to me. "They advised we should not have disturbed any of the locations, but they understand and thank us for our concern. They request the mummified bodies be returned to those places where we found them. It is important they be where they died. Second, they request all the fossilized remains be destroyed completely. They do not want to see their comrades intermingled with the Vandions. They would prefer it all be reduced to dust."

We hit a touchy area and we now had better do as they requested and complete everything they ask and make sure we do it right. "Bob please advise them we will carry out their desires to the letter immediately. Also request if there is anything else, we can do for them in regards to the care of their deceased?"

Bob had already received information for us. "No, they will care for them upon their arrival. Until then, they ask, we respect their position and leave them as they should be."

"Advise them that will be the protocol we follow."

"Joe, they ask about the other one thousand nine hundred seventy-one unaccounted for?"

324

"Bob, advise them those we told them about are all we have found at this time. Any other bodies or fossilized body we find will be processed per the protocol they have given us."

Just then Bob raised his right hand. "Joe, the Cubes just advised me there is a force approaching the base from the south."

I turned to Stan. "Do we have anything coming in at this time?"

Stan looked at Bob and I. "No, not that I know of.

Bob then added. "Joe, the cubes were specific, they said force. Force as in military."

"What the hell?" I reached out and grabbed Stan's arm. "Stan, can we get anything on that somehow."

Stan made a couple of calls and then turned to me. His face was almost gray.

"What is it?"

"It's a full battalion of the Brazilian Army advancing on the base with the sole intention of taking the base over for the country of Brazil."

I couldn't believe what I was hearing. That was the last thing I had expected and now we were in it up to our necks. "Please tell those people to advise their military not to do that. These cubes will cut them to ribbons if they attempt any armed takeover of this base."

Stan had a real worried look on his face. He was clearly confused by what was happening. "I did, Joe and their response was they could handle anything we tried to throw at them."

Now I was mad as hell. Those idiots were going to take on something they knew nothing about and they were going to get their butts handed to them. "Get back to those people and tell them it is not us they need to deal with, it's the cubes and they will not be able to handle anything they throw at them. They are already targeted and if the Security Cubes are activated, they will destroy them to the last man."

Stan checked and turned. "They don't believe us and are going to attack within the next five hours."

I turned to Bob. "Do the Cubes know that?"

"Yes, they do and they have activated the Security Cubes." Bob was nodding his head and listening at the same time. "Reports from our people are that the Security Cubes are in red mode."

I turned to Stan again. "Ah shit, Stan

tells those people to back off, they are to back off now. We cannot be held responsible for what is about to happen. Stan, you have to make it clear to them this could kill their entire nation if it goes bad."

Stan turned back to me after making the call. "No go, Joe. They're coming and that is that. They have been ordered by their president to take the base and place everyone on it under arrest and ship them out of here. This base belongs to Brazil and no one will be permitted on or near this base from now on. All technological hardware and data belong to Brazil and that is final."

"Bob, do the Cubes know the extent of their purpose?"

"Yeah, Joe, they do. I'll tell you this it's not going to happen. They have contacted the Demion ships in route to this base and they have received orders to reject any attempt to take control of this base. The Cubes recommend we move all of our personnel into the structure and buried ship for our own safety. When the Security Cubes cut loose, it's going to be death to all living beings within their range or the range set down by the Demion's.

"Joe, they're not going to hold back in

this. They mean what they say. We have opened a situation with the bodies we found that makes this place more a memorial to them and they will protect it even unto the total annihilation of the world."

That drove me into a cold sweat. "Crap, now the fat's in the fire."

I turned to Stan again. "Stan, call your contacts in the UN and at the President's office and tell them to back off or they will lose the entire battalion. Emphasize the Cubes can and will do it. If they push it any further, they could see their entire military establishment destroyed."

Stan was on his phone maybe twenty minutes when he finally put it down and turned to us. At first all he could do was shake his head. "They rejected my warning and advised me when they come in, all the leaders of this project will be arrested and tried for subversive activities against the sovereign state of Brazil. Joe, they are set to carry out their takeover of this base."

I knew there was little chance of changing their minds. "All right, get everyone moving into the structure and ship now."

My guts were knotted up and I could hardly move. This thing had just taken a turn we had tried to avoid. There was little we could do. "Bring everything they can carry and do it within the next two hours. The Brazilian military is three hours out, so move."

Over the next two hours, everything we could think of was hauled to the structure and hauled inside. We notified the UN and advised them of the warning from the Cubes. Several minutes later they came back with word Brazil did not believe us and was going to move in and take over the base.

We finally completed our move and closed the structure door and Bob advised the Cubes we were secure. Within minutes, the facility was taken over by the Cubes and the lighting was lowered and air treatment systems came on line to provide the needed level of air to the facility.

Then it hit me. "Everyone to the command center, we may be able to see the action from there."

I was right. As we entered the center, the main screen was coming alive with views of the base from several directions. The positions of each Security Cubes were located on the board and their respective level of operation shown. All were on red status.

It was then I noticed one of the screens was focusing on a region south of the base. It then zoomed in and I could see the line of tanks leading the advancing units. Over the tanks came a squadron of black hawk helicopters heading straight at the base.

"Man, Stan they don't have a chance. It's going to be a massacre."

Just then, I saw the helicopters all fire a salvo of rockets at the base. As the rockets came arching in toward the base, I could tell they were coming right at the structure we were in. They never made it. It was like something reached up and swatted them right out of the air. They exploded harmlessly short of the base. That was followed by several additional salvos and then the tanks joined in, but nothing reached the base. Not one round.

Just then, Terry yelled out. "The Security Cubes, they just went white!"

I swung around. "White, what the hell does white mean?"

"Stand by. You're going to see just exactly what white means and I have a feeling we will be happy knowing we're in here and not out there."

Terry was shaking with both anger and excitement. "This thing is going to be a turkey shoot."

He no sooner got that out when a white light blasted out from the base. It hit the squadron of helicopters and line of tanks at the same time and they disintegrated. It was instant and absolute death for anyone in or around those units. They didn't stand a chance.

Stan's phone rang. He listened and then looked at me. "They think we're controlling the weaponry being used against them."

I walked over to Stan. "Tell them we're holed up and have no control over anything that comes out of this base. They are fighting the Demion's Security Cubes and do not stand a chance in hell of beating them."

Stan did and then turned. "They don't believe me."

I threw my hands up. "Well to hell with them anyway. If they're so damn stupid not to listen to us then they are about to learn it the hard way."

Just then, the Security Cubes went into full attack mode. In less than ten seconds the entire battalion, about twelve hundred personnel, was totally destroyed. There was nothing left but ashes. But the Security Cubes were not done yet. This time a steady light generated out from the bass and started a sweep of the land beyond the base. I'm not sure how far out, but it was clearly beyond my sight.

They were clearing the entire area of any living life form. It was a sterilization that would leave even the soil dead."

A second call came in and it was from his UN contacts. They asked what the hell just happened. We advised them the Brazilian army had tried to send in a battalion to take over the base and the Security Cubes had made short work of them. In addition, they had also sterilized the land for an unknown distance out from the base.

Stan was talking as fast as he could so they would not have a chance of interrupting him. He then advised them they needed to contact their Brazilian contingency and inform them any further attempts to enter the base would result in far more serious consequences for them.

What these people did not realize was we were dealing with a society that was a billion years older than we were. With a billion years of technological growth beyond our current level of technology. Any more stupid acts like what they've done so far would clearly place us in a situation in which we would have no further control over our advancement. The Demion's were prepared to take over the running of the Earth and we would have little to nothing to say or do about it.

They were a month and a half out. We had been working with them to limit their involvement in our world business, but an act like this was not helping in any way shape or form. In short, Brazil may have queered any further attempts by us to get the Demion's to back off on some of their requirements over us.

We had gained considerably in the handling of their dead and the protocol they desired and then these people come in and may well have changed all our hard work to work of compassion but no gain.

It never changes. Some politician somewhere felt his or her power base is being threatened and so they are willing to kill any number of innocents to show their possession of whatever is in question. Damn, this whole thing had come down to a bunch of clowns in a meeting room in New York City fighting it out among themselves as to whether we should accept the demands of the Demion's and in the process of reaching whatever decision they made they would be demonstrating exactly what the Demion's were addressing. What a show.

Bob raised his hands and waved for me to come over to his desk. "Joe, Stan, they're preparing to take out the whole of Brazil."

I could hardly control myself and stood there looking at the ceiling. It was all coming apart and there was nothing we could do about it. It just came out of me. "What! Aw God man, this can't be happening. What is the key that will turn this action off?"

"Joe it's all up to the Brazilians. If they attack again, then they will pay the ultimate price."

"Stan, is there anyone we can contact that can intervene with the Brazilians and stop this madness?"

"Joe, give me a few and I'll see what I can do."

Five minutes later I heard Stan say. "Mr. President."

I knew he had gone to the highest level he could reach in trying to get this to stop. After several minutes Stan turned and shrugged. "The President has tried to get them to back off and they rejected everything he tried. In short, they are insanely angered over the loss of that battalion and are going to pay us back for it. They still think it's us and not the Cubes or Demion's. They don't believe there are any cubes or Demion's."

Chapter Ten

CUBES AND DEMIONS

The Brazilian Government had determined we were the responsible parties for the activities going on here at the Demion's' base. We had tried in every way possible to convince them they were wrong, but they had a blood lust going as a result of the loss of their army battalion. It had incensed them and no amount of reasoning was going to change their actions.

We advised the UN leadership who had sent us here we were, in effect prisoners on the Demion's base even though that was not the case. The Cubes were protecting us as well as their base. So far what they had demonstrated was a degree of aggression that made anything mankind had childish in comparison.

The UN had advised Brazil was not backing down and in fact several other South American countries were forming up as support for Brazil and whatever action Brazil decided to take.

That sounded ominous to us and if they did in fact make a move against this base it would probably be the end of Brazil as she sat right then.

I looked over at Bob and he was waving his hands over his head. I ran over to him. His face was ashen. "Joe, they did it."

He was scared white. "What, Bob, what did who do?"

Bob's eyes were wide open. "Brazil. They committed nuclear weapons. They're going to bomb this base with nuclear weapons."

I grabbed him. "How do you know?"

He was shaking all over. "The Cubes have detected it through the Brazilian radio transmissions that are being made. Those damn fools are going to try and nuke us."

I stood there watching him. "Bob, what are the Cubes doing?"

Bob looked scared as hell. "God, you

don't want to know. They're preparing to take the entire nation out, down to the last human being. The Brazilian government must back down or their entire nation will be sterilized."

This was a nation of over one hundred ninety million people. It is the fifth largest nation in the world by population and geographically.

Right now, they were on the verge of becoming the smallest nation in the world by population. If they did in fact attempt to use a nuclear weapon on this base, the Cubes would not stop until the entire nation was destroyed down to the last brick. This thing had the potential of expanding across the entirety of South America and possibly across the whole of the world. All that we had worked for was about to be lost.

Stan had been busy on the phone with his contacts in the States when he raised his hand. "We just got word that Guyana is staging the better part of its military at the border. They have determined they will assist Brazil in their taking of the base. In addition, Venezuela, Columbia and Argentina have advised Brazil they are readying their military for a full force push against the base."

I turned and looked at Stan. I must have

looked like I was crazy or something because the oddest look came over Stan as I started yelling at him. "Stan, we need to get the UN more active in intervening in this situation. Advise them we have intelligence that Brazil is preparing to use nuclear weapons and the other countries are aligning themselves to assist Brazil.

"Don't pull any punches. Tell it to them like it is. Brazil is either stopped or the Cubes will stop them permanently. There will be nothing left of brazil and possibly the others as well."

Stan was at a loss as to just what he should be doing. "I'm trying to get them to understand what is going on here. They're confused and don't know just who to believe."

"Damn-it anyway Stan. Tell them that the Cubes have absolute power to protect this base against any form of attack. They will have no qualms about killing every living thing between here and the Atlantic. Let them know these Security Cubes will never release this base even unto the complete and total destruction of this nation and any living being or creature around or near it."

By this time, I was almost standing on

top of Stan and just about ready to take the phone and let those dips at the UN know just what I thought of them. I was trying to calm down but we were looking at a fast track to oblivion and I had a personal interest in the issue right then and there.

"Listen Stan, they may want to let the Brazilians know after all is gone the cubes will still be here and operational. They are indestructible by any means available on Earth. What is happening is totally out of our hands. We have been trying to reason with the Cubes, but their protocol over-rules our attempts. We have tried to contact the Demion's, but that can only be done through the Cubes and they have cut that access off."

Stan then turned back to the phone and his contact and he laid it on the line and did not pull any punches. "Listen to me. We are able to work here because we are non-combatants. They have been protective of us and have assisted us in every venture we have taken.

The one thing they will not tolerate is weapons and especially weapons that are pointed toward them. You people in the UN had better get your act together or this nation will be absent from any future UN meetings.

Got that?"

I stood there looking at Stan. He had never talked like that before. This guy was not pulling any punches and if anyone could get through to them, he was the one. I was about to say something to Stan when he pointed past my shoulder toward the screens at the front of the command center.

"What the hell is that? Joe, do you see what I'm seeing?"

I turned and looked at Stan and he was shaking. His face was a brilliant red and angry, "Damn those no-good sons-a-bitches! Damn the ground they're standing on!"

I took hold of Stan's shoulder. "Take it easy. Come on and sit down."

He was looking at me. "Joe those bastards are killing their nation and there is nothing we can do about it."

Just then I looked back up at the screen. What the hell was that?" I looked over at Herman. "What the hell is that thing?"

Herman turned and looked at the monitor. "It's a dome. A transparent dome probably made of something that can withstand a nuclear blast. Better yet, it's a force shield and a big one at that. I'll bet it has been there all along. That's why the rockets

341

and artillery rounds could not penetrate. At the time, it must have been a low-level shield and was not visible. Now they are facing a nuclear attack and they have upped the dome to withstand it."

I was transfixed by what I was witnessing. "If a nuclear blast hits that shield, what will it do to this building and those of us in it."

"I would venture to say nothing. I think we are completely protected inside this base and building."

Stan interrupted. "Hold everything, guys."

"What's up, Stan?"

"I just got a message from the UN. They advise the Cubes have advised them the Demion's are asking that all nations shut down their military systems and walk away from them. They are telling us we, all nations, are to do this within the next twelve hours. Any nation who does not follow the instruction will be targeted by the Cubes and removed from being any threat to anyone."

I turned to Bob. "Bob, what's going on?"

"It's the information we sent them. They have come up with a way of separating the peaceful from the aggressor and it means our laying our weapons of war aside. They will deal with those who refuse to. They have set a time limit and at the end of that time they will start the process. Any nation or group of people who have decided not to abandon their weapons of war will pay the full price for their decision."

Stan had just stood up when there was a vibration that moved through the structure. It was not drastic, but we could clearly feel it. I turned to the screens and saw the white light coming from the direction of the dome.

"They nuked us." I heard Stan yell.

The power of the weapon was obviously great and it seemed to go on forever. Finally, it cleared away and the dome was still intact. Just then a band of green light appeared across the area above the bank of main screens. At that same time, someone called out that the Security Cubes have gone green light. We had never seen a green light on the Security Cubes and it could mean only one thing. All hell was about to cut loose on Earth and there was nothing anyone could do about it.

Brazil took the full effects of the Security Cubes' power. She was flattened in just a matter of minutes and there was nothing left. Not even a simple radio signal from anywhere across this country. Next it was Guyana's turn. Her entire army was simply swiped away. Anything of a military nature was destroyed.

When it started, I thought half the world population would die, but what was happening was the warring capabilities of each country or organization who refused to abandon its weapons of war were systematically separated from their war making capabilities. It was a selective process and it was devastating.

When South Korea had walked away from its weapons of war, North Korea took the advantage and launched an attack on the south. They had crossed the border and were making tremendous gains with no opposition when the Cubes hit. It started with the lead tank of their initial strike force and then spread from there all the way through the attacking army, on into North Korea and across the whole of the country, completely destroying everything that was North Korea.

There they were one by one being completely smashed and driven into oblivion never to rise again against anyone. It was a purging unlike anything the world had ever seen. It was complete. It was total, and it was without mercy.

Then, we noticed the after effects. In every nation, country or region, Security Cubes started appearing. They had done it, but they did it in a manner that separated the peaceful from the aggressor. Whether mankind liked it or not, we were going to live in peace or die. The Demion's had carried out their intentions, but had given us the opportunity to join them in a peaceful venture into our future.

Oh, one last thing. The Cubes won.

Chapter Eleven

THE ARRIVAL

It was around noon on a Saturday when we first saw them with the naked eye. There were ten of them. They were large ball like ships, which seemed to float into the area between Earth and the moon, and then started to move into their formation. They positioned themselves around the world at equal point directly over the equator. The interesting thing about them was the color. They changed from color to color in what appeared to be a random pattern. Each of the ten synchronized to the other nine.

The Cubes seemed to go into hyper drive as they came in to their orbit. The amount of traffic going between the Cubes and the Demion's ships was well beyond our ability to capture and keep up with.

It was about fifteen hours after they achieved orbit, we got the first signal from them. We had been busy making sure we had returned all the bodies to their rightful place and had pulverized the fossilized remains on the battle field. Our people were moving the final body when the signal came in.

Bob was our connection. It started with a greeting and a thank you for all we had done and tried to do. It apologized for the death of our personnel early on in our work at the site. Then they started to set down the protocol for their arrival at the base. It was nothing special. They simply wanted Bob there along with me, Stan, Terry and Professor Blumfield. Then they decided they wanted Melanie and Jennifer there as well.

There was no special line or assignments of positions, just that we be there and be ready for their arrival.

Meanwhile, in orbit at two hundred fifty kilometers above earth the Demion's were preparing to depart their primary ship and head for the meeting with the research team. A circle appears on the side of the main ship or lead ship and then a tube started to slide out from the ship. The tube was about seven meters in diameter and when it cleared the main ship it was around twenty-five meters long. It was a silver green color and appeared to have no windows in it at all. It then turned and started its decent to the base.

The ship did not descend directly to the Brazil base, but made a deliberate and detailed tour of the whole of the earth, specifically the populated areas and those areas where the population was more advanced in technology. It was at least three hours before they had seen whatever it was, they wanted to see and they then headed for the base.

We did not see it until it was about a kilometer up from the landing site. As it descended it made no noise we could hear and when it landed it landed flat on the ground, digging out a small trench the bottom of the cylinder settled into. There was no dust or debris thrown up by the landing.

About five minutes later the door, located at mid-ship, slid open and a set of steps came down out of the door way. The first to exit was a woman, not unlike any other woman on earth. I would say she was about the same height and weight as Jennifer. Her hair was white and almost transparent. Her eyes were a livid yellow. Her nose and ears were no different from ours. Her clothes were not much different from those we had seen on the bodies and in the living areas of the base personnel. Where those clothes were generally white and green in color this woman's clothing was all red.

She was followed by two men and then a couple of more women and then a number of men. A total of twenty individuals, their uniforms were all dark blue. The first man to exit was almost seven feet tall. His hair was the same as the woman's, white and almost transparent. Everything else was the same.

The woman stepped over to within a meter and a half of Bob and then motioned him to step toward her. As he got to her, she took his hand and was saying something to him we could not hear. I don't know if she was speaking English or something else.

After a few seconds, Bob turned and pointed at me and then Stan and Terry, and Herman, then Melanie and Jennifer. He then signaled for Stan to step over to them. Stan looked at me and then stepped forward and the woman took his hand. She spoke to Bob who then appeared to translate to Stan what she had said.

Next, it was my turn and as I walked up to her, she reached down and took my hand, not shaking it, but just holding it. She spoke to me but what she was saying I could not understand. After she said what she said, Bob translated for me. She had introduced herself as Delegate Tamile Tontonsoon of the Demion's Central Guidance Commission for the region of space we lived in.

She then met the other four and invited the seven of us over to their ship where a canopy had slid out of the ship. They had set up a number of chairs for us to sit in.

"What's up, Bob?"

"Joe they are preparing us to talk about what we have found so far and if we have any questions concerning what was going to take place over the next few days and weeks."

The first question to be directed to us was how we came to find this location? Stan then related how a geological survey team had found the anomaly in the foot hills of this range. They had found it to be so unusual they brought their findings back to the main facilities to be analyzed. That resulted in an expedition coming into the area and an in-depth search started in the area under the auspices of the United Nations.

She asked when we found the building. Stan laid that out including finding the cubes and the death of the two workers and multiple injuries that had been received by other workers. He then related Bob's condition and his relationship with the cubes and ultimately determining how they were to enter the structure.

Tamile became extensively interested in our excavation of the battle grounds and the finding of the body fossils. Stan again explained the process in which we discovered the weapons cartridges and had determined they were of two entirely different cultures.

At the time we felt one was Earth based because of the metal make up of it and the other alien for the same reason. We had assumed the Demion's were the Earth based unit and they were the ones this base was built by. The Vandions were the aliens simply by the makeup of their metals and appearance.

We were wrong about the Demion's being Earth based. By that time, we were in communications with the Cubes and we then had determined what had actually happened at the location. That was confirmed by our archeological dig that followed and the body fossils we found. We knew a huge battle had taken place at the location. It stressed us to be excavating it, but we felt for the welfare of those digging and the need to understand, we continued the dig.

We did not understand the reasoning for the battle at the time, but our feeling towards those who had been in that terrible situation simply overwhelmed us. We found tangled heaps of body fossils all over the main base area inside the three main cubes. After we had completed the dig, we left everything as we found it. We had no idea what to do with it or how to treat it. So, we simply left it alone as we had found it.

She sat there looking at us and then leaned forward and laying her hand on the back of Stan's hand she said and Bob translated, "Thank you for your sensitivity toward those who have passed. The Vandions have been an enemy of ours for many centuries. In time they faded and became extinct. It was not their fault, but the region of space they lived in. That area is out of bounds for any culture to venture into because of the number of Nova's that happened there and the damage from the Gamma releases that can be done to the DNA of a species, if they're not killed outright."

I then leaned forward and she recognized my desire to speak. I told her we had learned the base had originally had a total of four thousand seventy-one personnel on site. As we explored the base, we had found a total of two thousand one hundred Demion bodies. That meant there were one thousand nine hundred seventy-one missing.

We had discovered the schematic drawings of the base and knew there were several other structures still needed to be excavated and entered. As a result of learning you, the Demion's, were coming, we selected not to continue the excavation of those locations until you arrived and determined what you wanted to do. The rest of your people may well have been in those structures.

"Mr. Nash, we understand, and we'll address that shortly, but first we must deal with those you have found. We will be bringing several ships of this size, indicating the one by us, along with personnel who will enter the building you have been working in and retrieve the bodies from their locations. During this time, we ask your personnel leave the building and withdraw to your camp and let us carry out this task.

"Though those people had died almost a billion years ago, they still deserved the honor and care we give to any Demion who had passed. There was a process, a method in removing the bodies and preparing them for transit back to their home planet.

"On our home planet there was actually, a memorial to this base and those lost with it. When we seeded the planet that many millennium ago, we did not disturb this site or the dead because it was a show of respect for them. But, once you had entered in and done just that, we now afforded them the honors any Demion deserved for faithful service."

Stan then spoke up. "Truly we are sorry for violating the places of your dead, but we did not know, nor did we expect to find them there."

"No, no, we are not accusing you of anything, you did not know and everything you did was scientifically honorable. It's just, once disturbed, we must afford them the honors they rightfully deserve."

"We understand, but it still disturbs us considering what took place in this location."

354

Tamile leaned back in her chair and signaled one of the men. He stepped inside the ship and returned a short time later with a large metal box. A second man came out of the ship with a small table with three legs. They placed the table in front of Tamile and then placed the metal box on top of the table.

As I looked at the box, I could see it had the same type of markings on it the same as the cubes had. In fact, the box was, in itself, a cube. She then looked at the seven of us. "Of all the people we have talked to, had contact with, and observed on this world, it turns out you, the people of the base, who have been the most open and accommodating of all."

She swept her hands across the front of her indicating everyone on the base. As she did so she smiled at us and then continued.

"You have not forsaken your world and, in fact, you have done everything to support the welfare of your world. You have not been aggressive as the cubes have shown that clearly. Even during the assault by the native nation this base sits on, you attempted in every way to get them to stop, even having been accused of causing the problems and resisting their forces.

"It cost this country its life and that we regret, but our security cubes were doing exactly what they were instructed to do. In addition, they had you and your people to protect and they would never allow any of you to be harmed by that force, any force."

She paused and looked at each of us wanting what she had said to be clear in our minds.

"As a result, it has been determined you, the seven of you, shall be the ambassadorial representatives of this planet to the Universal Council. What you may or may not know is the Demion's are not the only culture in the Universe. We are one of several hundred other cultures who have matured and grown together to form a council to oversee the governance of the Universe as we know it.

"There are many planets such as yours that have been seeded by member cultures of the Council. And, there are many planets that were self-developed. They generated their own culture outside the help of any other culture. You are both treated the same and are selected to enter into the Universal Governance and to become active members."

By this time, we were all looking back and forth at one another. This had not been expected and I for myself was not too sure I wanted to be included in this situation anyway.

As she had been talking, she had been laying out a number of medals on the small table in front of her.

"Though you are not fully into space travel, you are on the verge and that makes you perfect for entry at this time. If you agree, then you will take your rightful place along with the rest of the member planets and cultures. You do not have to make that determination at this time, but it will be expected of you within the next one hundred years. During this time, your culture will be given all the support in building a social system that is both beneficial to all of you of Earth and clearly sets you up for inclusion in the Universal System."

Each and every move she made was calculated and deliberate as she followed whatever protocol she was acting under. She had set the box aside and was now looking at each of us one at a time individually.

"These medallions I have here are for you. They are special in that they designate each of you as an ambassador to the Universal System as representatives of your own world.

Your careers on this world are now ending and each of you will find yourself making numerous trips between the Universal Council meetings and back here to meet with your world leaders to prepare for the world's entrance into the system. Believe me when I tell you, your selection is not that of the Demion's, but of the Cubes."

As I sat there listening to Tamile I could hardly believe what I was hearing. Me, an ambassador? That was nothing close to what I had expected in this meeting. Then it dawned on me and it appeared to dawn on the others at the same time Tamile had said we would be attending Universal Council meetings and it suddenly hit me that attending those meetings meant space travel. God, I was going into space.

At that point I believe I stopped tracking with anyone or anything that happened. In the last few days things had just gone crazy and now it was simply over the top. I was going into space.

Chapter Twelve

CHECK AND CHECK MATE

Things had gone off the board at this first meeting with the Demion's. I can assure you I was being drawn both ways on this issue of Ambassador Designation. How was I or we going to get to these "Universal Council" meetings? I know I didn't have a space ship and neither did anyone else on this planet. At least not one capable of traveling the distance involved and I'm sure it was light years and not just days.

I figured I had better start listening to Tamile as she told us of our obligations and activities over the coming years. But, right now she was talking about the cubes and what they were and why.

"The cubes are a universal tool. Every member of our system has them and they care for each member world as if they were that cubes own special purpose. That is how we maintain stability within the system. This is the system you will have the opportunity to view, learn about and see in actual operation. It is this information you will be bringing back to your leaders to assist them in their decisions. As your parent culture it will be our responsibility to see you're at the meeting of the Universal Council and this means we will provide you with your transportation. This is a huge step for your world...

"Mr. Franklin, Larry Denton is here for you."

"Good, send him in Carla."

"Well, Bill, what do you think of it so far?"

"Larry, I was just now reading some more of the manuscript, it's one of your best, but I have some issues we need to work on."

As I sat down. "Look, Bill, right now all we need is the okay, and we can complete the book and get on with the publishing of it."

Mr. Franklin held up his hand. "Larry, it's not that simple this time."

"What's up, Bill? What are you trying to tell me?" I was getting that feeling something was really wrong here.

I got up and walked over to the window and then returned to the chair and sat down across the desk from Bill Franklin my publisher.

Here in L.A. offices of people this powerful are things to behold. His was no different. In size it was probably twenty-five by thirty feet. Being a twentieth-floor office, it was located on a corner and had the view of a lifetime. The furnishings were first rate with mahogany desk with a back desk and book shelves of the same wood. Naturally there was the finest of carpeting as well.

As I said, I sat down in one of the arm chairs across from him and then I put my feet up on the edge of the desk and laid my head back on the chair and closed my eyes. I wanted him to know he worked for me and not the reverse.

"Larry, your last book, and by the way it was great, had a few things we found hard to accept, but we went along with you on them. We can't, this time. Some of the information you presented in the other book was found to be information no one should have had possession of. We ended up being investigated by the FBI and there was even a Senatorial hearing on it."

I sat there listening to Bill and shook my head. One thing I didn't need at this time was a bunch of problems with my publisher and a delay in getting this book out.

"No, this time we want to make sure nothing like that happens again. No, this time we want you to take us step by step through this book and fill us in on where you got your information. For example, the Guiana Highlands, where the hell did you come up with that one?"

I sat up and spread my hand and looked right at Bill, I guess I was somewhat dumbfounded by the question he asked. "Bill, I was simply sitting at the computer playing around with Google Earth and there it was. I thought the name would work well in the new book I was starting to work on."

I had been there just five minutes and already I was getting irritated and pissed off. "Really Bill, that's all it was. There is no insidious movement behind it. It was just me, the computer and Google. That's all. Come on, you can't sit there and tell me we are going to have to verify my source for each and everything I put in this book. Good grief man. That could take weeks, and on top of that, it's only a science fiction book and nothing more."

Bill was not going to give in easily this time. He was going to require verification and that was all there was to it. "Larry, you're not listening to me. The last book nearly put us all in jail. Where did you get all the information you had in that book? Crap, man, they had me on the carpet for weeks. I thought for sure I was going to be visiting my wife at a federal prison before it was all over."

"Bill it was just out of my head. Just as I told you and the FBI and the Senatorial Committee, it was just out of my head."

That whole mess was simply a misunderstanding and everyone blew it way out of proportion. "It scared the hell out of me too you know. I don't know where that stuff comes from, it just does. I'm damned if I can tell you anything that will satisfy you on this thing. It just comes. I don't do any research, except to verify locations and dates. Other than that, it all just rolls out of my head and onto the page."

Bill was just getting started. "Larry, why did you use those two cities?"

"Bill they are the only two cities of any size close to the mountain range so I took those names to use as landmarks in my description of the location of this story. They were there, on the map, and I picked them. What the hell is wrong with that? Damn Bill what is wrong with that?" Now I was officially pissed off.

Franklin leaned forward. "Larry there is nothing wrong with it, I just wanted to know the ways and means you came about picking them."

I wasn't going to accept this at all. "Aw, come on Bill. We're not going to do this on every little thing I wrote into this book are we?"

"Yeah, Larry, we are."

Bill could see I was getting pissed off. "Maybe I should take my publishing needs elsewhere."

He shrugged his shoulders and pushed the manuscript across the desk toward me. "Larry, that's your decision, but I can tell you after the last book, every publisher in the world will do the same thing. None of them want the headache that last book brought us."

It was time for me to calm down and work with Bill and not push the issue any further. "Well, all right I guess it did stir up one hell of a situation, surprised the hell out of me too. Okay, how do you want to go with this thing?"

He reached out and pulled the manuscript back to him. "Look, I have some time right now. You ready to answer some more questions?"

"Yeah, sure go ahead." This was the last thing I needed and my frustration level was going up every second.

So, he opened the manuscript to a marked page. "Let's look at some of these names. For example: Herman Blumfield, do you know if there is a Herman Blumfield at MIT?"

Damn I wish I hadn't come here today. "I don't know. I just pulled the name out of the blue." Actually, I couldn't remember just where I got it from at that moment. "There probably is a Herman Blumfield somewhere in the world and there could be at MIT, I guess, but I don't really know."

"Well, how about your lead characters Joe Nash, or Stan Davenport, or Terry Huntington?" He continued to read out to me.

I was completely blindsided by his questions. "Bill they are all out of my head.

Yes, there are people in this world, right here in this city with those names. They are common and nondescript. They're just names." Damn this was getting nuts.

"No, Larry, they are not just names. They could be names of people in high places. Names you should know nothing about, that could well be involved in the activities you cover in this book. We'll have the names checked out." Bill was looking right at me and turning pages. "The Cubes?"

"What about the cubes?" I was ready to scream about this time.

"Where did you come up with that?"

My frustration was now turning to anger. What the hell was he up to anyway? "Bill, them out of my mind and you're driving me out of my mind. I picked a shape and used it. They could just as well have been triangles or squares or whatever. If you like I will change them to any other shape you want me to. Damn it to hell anyway."

Bill held his hands up to calm me. "OKAY, we'll let that sit for a while."

He then came up with the next issue. "What about the Demion's and Vandions?"

"What about them?" I was starting to raise my voice.

"Where did you get those names?"

"Where the hell did you get your name, Bill? That's where I got them, the same place, out of thin air. When I first used them, I had them reversed for the characters of the book. Then I decided to change them around."

Bill immediately jumped on that comment. "Why did you do that? What made you change the character's name positions?"

I was no longer sitting back in my chair. I had stood up and was now pacing the floor in front of the desk. "Bill, you're completely paranoid. You've lost your mind. This thing is driving you crazy. I reviewed the story and did not like the names in the first positions I put them in so I changed them around. That is all there is to it."

I walked over to the desk and placed my fist on the desk top. "God, the next thing you're going to want to do is pack up and go to the Guiana Highlands and see if there is a valley like the one in the book. I can assure you there is. There are valleys all over that area and all over any mountain range in the world. They are common, Bill."

Bill sat there calmly watching me pace back and forth. "Ya knows what Larry? I think you're right in that matter."

"What matter?"

"Going to the Guiana Highlands and taking a look around. We can get some photo shots of the mountains and use them in advertising for the book when we publish it. Yeah, I think we need to go. I just want to be satisfied in my mind there is nothing there and this book is really fictional."

I had stopped mid-step and looked over at Bill and just stood there. "You're actually telling me you want to go to Brazil and check out the Guiana Highlands to make sure I have not stumbled on to something like I did in the other book."

"I think so Larry. In addition, the board of directors wants us to go and make sure as well."

Bill put the page he was holding down on the manuscript and pushed his chair back and stood up. "That last book cost this company a bundle and we're not going to take that chance again. Larry, we want to publish your book. You are a money maker for us, but this time we want to make sure there is nothing anyone can come back at us on."

He then picked up the phone and told his secretary to get airline tickets to Normandia, Brazil for first thing in the morning. He then told her to book himself, me, two photographers and two research people. "Larry, check with Carla on your way out and be at the airport at the time she tells you tomorrow morning."

Just then Carla called back and advised the tickets were set for the first of the week, five days from now. Bill nodded. "All right, we'll be ready at that time."

He then turned to me. "In the mean time you will work with our people to determine just where and what we are going to be looking at and for."

I had moved back to the chair and sat down and looked at him for several seconds. I had this strange feeling in the back of my head telling me there was something else going on here. "Bill, have you told me everything?"

He looked at me and then sat back in his chair. I watched his right hand as he started to tap the desk top. He always did that when he was nervous. "Come on, Bill, give the rest to me. Don't make me find out about it myself."

He raised his hands. "All right Larry, we have already sent a team to that location to see if they can find anything out of the

369

ordinary and in line with your book. That was two weeks ago."

"And, have they found anything?

"No nothing, just forests and underbrush."

"Then why are we going?"

He looked right at me. "Because that's what the board wants. That's why and that's good enough for me."

The next four days were filled with us going over the book in detail setting up a listing of all the anomalies we would be looking for. The more we got into this, the more bizarre it seemed to get. I had never heard of a book being as second guessed as this one. It was almost crazy, the level of detail we were going into. But the board wanted it that way and so what they want, they got.

Hell, the book wasn't even done yet and they were pulling it apart. As an artist something like this is almost unbearable. I had invested the better part of a year in the book up to this point. I still had to finish the final three chapters and we were now going to Brazil and looking the Guiana Highlands over.

I guess I didn't have any problem with

taking an all-expense paid trip, it was just the fact they were tearing into my book like it was some form of evil virus. I was feeling this was one of those days when I should have stayed in bed and had this appointment after I had finished the whole of the book.

The fact was I had hit a dead point in my writing. I was at a loss as to where to go at that point in time and I needed some input from Bill to help me get moving again.

As strange as it felt I knew I should not have come here this day or any day. There was something going on here that was bothering me and Bill was not helping in the least bit.

Well, the fat was in the fire now and I had nothing else I could do but go along with him. After investing almost, a year in this project you just don't turn and walk away from it.

Up until five days ago, August 6, 2015, I would have never thought I would be standing here in the foothills of the oldest mountain range in the world. Yet, here I was and I really had no idea why we were here except Bill had gone crazy and decided he wanted to see for himself this place and the fact nothing was there.

The day before we had been met at the Normandia airport by the team leader Bill had sent down here three weeks earlier.

"Frank, how's it going out there?" As He and Frank shook hands.

"Well, Bill, we think we have found a location that matches the one in the book."

That got my attention. "What? What do you mean?"

"Hi Larry, yeah, it's a small valley that runs up against the foothill. Nothing there though, just trees and underbrush."

"Frank. How long does it take to get there?"

"Well Bill it's about a two-to-three-hour drive north on the state highway, about thirty-two kilometers from the Guyana border. Strange, as it turned out there was what appeared to be a logging road that turned off the highway going west and we took it. We found this small valley and that was it."

"How far did the road go in?"

"Not far Larry, maybe five or six kilometers and then it dead ended."

Bill was looking at his watch. "Let's see, it's almost three now and we are looking at a minimum of three hours including the logging road. What say we wait till tomorrow morning to head out?"

"Sounds good to me, Bill. That will give me a chance to get some supplies we need."

"Okay Frank, you do that and we will meet you in front of the hotel at nine o'clock."

"We'll be there, Bill."

Normandia is a small town located in northern Brazil. It is a town of around six thousand seven hundred population. The 202 Brazilian rail line runs through the town as does Brazilian Highway 401. The 401 runs kind of north bound in a meandering way and it would be that highway we would be leaving on in the morning for the Highlands valley.

The actual Guiana Highlands region covers parts of Brazil, Guyana and Venezuela. The area in question was located in Brazil between the two cities of Normandia and Uiramuta. Normandia was the primary jump off point for access to the Highlands.

I took the opportunity to do a walking tour of the main commercial part of the town and found the atmosphere to be both inviting and friendly. As a result, I got to my motel room rather late and a little on the high side to say the least.

The next morning arrived faster than I

had anticipated. Unfortunately, I was carrying a rather large hangover by this time and was not looking forward to the coming trip.

As I walked out of the hotel there was Frank and the car and Bill was already in the co-pilots seat waiting for me. I looked at Frank and he then reached over and opened the door to the back seat. That was the one place I didn't want to ride after spending the night out drinking and having fun.

I managed to get in the back door and settled in. Bill turned and looked at me and then handed me a hot cup of coffee. That was just what I needed to help me get through the next few minutes.

We were on the road within minutes of the nine o'clock schedule. The highway is not what we would call a highway here. It is more of a rural road, two lanes all the way. However, it was fairly well cared for.

As for traffic, there was little of it this time in the morning. The further we got away from Normandia the less the traffic. It wasn't long before we were on the road on our own and could then make up some time.

About two and a half hours out, we came to a logging road that spurred off the main highway and headed toward our valley location. A half hour later we were pulling into their camp site.

Strange, there was a familiarity to the place, like I had been here before. You know what I mean, that feeling in the back of your head that says, *yeah, I know this place but I don't know why.* It could just as well have been the hangover.

As I stood outside the car, I looked around a full three hundred and sixty degrees. It was all forest except for an area to my right and left made up of just underbrush over by the south side of the valley's entrance.

It extended all the way to the base of the mountains and then off to my left it just extended away, strange. Bill walked up to me. "What is it, Larry?"

"I don't know Bill, but."

"Come on Larry don't start getting goofy on me now."

"No, it's not that. It's just, the general layout and overtones of this place strikes a chord with me, just odd."

Bill stood there looking around. "All right, let's go sit down with the guys and see what they've found if anything."

He walked over by the main tent and pulled a chair over by the fire pit and sat down. I walked over and sat down and the team leader, Frank, started to fill us in on what they had been doing and how the area fit in with my book to that point. Over all, they had found nothing with a great big NOTHING. I relaxed and let them finish their report.

I turned to Bill. "We made this trip for no reason at all Bill. What say we head back and jump the plane in the morning and go home?"

"No, Larry, I think we'll stay just one more day. I want to give the photographer all the time he needs to get some good publication shots of this place."

About that time, I was just about fed up with the whole game. I had gone along with Bill's paranoia to this point, but now I wanted to just go home and let things happen. If the book was ever published it would be just fine, on the other hand if not, that would be all right as well.

One thing I knew I was relaxing here in this place. It was quiet and comfortable and I had not had a chance to just sit back and relax in a long time. As night came on it cooled down, but not to a point where it was not comfortable, in a word this place was perfect.

It was quiet and that made it easy to fall asleep.

The next morning, I was up with the sun and out walking around the camp-site. As I stepped out by the car, I came to a complete stop and stood there. There was something wrong here and I could not put my finger on it. I had this back of the head feeling again and this time it was heavy.

I started a three hundred sixty degrees sweep and was half-way through it when it hit me. No sounds. It was dead quiet. Not one animal was making any noise. This far out there should be monkeys, birds, ground animals, but there was nothing. Not even the sound of a bug flying by, nothing. Just then Bill walked up.

I turned to Bill. "Bill, do you see or hear anything?"

He stood there looking around. It was like watching someone who was trying to see the obvious, but missing it entirely. He shrugged his shoulders. "It's just forests and hillsides and that's all. There is nothing here other than us. No buildings, no tent, no people, no bugs, no animals n... What the hell?"

I looked at Bill and he seemed to go

away for a few seconds. "Bill, do you understand what you just said?"

Bill raised one hand and started shaking his head. "No, there is something else behind this. Maybe one of the guys got up ahead of us and is out in the forest doing his thing or something."

I started shaking my head. "Bill, I've been up and out here for better than an hour and none of the others are up and about. There is something seriously wrong here and I don't know what it is. Bill, you sent these people down here and you told them what to look for, now tell me. What have you gotten me down here for, really?"

Just then, Frank came out of his tent and saw us by the car. He turned and leaned back into the tent and then stood up. He started too walked over to us.

Bill was standing there with his hands on his hips and looking up at the trees around us. "Frank, he's figuring it all out. He knows what is going on here."

Frank looked at me and then back to Bill. "Are you sure? What has he said or asked?"

Bill started walking in small circles and kicking a few rocks around on the ground.

"You damn well better believe, I'm sure. You saw his book, and now he is looking around and figuring it out. I guess we made the right decision bringing him here."

Bill turned and looked me in the eyes. "You SOB, you knew all about this. Somehow you figured this out and decided to make some money off of it."

It was slowly starting to dawn on me there was something far more serious going on here than I ever possibly could have imagined. It was scaring me and I had a feeling I was on my own.

"Bill, I didn't, honestly. I don't know what you're talking about." I was looking at both of them and trying to come up with an answer. "No bugs, Bill, that's impossible. There has to be bugs, Bill. Na, this can't be happening." Now I was really scared and starting to feel a little faint.

My mind went back to the book and its description of this location in the Brazilian forest and it matched to the letter. This was impossible no it was crazy as hell. How did I know this valley was this way? If I was right in my book then the valley was void of any biological life except for plants. With the lack of any observable animal life, I was beginning to feel everything I had written was true.

I started backing away from Bill. He had this damn scary smile on his face. He knew something was going on.

Frank moved around between the two of us. "Bill, relax. He's here and he's not leaving. We need to deal with this on a rational basis and not based on anger."

Bill stopped and stood there. "How could he know all he put in that book? He has never been here, yet he knew."

I leaned around Frank. "What the hell are you two talking about anyway? Frank, I'm getting a little scared here and a little pissed off as well. Someone had better start talking to me and soon or there will be hell to pay."

Frank spun around facing me. "What do you mean by 'hell to pay' Larry? There is no 'hell to pay.' You're not here to pay hell or see anyone else pays hell. You're here because you know too much. How, we're not sure, but before you or anyone else leaves this place we're going to find out."

I began backing up and bumped into something hard. I turned and pushed the brush away from it and saw a sharp edge to an object. I pulled the brush away from it. "No, no, it can't be."

I turned and looked at Bill and Frank and they just stood there nodding their heads at me. I turned back around and pulled more brush away and saw the side of the object. My heart sank in my chest. It's a cube, just like the ones in my book, but how? How the hell did I know these things really existed?

I looked again, yeah it was a meter on all sides and the vertical sides had markings on them and they had a soft light blue glow to them. No way, how can that be? I had no idea what was going on, but one thing I did know, I was in deep trouble and there was no one around who could help me.

Just then, several more men came from their tents and made the walk over to where we were standing by the cube. They said nothing, just made a circle around me and the cube and then just stood there.

"All right Bill, fill me in. Are you the Vandions or the Demion's?" I had that sick feeling in my guts, not just because of the cube but because of the fact I was obviously out here miles from nowhere and all alone.

Bill finally stepped toward me. "Larry, much of what you had in your book was right on the money. However, you did get a few things wrong.

"First of all, there were occupants of the Earth some nine hundred million years ago. They were the Vandions, the original natives of this world. Their society had developed fairly well over the years they existed, but it was nowhere near that of ours. They fought us well for the first few months and eventually they could not withstand the level of technology we brought against them. It was clear we would have to purge the whole of this world, leaving nothing of them and their existence behind, not a single sign."

He paused for a moment to let that information sink in and then continued. "What we did not count on was their finding this base and when they did, they threw everything they had at the garrison manning this base. Our people, the garrison, could not hold them and in the end, they had to use the cubes to annihilate both the Vandions and the garrison to ensure that no one got away.

"Few worlds have been able to withstand us as this one did. But, in the end, it cost them everything. They could have surrendered and lived a wonderful life under our rule, but they chose not to and that was their end."

"Then you are the Demion's and you

did seed this world, right?"

I was beginning to realize my life was worth less than any single rock lying on the ground. I felt my heart sink as I finally realized just what my situation was.

"That you have right. We are your parents as you stated in your book. But we have run into opposition here and are having a difficult time getting you people to understand you are of us and with us. Then you came up with that damn book and it could have been a real problem if it had not been for your prior book which had caused so much trouble for the publishers. We don't need that kind of trouble right now."

"Can I ask a question?"

Bill stood there waiting for my question.

"How did you eliminate any and all evidence of the Vandions presence on this world?"

He took several seconds to prepare his response to my question. "By the cubes, we simply finished the preliminary cleanup work and then left the cubes here to carry out the complete cleanup of the mess that was left. They sterilized the world from one end to the other. Nothing was left, not a single cell.

Where we messed up was this base. We could not return here because of the level of clean up the cubes were carrying out. We could not have survived it, so we left it hoping someone would never come across it and no one ever did. That is until you wrote your book.

"Now we need to know how you came about your information on this base and its layout. That is our purpose here and now. You could never have just dreamed this up, you had to have some information from somewhere and we need that source."

I stood there looking at them. I had no place to go and would never be able to physically handle all of them. "Bill as I told you before, I have no idea. I just sat down and started writing and this is what came out."

Just then I felt a surge of pain through the back of my head and it almost knocked me to my knees.

Bill saw me winch in pain. "What's wrong, Larry?"

"Look, you guys, you don't have to resort to force to make me talk. Damn that hurt." I was looking around at them.

"Larry, we didn't do that."

"Then who the hell is hitting me in the

back of my head with all the pain? Crap it keeps coming and it's getting worse by the second."

Frank and Bill turned and looked at each other. Just then, I looked down at the cube and the markings on it had turned red. Everyone seemed to be in shock when they saw the cube in a red mode. I looked at Bill. "Was I right about the cubes' modes?"

By this time, they were all backing away from me.

I continued asking. "Come on guys, it's your cube. What the hell are you afraid of anyway?" I was taking a little pleasure in seeing the look on their faces as they backed away from me and the cube. They were clearly scared and confused at the same time.

Bill held up his hand and started to say something when it hit me. It was a shock that grabbed me by the back of my neck and slammed down through my body and into the ground. I had never felt a force like that before. It numbed me.

I looked over and all the rest were lying on the ground. Bill looked over at me and tried to say something when the next shock hit. That one knocked me to the ground flat on my back. When my vision cleared, I was looking straight up and at the belly of a round cylinder type structure around twenty meters in diameter and maybe thirty-five meters long. It moved over the top of me and then continued toward the mountains before starting to land. It settling down just about thirty meters from us, and it was not making a sound of any kind. While setting down, it dug a shallow trench in the ground it settled into.

Bill jumped up and ran to the ship and waited for the door to open. As it opened, a set of steps slid down out of the ship and was followed by a man. He stepped on to the ground and turned to Bill. They talked for a few minutes and then the man turned and looked at me. Right then I knew in the next five to ten minutes my destiny would be decided by these beings.

Finally, the man turned and walked over to me and reached down and took my hand and pulled me up to my feet. He looked me over and then looked at the cube, which was still in the red. It immediately changed to light blue and the man returned his attention on me.

He started to speak and it was in perfect English "Mr. Denton my name is Devlon. You have become a serious problem for us."

I immediately challenged him. "Who are us?"

He stopped and looked at Bill and then back to me. I immediately knew I had said the wrong thing. I had better start thinking or this place in Brazil will be my last place anywhere.

"We are of the Demion culture. This planet is ours and has been for the past billion years. In effect, anything that originates on this planet is also ours. You, as a subculture, are clearly our property and we will deal with you as such."

That sent a cold chill down my spine. These beings were so far advanced from us we were simply a subculture and that meant trouble for the people of Earth.

I guess I became a little defiant. "Then why don't you just kill me? What the hell you waiting for?"

He smiled and glanced over at the other again and then continued. "That would be a simple solution to the problem, but it would not be the right or preferred answer to the problem. No, we must deal with you in a different manner. There is value to you and that is the life within you. Though a subculture, you are still of us in that we seeded you so many millenniums ago. No, death is not an option."

Damn that felt good, at least I was going to leave this meeting alive, but I still needed answers. "Why am I a problem?"

"It is simple, Mr. Denton. The people of Earth do not know of us and it is best they not know of us at this time. In due time we will approach this world and bring you into your rightful place in the Council of the Universe, but that is not to be at this time. You still have a lot of growing to do."

"Growing? What do you mean by that?" Now things had changed and we were into something different.

"Your world is a violent place. You spend much of your time killing one another and not enough of your time helping one another. As an aggressive and violent culture, you are not welcome among the Universal Cultures. They simply will not accept you. Their alternative in order to stop your expansion into space is to kill you, which will still remain an option. No, this world is not ready for the Universe and we are not going to let you come into our realm.

"So, Mr. Denton, I am faced with a dilemma and that is, what we should do with you. You are way too independent for us to just let you walk off. That makes you a real problem. We want to keep your life vital and living, but just how to do that is one big dilemma."

"Well, if I can help, I have an idea."

"And, what is that?"

"Why don't we just forget this whole thing? I'll burn my book and move somewhere I can live my life without ever thinking of this again."

Devlon looked at me and shook his head. "No, that would not do. Let me offer you an alternative, Mr. Denton. How would it be if we tagged you?"

I looked at him. "What? Like a fish? I don't think I would like that."

"No, like a man who should live, but is a high level of hazard to us and our system in the universe."

"Well based on that, it sounds just fine." Hell, I didn't know what I or Mr. Devlon were talking about anyway.

He then continued to explain the situation to me. "Let me warn you, Mr. Denton, tagging is not just a little marker placed on or in you. Tagging is a system of tracking. Your monitor will know where you are every second of your life. Your monitor will know everything you say, think, or do. Your monitor will watch you day in and day out. It will never be away from you nor can you get away from it. We place nothing in your body, we don't have to. Your monitor will do everything and you will never, ever be able to get outside its presences and authority. And, if you really try, your monitor will kill you in a second."

Oh boy, that didn't sound like something I wanted to be a part of. Kill me in just seconds? Crap, with a mouth like mine I could get myself killed faster than my monitor could think. No, maybe this was not what I wanted.

Devlon continued. "Live your life and have a career. Write all the books you want and become famous and wealthy. Do anything you can think of. Live freely. But, violate this mandate and you will never get the second word out.

"Your mandate, to say nothing ever again about your book, this place, Demion's, Vandions or anything in relationship to the past before recorded time. If you agree to live this way, then you will be free to do as you wish and go where you please as long as it never violates this mandate. Do you understand?"

Now when I stood there considering the alternatives, Mr. Devlon's offer started to look more and more appealing. "Yes, sir I understand."

"Are you willing to live under our authority?"

"Yes sir."

"Can I trust you?"

"Yes sir, one question?"

"Yes, go ahead."

"Who is my monitor?"

He looked at me and then raised his right arm and pointed his finger at the cube sitting three meters away.

"Ah, man!" This was going to be impossible. Just then all I had written about those things charged through my mind and I knew if they were anywhere near that level of capabilities, I was in real trouble.

"On the contrary, Mr. Denton, it will be just fine. Live, please live a good life." Replied Devlon and then he said. "Oh, one other thing you should know.

By now there was nothing else that could make me any more nervous than I was right then. "What is that?"

"Your monitor is also your protector. Nothing will happen to you or hurt you under its care. That will be true for your mate, if and when you have one and any offspring's. Again, have a good life, and forget everything you've seen here."

I took a deep breath. "Yes sir."

For the longest time we all just stood there looking at one another and not saying a word. They were waiting for something and I was waiting for more information as to what was going to happen in regards to my being monitored.

That is when the pain in the back of my head increased about tenfold and then subsided. In no time it was completely gone and there was a soft vibration in my mind. It was not an irritant, but was comforting.

Then the cube introduced itself to me. Yeah, that's right it introduced itself to me. Not like, "Mr. Denton, I'm so and so, I'll be your mentor from now on." No, it was more like, "Hi, I'm here, if you need anything, just think it." And, that was it, my mentor was installed.

Devlon then took my hand and walked me over to his ship. "Would you please enter?"

Now that scared me. I looked at the door and then back at him and then back to the door. He was wanting me to enter his space ship and for what reason I had no idea. Needless to say, I was not really interested in entering his ship, but on the other hand what the hell was I going to do out there anyway.

"Where are we going?"

"Well, Mr. Denton, there is no reason for you to remain in this area now is there?"

I found myself nodding my head in agreement. "Well, I guess not."

"Then the only really considerate thing we should do is give you a ride out of this area and to some place that will be more to your liking, right?"

What could I say except? "I guess so."

"Please step on board."

As I entered the ship, I noted it was not a plush interior. In fact, it was a simple and matter of fact kind of a place. The seats were comfortable and there was lots of room, but for style, well, who was I to complain. For a society more than a billion years old you would think design and decoration would have a place.

I had no idea when we lifted off. All I know, before we got to the destination, they had selected for me it was dark out. That meant we had traveled west, but how far, I had no idea.

I remember nothing of the landing or putting me off the ship. Things just went blank. I had not had anything given me; I just went out. Right, the mentor, had put me out so I would not know where I was going at the time. They landed and took me off ship and left me there. They were kind enough to leave me with assistance after they left.

I woke up sitting against a palm tree on a white sandy beach on the island of Maui, Hawaii. It was wonderful, so I decided to stay there for a few weeks. As I checked my pockets, I found a bundle of money. It turned out to be fifteen thousand dollars. With that amount I could be as comfortable as I wanted to be for as long as I needed, within reason that is.

Later on, that day, as I was searching out my current situation on a hotel computer, I found, while checking my accounts back home, my funds had increased to twenty million in one account and thirty-five million in another. Wow, I was now a multimillionaire.

Just then it spoke to me. "How are we

doing Larry?"

At first, I started to look around and then realized it was in my head.

"Oh, just fine, by the way do you have a name?"

"I am designated as a Tempura Four Seventy-five Multi."

"No that's too long a name. What would you think if I called you John?"

It, he, replied. "John? That would work just fine. You can call me John and I'll continue to call you Larry. That will be just fine."

Yeah, I'll be able to live under those mandates after all. If I can't then I'm the idiot, not the world. I'm on a first name basis with my monitor. And, yes, it's there all the time. I can feel it in the back of my head. It keeps me aware as to what is going on around me and across the world.

We make a great team when it comes to me investing my money. It's actually building and should pass the one hundred million marks by the end of the year. We have not missed on one investment it's great to have an inside track. We have become one and this living with its presence is going just fine.

After all, I'm a non-combatant.